ALSO BY MARK SPRAGG

*An Unfinished Life*

*The Fruit of Stone*

*Where Rivers Change Direction*

# BONE FIRE

# BONE FIRE

## Mark Spragg

Alfred A. Knopf · New York · 2010

THIS IS A BORZOI BOOK
PUBLISHED BY ALFRED A. KNOPF

Library of Congress Cataloging-in-Publication Data
Spragg, Mark, date.
Bone fire / by Mark Spragg. — 1st ed.
p.   cm.
ISBN 978-0-307-27275-1
1. Domestic fiction.   2. Wyoming—Fiction.   I. Title.
PS3619.P73B66 2010
813'.6—dc22   2009029645

*Book design by Robert C. Olsson*

Manufactured in the United States of America
First Edition

*For Virginia,*
*because of Virginia,*
*always,*
*and*
*for Harriet Bloom-Wilson*
*and Richard Wilson,*
*with my love*

In fact, the absolute is available to everyone in every age. There never was a more holy age than ours, and never a less.

—Annie Dillard, *For the Time Being*

# BONE FIRE

# One

SHE LUNGED THE HORSE forward because that was all that was
left to them, the slope too sheer to turn him, the shale his hooves
struck loose skidding away, wheeling downward. She felt him slip
from under her, struggling to regain his feet, the air snapping with
the sound of stones colliding, echoes rebounding against the head-
wall of the cirque. It was the second time he'd come close to
falling, and now he stood bunched and quivering, his ears flattened
against his skull. They were both breathing hard.

She glanced back over her shoulder. Below her the ridgeline
rose up sharp-edged, spangling in the sunlight, seeming to beckon
as madness is sometimes said to. The bands of muscle in her back
and shoulders burned, and her mouth had gone dry.

She inched higher against the long run of his neck, careful not
to unbalance them, whispering, "Just this" to urge him forward
again. She felt him gather his weight in his hindquarters, heard
him groan. He still trembled. "Just this," she whispered again, and
there was the chopping of his iron shoes against the broken rim
and they were over all at once, unexpectedly, the horse staggering,
standing finally with his legs splayed, his head hung low, braced up
against the suck of his own breathing.

She slipped to the ground, tried to walk and couldn't, then
squatted with her arms thrown over her knees. She smelled like

the horse: salty, souring, indelicate. Her hands shook when she held them in front of her face. She'd acted like a goddamn tourist bringing them straight up out of the head of Owl Creek, ignoring the game trails. Sweat ran into her eyes, down the beaded course of her spine.

She shaded her eyes, looking southeast over Clear Creek, Crazy Woman Creek, across the Powder River Basin toward the Black Hills, the horizon a hundred miles away, faintly edging the dome of blue sky. This was the secret she'd kept from her East Coast classmates, the exhilaration of this perfect air, filtered clear—as she has believed since childhood—by the rising souls of the dead. In her early teens, she even imagined she could feel the press of them in their passing, those assemblages of spirits retracing the very same watercourses that flow east and west from this divide, much as salmon would climb them, single-minded in their desire for homecoming, lifting themselves toward the advantage of heaven.

She straightened her legs. The insides of her thighs prickled from the chafing of the climb. Her belly hummed and she pressed a hand against her abdomen, turning to check the horse where he stepped carefully through the lichen-covered stones bearing the imprints of Cretaceous fishes. His name is Royal, and except for days like this when they're at work, she rides him bareback. Always. She trusts him that much. He nickered softly and she watched her reflections in the dark globes of his eyes. She smiled and her reflections smiled, and she thought there's joy in a horse, laughter in its movement, even at this point of exhaustion. She stood, stomping her legs until they were just shaky.

Her grandfather had asked her only to check the new grasses before they pasture the cattle on these Forest Service leases, but she was concerned—as she has always been—not to disappoint him, not to waste his time with her carelessness. So she and Royal have weaved among the cows where they've found them collected in the timbered undergrowth, alert for signs of illness or accident.

They've walked the fences where they could, and lastly, when the job was done, made this break for the toplands.

She knelt in the soggy cress that bordered a seep and bent to the water and drank. Then she peeled her shirt and bra over her head, splashing the water against her neck, shoulders and breasts, finally sitting back on her heels to stare at a contrail that halved the sky above her.

Her mother had asked, "Are you still stringing that Indian boy along?"

They were seated across from each other in the new café in Ishawooa. Salads, meatless soups, herbal teas. A sandwich board on the sidewalk out front, its legs sandbagged against the wind. It's their habit to eat together once a week, as testimony that they truly are mother and daughter.

Griff scooted forward on her chair, against the table's edge. "I get really sick of you pretending to be a racist."

"Saying he's an Indian is just a fact."

"So is his name."

Her mother cleared her throat. "Are you still fucking Paul Woodenlegs?" Louder this time, a woman turning at another table rearing back to stare through the bottom half of her bifocals.

The blood rose in Griff's cheeks, her mother nodding conclusively, the gesture women commit in church in lieu of speaking *amen.*

"When your dad and I were your age," Jean said, and smiled, unconsciously reaching inside the open throat of her blouse, straightening a bra strap, "it meant something then."

"I love him." She knew the statement was heard as excuse, and therefore feeble.

"Love must be different now."

And there it was, just a hint of the sour, woody smell on her mother's breath, and Griff wondered when she'd taken her first bourbon this morning.

"Your dad and I never wanted to be apart. Not for a single day."

"I'm not like you."

She watched her mother's hands pick up a menu, holding it open. She hung her own weather-roughened hands out of sight, finding it impossible to admit that when she and Paul are making love it's the grinding of their bones she hears, the clamor of one animal moving against another. Not always, but often enough to convince her that nothing remains unbroken forever.

"Is he the reason you're not going back to school?"

"He won't even be here this fall. He's finishing graduate school in Chicago."

"In what?" Jean held up her empty glass, trying to catch the waitress's attention.

"Didn't we already have this conversation?"

"Tell me again."

"Public health."

"Isn't that something?" Her mother's eyes remained calm. "Just think of the career opportunities he'll have for scrubbing bathrooms in some reservation casino."

"Yeah, Mom, I'm sure that's what he's shooting for."

"I remember that we've talked about this now." She dabbed at her mouth with a napkin, though they hadn't yet ordered any food. She folded the white linen over the berry-colored smear of lip gloss, leaning forward on her elbows. "You know it's what dropouts always say. 'Just this fall.' " She rested her chin on the heel of a hand. "But it always turns out to be for the rest of their lives."


She spent the afternoon wandering through an acre of chert and obsidian chippings, in places half a foot thick, imagining the ancients squatting here so near the sun, raised above the worst of the summer heat and flies, fashioning their spear points and arrowheads. Twice she scooped up handfuls of the glittering spall, tossing it upward, watching it plume in bursts of refraction as crude fireworks would, then rattle back to earth.

In the late afternoon she found the butt of a broken Clovis point and, later, the skull of a bighorn ram. This she lifted out of the scatter of bones strewn by predators, wind and snowmelt, and carried it to where Royal grazed, securing it behind the cantle with the saddle strings.

She caught up the reins, and led the horse onto a trail that descended through a thick copse of aspen, weaving him down through the slender white trunks and stopping in the last throw of shade. She leaned against his shoulder, staring along the curve of his neck into the evergreens crowded before them.

The spring had stayed wet through the front part of June, and now, in this heat at the end of the month, the firs have shrugged their mustard-yellow pollen in a day, staining the air as a ground fog would, luteous, and in the late and slanting light seeming to glow from within. She extended her arms over her head, walking forward, the horse following.

At dusk they were out on the open foothills, winding down through the cows and calves scattered and grazing in the cooler air. And far below them—along the creek, arranged among the old homestead cottonwoods—the house, the barn and outbuildings.

She breathed in deeply, contentedly, pressing her tongue against the roof of her mouth to better taste the perfumed air flavored by fertility, by promise, by this country she has lived in for the best half of her life.

# Two

Aт NIGHTFALL Einar was dozing in a porch chair when the cow elk in the timber above the pastures started barking like a mob of ill-mannered dogs, and the surprise of it roused him so thoroughly he tried to stand right up and his balance crumbled and he sat back blinking. He felt weakened, unnaturally insubstantial, and wondered if he was coming down with something, maybe the flu, and then it occurred to him that he hadn't spoken aloud since breakfast, and that in past spells of frailness conversation had acted as a palliative. He tried to think of a rousing declaration but nothing came to mind, so he simply muttered, "Not ready yet," and that proved enough to get him to his feet. This wasn't anything. It wasn't like when he'd woken up in the garden with Griff kneeling at his side and for a time couldn't remember his full name, or which rows he'd seeded, feeling tired enough to fall back asleep right there on the warm earth. This wasn't like that at all.

He came in the house and stood at the kitchen counter. When he thought of it he ate a dozen soda crackers, staring out the open window above the sink, the landscape gray and indistinct, as most of the world was for him now, the barn standing at the farthest reach of his sight, merely a black cube in this darkening scene. He stopped chewing for a moment to listen and no longer heard the elk, so he supposed they were bedded down for the night.

After two glasses of tap water he felt reassuringly just hungry and found the new jar of peanut butter Griff had placed directly under the bulb in the refrigerator so he could spot it straightaway. He stood with the door propped open against his hip, enjoying the cool draft and eating from the jar with a tablespoon. They both preferred her cooking, and he expected the crackers and peanut butter would help him hold up until she got home and could start their supper.

He went back out on the porch to wait for her. The evening had progressed enough that he couldn't distinguish the barn at all, or any of the outbuildings, just the greater dark of the earth rising into the slate-colored sky, shouldering the last of the light upward into the brightening stars. Some time ago she'd made him promise not to turn on the yardlight unless they had visitors, so on these summer evenings they could sit by themselves and watch the stars ripen above them like some crop of incandescent fruit, and that's what he was thinking when he heard the suck of Royal's hooves in the irrigated alfalfa of the lower pasture. He was considering how much she'd altered his life in the past ten years, and then there was the drumming of the horses circling in the corrals, nickering, excited, as they always are for any sort of reunion.

He listened to Royal roll, once, twice, three times on the raised hardpack at the center of the main corral, finally standing, shaking, and then all of them crowding into the barn, the noise of their hooves booming on the worn boards, striking out a rustic tune as if from the box of some good and primitive instrument, and then the orderly rhythm of the girl pouring their separate measures of grain in the feed boxes, the settled and contented chorus of their feeding. He could feel every part of it in his hands, in his shoulders, and when he swallowed there was the taste of oats and horses.

Sitting with his better ear cocked forward, he imagined her pausing in the barn's doorway, hands on her hips, coaxing the stiffness from her back. When his eyes had been better he enjoyed watching her work through her chores, concentrating on each task as it came up before her. She'd adopted many of his mannerisms, his attention to detail, and he'd taken his time over the years to teach her what he knew for sure: how to move among the horses, the operation of the combine, the swather, the baler, the front bucket on the tractor and the backhoe attachment that's gotten more use than he thought it would when he bought it at auction. To the best of his ability he's taught her when to be wary and when to be bold among the bulls, where the constellations set on the horizon, the indifference of the seasons and of God. But he's never demanded that she become devoted to his manner of living; that's just how it's turned out, as though it was an inevitable aspect passed down from him to his son, Griffin, and so on to her. And he doesn't regard the imperatives of blood as anything for which a man can take much credit.

After supper she stacked the dishes in the sink, and when he lit a cigarette she brought him the glass ashtray from the cupboard over the refrigerator.

"I don't know how you can smoke just one and not want another." She reached forward with a wadded-up paper napkin, brushing a crumb from the gray-and-white stubble on his chin.

"I wish I enjoyed it more." He scooted his chair back enough to cross one leg over the other, biting down on the filter and adjusting his glasses so he wouldn't miss the ashtray. "I feel like I'm letting him down."

There was the rich smell of ground coffee, the fading odors of their meal, the peppery scent of tobacco. She was leaning into the counter watching the blue smoke rise into the still room, her weight over her left hip, her arms gone slack—a posture she affects when she's worn down and the day's not yet done. It's how a horse stands, resting, and how, as a young girl, she'd been standing in Mitch's cabin half listening as the doctor told him that nothing else he had would outlast his lungs, that his kidney would most likely be what quit him first. Mitch winked at her, working his shoulders back against the pillows to get himself more upright in bed. "This here," he gestured toward the doctor, "is a blessing." And then: "Lucky Strikes is what I like. Maybe next time Einar gets to town."

She brought two cups of coffee to the table and sat across from her grandfather, pulling the cigarette from between his fingers. She took a drag, then another, and handed it back. His eyes appeared yellowed and outsized behind the thick lenses of his glasses.

"The fence is down on the south side of Owl Creek." She sipped her coffee.

"Down bad?"

"I'll get Paul and McEban to help." She picked at the cuff of his shirtsleeve, and tapped his wrist and stood up from her chair. "You're missing a button there."

She rummaged around in the tool drawer in the kitchen, and when she sat back down she had a packet of needles and a spool of thread and a spare button. He stubbed the cigarette out and folded his glasses into his shirt pocket, keeping his elbow tucked to his ribs.

"You ready?" she asked, and when he didn't look at her she asked again. He seemed older to her now, more diminished than he had even nine months ago. She puffed her cheeks and blew out, waiting. "I'm sorry you can't take care of your own fencing. I'm sorrier than you are."

She dragged her chair around, waiting until he was done pouting to lift his arm away and settle it on her knees. "At least we'll be fencing more grass than we need." She spoke with her head down over the mending, and when he didn't respond she bit off the thread above where she'd knotted it and replaced the needles and thread back in the drawer, then started the water in the sink.

"Your mother called this afternoon." He was fingering his new button, testing it.

"Does she want me to call her back?"

He sipped his coffee, grimaced, then blew on it. "I believe she just called to tell me you'd lose your scholarship if you don't go back to school."

"Well, she's wrong." She felt her face flush and turned back to the dishes.

He tried his coffee again, then set it back down. "My sister might come for a visit."

She shut the water off and stood drying her hands. "Really?"

"McEban found an article about her on his computer. Then he found her phone number."

"And you called her?"

He nodded. "Last week."

She watched him turn toward the living room, perhaps imagining he'd heard someone there, and thought she might get a dog again, if only for the noise a dog would make. "Do you think she'll come?"

He was still looking into the other room. "You mean Marin?"

"Yes."

"I couldn't say." He pushed back from the table, squinting at her. "I'm ready for bed now."


She helped him take his boots off, leaving the room so he could get out of his clothes. When she returned he was under the bedcovers, propped up against a drift of pillows. He'd swung a foot-wide magnifying glass between his face and the book he held open at his waist, the lens attached to a hinged metal arm mounted to the wall above his nightstand.

"I could get you large-print books from the library," she said.

"That doesn't have to happen just yet."

He lowered the book to his lap and she pulled a chair close to the bed, thinking about all the hard conditions under which old men can die, but mostly of Mitch, lying for two years in his cabin just thirty-seven steps out the mudroom door. Reading his John D. MacDonald novels, reading them over again, enjoying his Lucky Strikes and the coffee and chocolates she brought him each morning. Their regimen of small pleasures to provide some relief from the constant speculation about which organ might fail enough to cause them all to cave in.

Einar folded the magnifying glass against the wall and a coyote started up with a series of high-pitched skirlings. They both stared at the window until the animal was done, then he closed the book and held it against his thighs. "I'll sell this goddamn place and move into the county home before I'll see you drop out of college to nurse me."

She placed a hand on the blue-and-red dragon wrapping his forearm from wrist to elbow, but it felt too intimate a gesture and she brought her hand back to her lap. "Is that why you called your sister? Because you don't think I can take care of you?"

"Marin's had some trouble. That's all there was to it."

He stared at her, unblinking, and she'd always wondered what he saw when he looked so long, searching her face. "I was frightened," she said.

"Of what?"

She walked to the window, leaning against the wall to the side of the frame. She hooked her hair behind her ears. "The noise." Her reflection in the glass made her uneasy, so she stepped away. "It was like what Paul told me about the summer he worked on an oil rig. All clank and strain. That's what Rhode Island sounded like."

She raised the bottom sash higher and the room swamped with cooler air and she came back to the bed, bending over him. She pushed a fist into the mattress on either side of his hips. "I'm sorry if you think I wasted the money you gave me."

When that was all she said he expected her to kiss him good night, but she just held her face close, taking shallow, steady breaths.

His eyes stung and he closed them, the memories of when he was her age and gone from home for the first time coming up clearly. The weeks at Fort Jackson in South Carolina, the loud, drunken nights in Columbia or Charlotte, the constant soul-grating wail of his thousands of new neighbors, like a dental drill in his sleep, but he'd had Mitch and a red-haired boy named Ferguson from Colorado Springs to share the dislocation when the panic set in. When the press of the overly treed horizons and the too-wet air made it hard to breathe, he had friends who could help conjure the wind and distance and silence of the Rockies, and then they were shipped on to Inchon.

"Have we got any ice cream?" he asked.

She smiled, shaking her head, and when her hair came loose and fell against his cheeks she straightened up and scooped the hair away from her face. "I'll get some tomorrow."

He opened his eyes. "I don't want you to worry about what I think. About you not going back to school."

"I'm not worried."

"I believe you are, just a little. And I don't want you to worry about Marin, either."

She looked down to where her hands were clasped at her waist, letting them swing free, for a moment imagining he might guess how often she's prayed he'll die all at once, like a young person does, without expecting it. She doesn't want him to suffer like Mitch had, slipping away with no last statement of regret or summation, no parting smile or gasp, just a single weak exhalation. She'd been sitting with him in his little cabin, and when it was clear that he was gone she'd walked outside, staring into the vaulted sky, turning slowly under the silent witness of Cassiopeia, Andromeda, every point of light where she expected it to be in its seasonal progression, Orion with his shield tilted against the earth as though to safeguard the heavens from our accrual of grief. She'd expected some sort of revelation, but there was none. The night sky remained free of circumstance.

"You need a glass of water?"

"I'm better off if I go to bed thirsty."

"All right." She moved the chair back against the wall. "My mom said that if I wouldn't go to school, she would."

"When did all this happen?"

"She said she's going to take classes this summer over in Sheridan. She'll be a nurse's assistant."

"That's not something I'd want to do, but good for her." He switched off the nightstand lamp and they waited for their eyes to adjust. "We both know I haven't paid for squat," he said. "Your airline tickets were the only thing I even helped with."

"I'm going to call Paul now." She moved to the doorway and stopped, standing silently, and when he reached to turn the light back on she added, "I should've told you I wanted to come home, but I didn't want you to think I was a quitter. I didn't want to think of myself like that."

He brought his hand back from the lamp switch, staring into the darkness. But he couldn't distinguish her silhouette, and then he heard her walking evenly in the hall and the front door open and close. He tried to remember if she'd wished him a good night.

"Don't think I believe it was only the noise," he whispered. "Not for one single minute."

# Three

CRANE STEPPED OUT of the county cruiser and eased the door shut, holding the handle up to avoid the metallic click of the latch. He'd turned off the radio and headlights at the highway, idling in under a moon three-quarters full, and now stood hesitantly in that just sufficient light and when it occurred to him tipped his silver-belly stockman's hat off, reaching in through the open window to place it on the seat. The hat attracts moonlight like cumulus, and he wondered what else he hadn't considered that might get him killed. He studied the timber at the edge of the clearing for threat but saw only a dove-colored border of shadow, pendulate and hypnotic, and had to lean unexpectedly into the windowframe to keep his balance, focusing on the shotgun in its bracket between the seats, until his sudden rise of vertigo quieted.

He raked a hand back through his dark hair, wondering if blond or white-headed sheriffs made better targets in nighttime shootings, promising himself to look on the Department of Justice website when he got back to the office.

He unsnapped the leather strap over the hammer of his pistol and lifted it out of the holster, holding it at his side. It seemed heavier than it should, pulling on his shoulder, and he switched it to his right hand. Sweat ran down his ribs and he plucked his shirt away so it wouldn't stick.

In his experience violence arrives when it wants to, and if it wants you it'll find you, just like lightning. It's the frail woman hardly noticed, quietly nursing a glass of wine until the wine spills and she has a steak knife in her ex-husband's new wife, or the big, sorry boy out of the oilfields gone apeshit in a fight, or the fresh butchery of a car wreck, and this deal tonight might not be anything at all. He was stalling. So far this was only a call-in from Denise Rickert about something that didn't sound like it should, but then Denise has lived thirty-nine years with old Bobby Rickert and never said hi, bye or kiss my ass about that arrangement, so whatever else she might be, it sure as hell isn't prone to complaint.

The side of the trailer reflected dully in the moonlight, and he stood there for another minute. There was a lamp on in what he imagined was the bedroom, but the orange drapes were drawn. A radio was playing country music, faintly, though it wasn't a song he remembered having heard.

He stepped out of the gravel and into the overgrown meadow grass to the side of the drive so his footfalls wouldn't give him away. His heart raced as he thumbed back the pistol's hammer, taking in three deep breaths. That's the part he always forgets. To breathe.

He stopped next to the trailer, just below its wooden stoop, and breathing wasn't a problem anymore. He sucked at the air as though he'd gained altitude, feeling the heat against his face and smelling the jumble of what remained: the sharp, acrid scent of burned chemicals and plastics, the sweet, sewer reek of propane, all of it seemingly extinguished by gallons of cat piss. And tonight there was something else, the odor of a branding, of burned hair and flesh.

He pulled the gas mask from his service belt and fit it over his head, thinking of the rookie deputy who got charged up last year and stormed a lab like this, inhaling enough of the fumes to have him drawing benefits from the county for the rest of his sicker-than-shit life.

At least there wasn't a dog. Not yet, that is. He'd hate to have to kill a dog.

The door stood ajar and he pushed it back slowly with the barrel of the pistol, holding it up between himself and whatever was going to come at him. Nothing did. "Sheriff's office," he called, but most of that announcement echoed inside the mask.

The sound of his breathing filled his ears when he stepped through the doorway and he clenched his teeth. There was enough light from the bedroom that he didn't need a flashlight, and he swung the pistol to his left and right, and when there was nothing but the still-smoldering squalor of the front room and kitchen he moved to the windows, lifting them open in their aluminum frames, keeping the pistol trained down the hallway, thinking, *That's the sweet thing about trailers, no surprise in the layout.* He started toward the back as quickly as he could without stumbling in the debris, and when he reached the bedroom there was just the light on the nightstand where the radio was playing. He sat on the bed with both arms hanging between his knees. His shirt was stuck to his chest and across his shoulders, and when he eased the mask off the sweat ran into his eyes. He dragged a forearm across his face and switched off the radio. His hands were shaking and he slumped forward and stayed there until he steadied. Then he laid the pistol on the orange bedcover and took the handheld radio from his belt. He mopped at his forehead again before he called the office, and Starla's voice came through cheap and tinny.

"This is Crane."

"Hey, boss." She snapped her gum, and he tried to remember if he'd ever heard her say anything with her mouth clear.

"I need an ambulance out here. I need one right now."

"Are you hurt?"

"I'm fine, but there's someone here who isn't."

"Oh, God."

"Let's just stick with being glad it's not me." He heard her hit the speed dial for the hospital on the office console.

"You still out on Cabin Creek?" The gum snapping was like static.

"I'm in that trailer Jake Croonquist put out for his foreman. Where the road turns to gravel past mile marker twenty-four."

He listened as she repeated the information to the dispatcher at the hospital, setting the handheld down by the pistol, shaking his left arm over the side of the bed. It felt like it had gone to sleep.

"You need me to locate one of your deputies?"

He grabbed up the handheld. "Say again?"

"Do you need backup?"

"I'm all right." He shook his arm harder. "Have those boys pick up Dan Westerman on their way out."

"Oh, my God, Crane. Tell me this isn't something you had to do."

"Somebody else did it before I got here."

"But you're sure?"

"I believe I'd know if I killed a man."

"I mean, are you sure you need the coroner?"

"Jesus Christ, Starla."

"Oh, God."

"I wish you'd stop with that."

"You want me to call Jean?"

"No," he said, "but I'm going to need a DCI unit before I can leave."

"Is that everything?"

"I guess Jean'll see I'm okay when I get home."

"Roger that."

He sat for a minute longer, then pulled a pair of latex gloves from his shirt pocket and snapped them on. He pushed against his knees to help himself stand, holstering the pistol when he noticed it lying on the bed.

He went back down the hallway, turning on the lights as he found the switches, and stopped in the kitchen. He opened the refrigerator. Half a pizza, a carton of Marlboro Lights and three bottles of decent lager from a brewery in Red Lodge, Montana. He twisted the cap off a beer, draining it without taking a breath. He set the empty bottle on the countertop that separated the kitchen from the living room and opened another beer, carrying it to the couch that sat squared against the far wall. The dead man lay curled on the floor at the end of it, with a ruptured propane bottle right in front of him and the rest of the floor strewn with melted and misshapen containers that once held benzene, Freon, white gas and black iodine. The rest of the mess was the tubing and pans, here and there the charred foil discarded from dozens of cards of cold tablets. The TV was turned on its side, next to a fire extinguisher with the pin pulled.

He wedged the beer between the cushions of the couch and knelt by the body. The head, shoulders and chest were badly burned, the flesh puckered, crusted black, frosted with foam from the extinguisher. When he noticed the sweep of blood leaking back toward the wallboard he gently lifted the head out of it, turning the misshapen face toward the light. There was a hole punched in the left temple, and he could feel the lack of skull in his palm, where the bullet had exited at the top of the spine. He lowered the head back into the blood, slumping back on his heels, his hands on his thighs, palms up and smeared.

"Fuck me." He could smell the beer on his breath when he spoke, and peeled the gloves off.

He worked a billfold out of the dead man's jeans, and when he heard the ambulance turn off the highway and cut its siren, and then the crunch of tires in the gravel drive, he was sitting on the couch with the wallet in one hand and the beer in the other. "Come on in," he called.

"Is that Crane?"

"Yeah, it is."

Dan Westerman stood in the doorway. "You need all of us?"

"We better start with just you."

Dan stepped in gingerly, lifting a foot to check the sole. "Is it safe?"

"I believe it is, mostly. Just watch where you walk, and I'd hose off when you get back home."

Dan wore dark green shorts with cargo pockets, a yellow knit shirt, white cotton socks and slip-on Birkenstocks. He held a small green duffel at his side. They were both staring at the body.

"The kids are home for the summer," he said. "We were up talking when Starla called, and I didn't have time to change."

"I'm sorry to get you out here for this."

Dan stepped to the body and squatted, pulling on a pair of gloves and zipping open the duffel, and Crane closed his eyes against the series of camera flashes, then watched while Dan bagged the hands and examined the bullet wound in the head, finally standing away.

"I'm not going to be able to tell you a whole lot out here."

"I didn't expect you to."

"I thought they were cooking most of this shit in Mexico now and trucking it in. The skin that's not fried on this poor bastard's too pale for a Mexican national."

Crane held up the wallet. "He's from over in Sheridan."

"You know him?"

"I know his parents, though now I wish I didn't. He was only nineteen."

Dan looked back at the body as if it appeared younger to him. "That's just getting started."

"That's all it is."

"When I was a kid the most I could get my hands on was Coors beer and weak-ass reefer." He zipped the duffel shut and lifted it up.

"It's not like that anymore. We've gone miles past that."

Dan just nodded, still staring down at the body. "Something like this, you might never find out who else was in here."

Crane struggled out of the couch and walked to the kitchen, taking the last beer from the refrigerator. He lined the second empty next to the other on the counter. "Contaminated evidence," he explained.

"You all right?"

"No, I'm not." He leaned against the counter. "Whoever shot this boy's ruined his own goddamn life too. That's what I'm thinking." He sipped the beer. "Whether I find him or not, this here isn't something you just forget you did."

"I don't think I could." Dan called to the two paramedics standing beside the ambulance and they pulled a gurney from the back, righting it in the gravel. A body bag was folded on top. He took a step into the kitchen so they wouldn't have to go around him. "You sure you don't want to keep him out here so the investigation team can have a look?"

"They can look at the pictures." They watched the men start toward the trailer with the gurney. "I need to come in and see you next week if you've got a spot."

Dan turned back to him. "You think something's wrong with you?"

Crane extended his left arm, drawing the hand into a loose fist. "I've got no grip left."

"That could be a lot of things."

"Well, it feels like something's broke, that's for damn sure, and this here"—he pointed at the dead boy with the hand that held the beer bottle—"is just the kind of thing that can get to a man's heart."

# Four

Aᴛᴛᴇʀ ѕʜᴇ ᴅɪᴅ the breakfast dishes and Einar said he might soak in the tub, she slipped out past the barn to her studio, thankful to have an hour just to herself. She wedged four mounds of clay onto the worktable and kneaded it to the consistency she preferred, wrapping it in plastic so it wouldn't dry out. She knew it might be a day or two before she had the time to get back to it.

She was returning to the house, wiping her hands on a scrap of rag, when Paul turned the Rocking M one-ton into the yard. McEban rode with him, filling the passenger side of the cab so completely that it appeared they'd bought the truck a size too small. His arm hung out the window with the hand spread against the door panel, holding himself, as best he could, away from Kenneth, who sat squeezed between the two men. They were pulling a four-horse gooseneck trailer and parked in the shade of the cottonwoods.

She watched from the porch as they stepped the saddled horses out, tying their leadropes off to the trailer, the last of them a rangy bay wearing a packsaddle. The air was grainy with pollen and insects and the settling dust.

"Who's here?" Einar called from the dining room.

"My fencing crew."

Kenneth moved among the horses with the seriousness of a

newly hired man, careful not to get kicked or cause an accident, but when McEban started toward the house the boy came apart, jostling a shoulder against McEban's hip and bouncing away, turning back into just an unbullied and sweet-natured kid who'd gotten a good night's sleep.

Paul stayed with the horses, and when McEban was close enough she called, "Coffee's still hot."

He stopped short of the steps, thumbing his hat back from his face, Kenneth doing the same with the bill of his cap. They both were smiling. "I'm all coffeed up," he said.

"How about you, Kenneth? Would you like a glass of milk?"

"I'm all milked up."

He was grinning clownishly, and she had to ask him to repeat himself because he'd become so tickled he hadn't gotten the words out clearly on the first try. Then she said, "I'll be ready in a flash."

"You can take your time if you want." McEban checked his watch. "It's early yet."

Einar stepped through the screen door behind her carrying the sack lunches she'd packed and left on the counter. His shirt was neatly buttoned at his throat and he wore his town hat, walking more assuredly, less stooped, than when it was just the two of them. He thrust his jaw toward McEban. "I see you're still about as thick as a skinned ox."

"Hey yourself, you old bastard." McEban plucked a can of Copenhagen from his shirt pocket and pinched out a dab. "You operating a catering business now in your dotage?"

Einar held the bags out to Griff, who took them in both hands. "I'm her silent partner," he said, lowering himself into a porch chair. "My part of the deal here is to keep quiet and watch her get the work done."

McEban settled the tobacco behind his lip, brushing his fingers against his pants while Kenneth worked his tongue around his bottom front teeth like he was adjusting a chew of his own.

"That must be Mr. Kenneth you've brought with you."

McEban stared down at the boy as though surprised to find him there. "Why, yes sir, it seems like it must be."

"Say something so I know McEban's not lying."

The boy stepped up onto the worn timber of the lowest step. "We got a new colt at the sale barn in Sheridan last week," he announced. "If he works out he's going to be mine and nobody else's."

He looked back at McEban, making sure the statement wasn't inflated, and Griff started toward the horses, pinching the boy's arm as she passed, feeling lucky to have always enjoyed the company of men.

McEban dragged a chair next to Einar's and Kenneth sat up on the railing, straight-backed and attentive, swinging his legs.

"She ask you about coffee?" Einar asked.

"I guess I'm over the coffee part of the day."

The early light made their hands and faces appear glassy and little used, and Einar strained over his lap to have a better look at the boy, finally relaxing back into the chair, pulling his glasses off and holding them against his leg. The kid's image held clearly in his mind and he wished Mitch was sitting here with him, with his better eyesight and easy humor, and then he felt embarrassed that this good morning wasn't enough for him without summoning the dead. He closed his eyes, trying to remember anything of what it was like to have been a boy, and what came to him was how each day had emerged as though freshly coined, and endless. He remembered the safety he'd felt under the care of his parents, and the cowboys who'd worked for them, primarily Simon Samuelson, but also Karl Tibbetts and J. L. Manz. He remembered the hours spent studying those hired men, listening to damn near everything they cared to say, supposing the example of their lives would offer up a blueprint for what it might take for him to become a man. He still missed every one of them but had no expectation of joining their number. It was his belief that those who were gone convened in the minds of the living as merely flashes of familiar light. He didn't imagine heaven anything like his mother had, as some potluck in the basement of a Lutheran church, but he maintained specific memories of those he cared for and expected Griff to remember him. If she did, he thought that might prove sufficient in terms of an afterlife.

He heard the boy whisper a question and McEban stand out of his chair, spitting over the railing. "I don't know," he said, "I guess you could go in the house or just down there off the end of the porch if you can't wait."

Einar watched the boy wriggling away from them, working at his zipper. "When I was a young fella," he said, trying to make it come out as simply informational, "I used to have to hook it under that railing not to piss in my eyes." That was how J. L. Manz had told it, with just a hint of regret in his voice. "Now I'm left with laying it across the top rail so I don't piss on my shoes."

The boy tried out a laugh but wasn't completely sure what had been funny, looking at McEban for a clue. He was standing knock-kneed, hunched over his belt buckle.

"Just go on," McEban said. "We can talk about it later." And then, to Einar, "I don't suppose I'll have to explain gravity to him ever again."


Paul led the bay through the corrals and Griff fell in beside him. Against their silence, the resonant bass of the creek, the ascending notes of a single meadowlark and the soft, fleshy chitter of the cottonwoods kept lively in the morning downdraft. She thought to reach out to take his hand but wouldn't, and that set up an itch, a slight but specific panic like wanting a cigarette and not having one. It was a feeling she liked.

Royal stood ahead of them, saddled and tied to a rail where the corrals met the corner of the barn, nickering at their approach. Leaning against the side of the barn were two wooden posts, a length of four-by-four-inch lumber for a cross brace, a bundle of steel posts and, tucked beneath them, two box panniers with a packcover and lashrope laid across the top.

She'd been out at dawn, packing the panniers with a half-used spool of barbed wire, sacks of staples and clips, a come-along, the Swede saw, spikes, a hammer and chisel, fencing pliers and a driver for the steel posts. She'd stood quietly picturing where the fence was down and exactly what would be required to mend it. Then she'd repacked each pannier, padding all the loose tools with burlap sacking, hefting first one and then the other to balance their weights.

Now she held the packhorse while Paul lifted the panniers up on each side of the animal, adjusting their straps over the bucks to level them.

"It'll be a light load." These were the first words he'd spoken to her.

She heard Kenneth giggle from the porch and wondered which man had made him laugh. Hearing Einar laugh too, she thought she should have people over more often.

"Is your sister home?"

"Should be next week." He was balancing the posts on top of the panniers, positioning them where they belonged, making sure they wouldn't rub against the horse's shoulders. "You can drop that leadrope," he said. "He's not going anywhere."

The gelding stood solidly. He didn't even shy when they shook the packcover over the posts and it bellied in the wind before they could tuck it behind the sides of the panniers.

"She bought a color printer in Denver," he said. "Had it UPSed up to the ranch." He was uncoiling the lashrope. "So she can print up diplomas for the white women who take her classes." He stood back from the horse. "I'm not tall enough to tie a hitch over all this."

She went into the granary and returned with a five-gallon

bucket, turning it up by the horse's side, and he threw the lashrope over and stepped onto the bucket. He steadied himself against the pannier, looking down at her. "She had Kenneth help her think up fake Indian names like Lightning Flower, or Crystal Walker, or whatever she thought might get her a tip on top of tuition."

Griff handed the cinch back under the horse's belly, taking up the slack, slinging the pannier on the offside, and taking the slack again. She held tight while he finished the hitch, and when he stepped down from the bucket they backed away to appreciate their work.

"Doesn't that look exactly like a load of shit," he said.

"You want to do it over?"

"I don't know how I would. I guess it'll look better after we get those posts off and set." He led the bay in a circle, walking backward to see how the pack rode. "Rita says everybody wants to be Indian if they're not. You all set?"

"I guess."

She brought Royal around and they led the horses back through the corrals, stopped at the gate and watched as Kenneth jumped down from the porch, racing to the Russian olive by the corner of the house. He was ducking and feinting, keeping his left arm extended, reaching over his shoulder with his right hand, bringing it forward as though plucking some invisible harp.

"What's he doing?" she said.

"Killing Orcs. McEban bought him the boxed set of those Middle Earth movies. They've watched them six or seven times."

The boy started to make arrow sounds, the sounds of arrows striking Orcs.

"You think this'll take us all day?" he asked.

"Are you still mad?"

They were sitting back against the wheel fender now, waiting for McEban to notice and say his good-byes.

"No, I'm okay."

He was kicking a boot heel back into the divot he'd made in the soft ground in front of the tire. It was something he used to do as a kid, ten years ago when Rita had moved them in with McEban.

"I know RISD isn't the only art school in the country," she said. "If I thought I could go back to school I'd find something in Chicago."

"Right."

"I would."

"It's too nice a day to fight about this."

"Or you could stay."

"In Wyoming?"

"It'd make McEban happy."

He stepped a boot up against the tire, tightening his spur leather on that one and then the other. "I like it in Chicago."

"Because the grass is greener?" She couldn't keep the taunt out of her voice.

"Sometimes the grass is greener."

"Define greener."

He turned toward her, leaning into the truck's sidewall. "Greener's being able to go out for a beer and not have the rest of the bar waiting for Tonto to get drunk and piss his pants, or pull a knife and go to scalping, and you know goddamn well that's how it can feel for me here."

"You got us all ready?" McEban called, coming down off the porch.

"Just waiting on you," Paul called back.

"You're right," she said. "It's too nice a day."

She stepped to the packhorse while he pulled his chaps from where he'd draped them across the seat of his saddle. He belted them and bent to buckle the leg straps.

"I love you," she said, watching Kenneth fall in behind McEban, covering his back against attack, Einar standing there at the railing looking on. She knew all he could see were the shapes of them, the movement.

"I know you do." He stepped up onto his horse.

They worked in pairs, McEban and Kenneth, she and Paul, repairing the small defects in the fences running west up through the foothills, tightening, splicing, hammering in new staples where they were needed. By late morning they'd gained the bench to the south of Owl Creek, where the elk had crowded up out of the steep drainage, and for the next two hours they all worked together replacing the corner brace and restretching the wire.

Kenneth sliced his palm with the wood chisel and McEban bandaged it with his bandanna and the boy paraded the bloody hand like a gift. They were sweated out and hot, all of them, and the day remained faultless, a dozen swollen white clouds to break up the blue, the wind steady enough to keep the flies down.

"How we doing?" McEban asked. He took a plastic Pepsi bottle filled with water from a saddlebag, drinking half and then passing it over to Kenneth.

"The top two wires are down for about a hundred yards just half a mile west of here," she told him. "And the corner brace is rotted out."

"That's it?"

"That's all of it."

"Well, shit. I don't see why you couldn't have managed this by yourself."

"I was lonely." She winked at Kenneth.

"Me too," Kenneth said.

"You were?" McEban knelt in front of the boy, rewrapping his hand. "Well, then, that's another matter altogether."

They led their horses to a shaded spring set high in a depression grown thick with wildflowers, holding the reins away from the animals' front feet while they drank, pulling the bridles off so they could fan through the tall grass, trailing their halter ropes as they grazed.

They ate their lunches spread out around the spring, and when they were done McEban lay back with his hat tipped over his eyes, his hands laced behind his head, and Kenneth, lying back against him, pretended to sleep, watching Griff and Paul where they sat together in the sun against the sidehill across from him.

Paul leaned back on his elbows. "Did you hear about the guy Crane found dead in the trailer house?"

"My mom said Crane knows who he is but wouldn't tell her. She said it was a meth lab."

"I always thought that could've been me," he said.

She shaded her eyes. "You've never done drugs in your life." She watched him turn the stem of a weed in his fingers, tying it in a knot.

"I mean I expect something like that. I don't know. Something sudden."

She hooked a finger in one of his belt loops as though she was afraid he might fade and then vanish entirely, lying back against him, resting her head in the curve of his hip. "From now on I want you to call me Divine Tiger Woman."

"You want what?"

"Divine Tiger Woman."

He chuckled, genuinely surprised. "You think that sounds Indian?"

"I think it sounds more Indian than Lightning Whatever. Anyway, she was *East* Indian."

"And here I was thinking you pulled the name out of your butt."

She was watching the clouds scud to the east, and their movement made her feel as though she were rolling slowly away from him. She put a hand down to steady herself. "Every man who ever made love to her never had to come back to a lower life."

"You mean like a prairie dog? Or a worm?"

"You've got it."

He laughed again, enjoying himself, easing out from under her, getting up on his knees.

She squinted against the sun. "You don't always have to say the whole thing. When we're around other people you could shorten it to DTW. Everybody wouldn't have to know how lucky you are."

He leaned over her, casting her face in shadow. "What do you think, Kenneth? You think I ought to kiss her?"

When the boy nodded without lifting his head from McEban, Paul kissed her and sat back on his heels.

"I can't leave him," she said. "Not the way he is now."

He pulled a notepad and pen from his shirt pocket. "You understand he could live a lot longer."

"I hope he does." She cocked an arm under her head. "You writing me a poem?"

"I'm writing down what we did today." He waved a bee away from his face, watching it dip and sputter toward the creek. "Something about where the fence was down. When we got thirsty and how our mouths tasted like wood. How the horses made out." He looked across at McEban and the boy. "Maybe something about when Kenneth cut his hand."

"Like a diary?"

He held the notebook against his thigh, writing. "For Einar. So I won't forget to tell him. It's not like he can get out here with us."

She lay back in the warm, sweet grass, after a bit throwing an arm across her face, over her eyes, in case the tears started. Because sometimes they did when she was filled with the certainty that he was here mostly just for her, to get her started out right, and she's never once felt it would last her whole life. She rolled her arm just slightly, so she could see his outline against the sun.

# Five

CRANE SHIFTED his weight against the chairseat, working his knuckles down the tops of his thighs and back along the outsides, and when that didn't help he stood and paced along the east wall of the waiting room. This new cramping seemed to twist at the muscles deep inside his legs, usually when he was tired or uneasy. He sat down again and leafed through a three-month-old *Smithsonian*. Pictures of a South American rain forest, melting icepacks, the statuary at Angkor Wat. Then the discomfort started tapering off and he tossed the magazine on top of the low table beside the chair.

Two young mothers sat across from him. When he caught their eyes they nodded, smiling earnestly, as people always do with cops, then leaned back together in conversation, lowering their voices, glancing now and then to where their children played in a carpeted corner of the room. Two boys and a girl, all under six, crawling in and out of a high-impact-plastic playhouse, rising up out of the scatter of high-impact-plastic toys, the distraction provided to keep them occupied and forgetful about what was going to come next. Old man Houle was curled forward on an orange plastic chair by the row of windows overlooking the street.

Under the Muzak and the constant squabbling of the children he could hear the hum of fluorescent lighting and closed his eyes, trying to remember how the old Heyneman Building looked just a year and a half ago, before Sheridan Memorial had it gutted and renovated into this satellite clinic. He could still smell the paint, or something like it, maybe just something antiseptic.

When he'd told Jim and Nancy Tylerson their son was dead, that his body had been terribly burned, that he'd been shot as well and possibly hadn't suffered too much, not as much as he would've if the fire had been what killed him, Nancy slumped against the doorframe of their home and vomited over the front of her sweatshirt. Then she collapsed on the concrete stoop beside the worn brown welcome mat. Jim knelt next to her, holding her until there was nothing left in her stomach. He held her even when it was apparent she had no intention of getting off her hands and knees, or out of the soiled clothing, or of wiping her face. She was wagging her head back and forth, with streams of spittle hanging from her mouth and tangling in her long hair, and Jim said, "I'm going to need some help here."

It took both of them to get her up and into the house, finally onto the couch in the front room. She flailed and moaned, seeming to weigh twice what he might have guessed, as though her grief had somehow intensified the pull of gravity, drawing her away from them and into the earth.

He sat with her while Jim went into the kitchen to find a damp cloth to clean his wife's face. For a short while she sobbed quietly, then stiffened and began clawing at him, and he was forced to grip her wrists, pinning them crosswise in her lap, and still she twisted and shrieked that she hoped he'd die just like her son had. Then she spat in his face.

Jim got her to swallow a sleeping pill, and when they felt they could briefly leave her lying on the couch with her eyes wide but unfocused, they went back outside and walked to the curb. They stood by the cruiser, staring into the sky, and he told Jim again how sorry he was. He said there'd been drugs involved and that he didn't want him to read about it in the paper without already knowing. Jim nodded, once, then he sat down on the curb. He didn't weep or curse, just sat there with his head bowed, and after a while he got to his feet and looked back at the house. "I don't know what I ought to do now," he said. "I haven't a clue."

When Crane heard his name called he got out of the chair. A thick, mannish-looking woman stood in the doorway beside the receptionist's cubicle, lifting her chin to indicate that he was next, and he followed her down the single hallway and into a windowless white room. She had him step on a scale, then he sat on a stool so she could take his blood pressure and temperature. She asked him to roll up his sleeve.

She thumped at the blood vessel on the inside of his arm and inserted the needle, loosening the rubber tubing she'd cinched around his biceps. They both watched as she filled three vials with his blood, then she had him fold his arm back against a cotton ball.

She got a light blue hospital gown from a drawer and handed it to him. "You'll need to put this on," she said.


He had a leg crossed on his knee and was examining a mole on his calf, comparing it to the stage-four mole on the skin-cancer chart hanging on the wall, when Dan walked in, apologizing for the wait.

For the next half hour they talked about their inability to afford the homes they wanted, the sorry rise of evangelical right-wingers and how video games were turning out a generation of surly clerks, while Dan listened to his heart, looked in his ears, eyes and throat, pushed and prodded his abdomen, checked his reflexes, finally pricking him here and there with a pin and asking if he could feel it. Or that's how it came to be lumped together in his memory, as a single blunted and humiliating episode, but about a hundred times easier than telling a man and woman that the child they'd loved and raised was now lost to them.

He then sat on the end of the examination table, watching Dan at the sink in the corner. He made a fist with his left hand and the grip seemed improved. His arm just tingled, and his legs weren't cramping anymore.

"Why don't you put your pants and boots on and we'll see what your heart's got to say." Dan was drying his hands.

"Not my shirt?"

"You'd just have to take it off again."

He followed Dan to a room at the end of the hallway where a young, pale nurse stuck electrodes on his bare chest and guided him onto a treadmill. "It goes easy like this if you don't have much hair on your chest," she said, her voice sounding more like chirping than speech.

Dan stood at the head of the machine, studying the readout while they worked him into a trot and faster still, until he hardly had enough air to shout that he ought to be allowed to quit.

Dan tore the printout evenly away from the machine, folding it back upon itself as he started for the door. "Come on down to the office when you've got your breath."

Crane stood crosswise on the inclined tread, gripping the handrail, red-faced and gasping, and the nurse helped him off onto the tiled floor where he stood leaning into her. She was strong for her size.

He sat across the desk from Dan, still overheated, only half-listening to the telephone conversation Dan was having with a doctor at the Billings Clinic. He pulled off his right boot and sock, and when Dan hung up, writing something on a notepad, not saying anything at all, Crane said, "My foot's blistered." He moved the pad of a thumb over the blister forming on the ball behind his big toe.

Dan held a slip of paper pinched up in front of him, both forearms resting on the desktop. "I should've told you to wear tennis shoes."

"It's not my heart, is it?"

"No, your heart's just fine." He leaned forward in his chair, and Crane took the slip of notepaper he offered. "Bill McCarthy's a good guy," he said. "He's up in Billings but well worth the drive."

Crane nodded, folding the paper and slipping it behind the bills in his wallet. He saw the appointment was scheduled for one-thirty in the afternoon, so he wouldn't have to wake in the dark to get there in time. He hated waking up at night. "Should I wear tennis shoes?"

"No, you're done with that. McCarthy's a neurologist."

Crane nodded again, pulling his boot back on.

"This doesn't have to be what you think it is," Dan said.

Crane stood out of the chair. He put his hat on, squaring it. "You don't know what I'm thinking. You're not that kind of doctor."

"But I know you never thought it was your heart."

He didn't sleep well that night, or the next, or any of the nights before he told Jean he had to escort a prisoner to Billings and drove by himself to the clinic.

That had been a week ago, and this afternoon he was standing on the screened-in porch off the east end of the house, watching Jean work in her garden. He was on the phone. First it'd been McCarthy's nurse, but now it was the doctor.

"There're a few more tests I'd like you to consider."

McCarthy's voice sounded farther away than Montana, as if he were calling from somewhere overseas, and Crane wanted to ask, "Did I flunk the others?" or something smart-ass like that, but he hadn't been able to finish his cereal that morning, his left hand wobbling so much he couldn't keep the spoon level. He asked, "Is there a problem with the tests we already did?"

"No, Mr. Carlson, the other tests were conclusive."

"You can call me Crane."

"Then how about Monday, Crane?"

Jean was dragging a cardboard box behind her, filling it with weeds. When it got too heavy to drag she'd empty it into the wheelbarrow.

"If you have something to tell me I'd rather hear it now."

"I'd prefer to discuss this in person, Crane."

"I'm not coming back up there."

There was a pause on the line, the sound of papers being shuffled. Jean scooted a foam pad ahead of her in the row, kneeled on it and pulled the sodden box along. The bottom was stained dark and looked about ready to tear.

"Your electromyogram indicates certain abnormalities, and along with the other—"

"It's Lou Gehrig's, isn't it?" He moved the phone to his other ear, watching Jean staring up at the sun, checking the advancement of the afternoon. It seemed clear to him how alone she must feel, how little he'd done to fill any part of her life.

"Yes, it is. It's ALS."

He sat back against the edge of the wrought-iron table, heard its legs scrape on the redwood and then catch, holding his weight. "Well, goddamn."

"I'm very sorry, but I think it's important for you to come in and—"

"I don't suppose you've got a cure now?"

"What I'd like to talk about are your treatment options, Crane. We need to set up a schedule to monitor the possible progressions I believe you can expect."

Again, the shuffling of papers.

"What I can expect is to lose more control of what muscles I've got, until a year or two from now when I'll die choking on my own spit."

"That isn't exactly how I'd choose to characterize it."

"It's what killed my granddad."

At the funeral for the Tylerson boy he'd sat in a back pew, and when Nancy came in, walking very straight with her hands forming fists at her sides, she'd stopped at the end of the row, staring directly at him. Her mouth hung open slightly, like she might be about to speak, or else just didn't care about closing it anymore, and even though it had only been a little more than a week since he'd seen her, she appeared older, like she wasn't there at all and had sent her mother instead.

"I'm not finding that in your medical history."

"I didn't put it down."

"There's a great deal that's changed, Mr. Carlson. With nasal ventilation, patients can now expect—"

"The same thing they always could." He hung up, set the phone on the table and pushed through the screen door, standing on the apron of gravel below the stoop. He couldn't remember if he'd intended to go any farther, but at least he was away from the phone.

"Who was that?" Jean called.

"Work," he said.

"I thought you were taking a long weekend."

"I am. Starla was just checking in." His sunglasses were resting on the top of his head, and he pulled them off, cleaned the lenses with his handkerchief and put them on. The sky fell a deeper blue. "You want to go for a drive?"

She stabbed her gardening trowel into a hump of dirt and stood. "I can't. I need to study for my exam." She placed her hands on her hips, pushing them around in a tight circle. She was wearing flowered gloves.

"When's that?"

"Next week, but I'm behind."

She peeled the gloves off, tossing them beside the trowel, and pinched a joint out of her shirt pocket and lit it. She took a drag, holding the smoke in.

"I thought you'd quit that." He tried to spit but his mouth was too dry. He watched her exhale through her nose.

"I did for a while. I decided I didn't need to quit forever."

He turned toward the neighbors' house to see if they were out in their yard, and when he looked back she was holding the joint up in front of her face, examining it like it was a bug she'd never seen before.

"Don't you just love the shit out of Rose?" she said.

"Rose Bauman?"

She nodded, clenching the joint between her teeth, squatting to get the weed box cradled up in her arms. "Her son sends it to her from San Diego." Her head was tilted back to keep the smoke out of her eyes and she lurched forward, kicking out with her feet until she hit the wheelbarrow. She dropped the box in just as the bottom came apart.

"I can't hear you when you've got something in your mouth."

She cupped the joint in her left hand, bending the hand forward to rub at her eyes with the back of her wrist. When she was done she said, "It helps with Rose's glaucoma."

A hummingbird hovered for an instant between them, its wings buzzing as it banked away, and the sudden lack of sound produced the effect of a greater silence. Then a dog barked, a car passed in the street, someone started a lawn mower down the block.

They both stood watching the hummingbird arc back over the house, returning to a border of marigolds.

She took another hit, holding the smoke in, pointing back at the wheelbarrow. "Could I get you to empty that for me?"

"Sure."

He stepped past the tomato plants starting up lush and bushy in their wire cages, and carefully over the deep green peppers, lifting the handles and pushing the wheelbarrow through the soft dirt to the northwest corner of the garden, where he'd dug a compost pit in the spring. He turned it up, tilting it over onto the heap of decomposing weeds and kitchen waste. The wheel was caked with mud and spun slowly in the air, and the bottle flies rose from the soggy mulch in a high-pitched drone.

"You hungry?" she called. She held the screen door open but hadn't yet stepped up onto the porch.

"I'm good for now," he said. "But maybe after I take my drive."

# Six

KENNETH FINISHED clearing the table and when he had the oil-cloth sponged clean he joined McEban at the sink. He shook a dishtowel out and dried the plates already washed and leaned up edgewise in the rack, and then they shelved them away in the cupboards and slotted the silverware back in the drawer. They left the pans to air-dry, tilted so they'd drain. It's how they clean up every evening, and the boy will be eleven this winter and they never have treated each other like father and son, they've always managed better than that.

He pushed their chairs in at the table, draping the towel over the backladder of a chair. The screen door to the mudroom stood open but the outside door was still closed against the day's heat.

"It'll go quicker with both of us," McEban said.

The boy glanced down the hallway, where they could hear water running in the bathroom. "It's your turn," he said. "I got to go to town with her this morning." He smiled. "Anyway, she's just my mom."

McEban stripped off his yellow Playtex gloves, hanging them over the edge of the dishrack, and opened the window above the sink. He leaned back against the counter, looking down the hallway himself. "I don't need to see her tonight. I can spend all day tomorrow with her."

They heard the water shut off and the pipes knock behind the wallboards and stop, leaving only an argument among the grackles in the windbreak, the distant lowing of cattle.

"She might not be here tomorrow," the boy told him.

McEban nodded, digging his pocketknife out of his jeans. He cleaned a thumbnail, slipping the knife back into the pocket. "I guess you've always known more about it than I have," he said.

The boy moved to the mudroom and sat down on the bench to pull a pair of hip waders on over his boots. The waders were faded a blotchy gray and patched and too big for him and he had to cuff the tops down twice. When he stood in the doorway he looked like a shrunken and shoddy musketeer.

"I should get used to changing the water by myself," he said, then shrugged as if to underscore the obvious. "So I know I can."

He drew the door shut against its broken spring, his features clouded by the screen. McEban thought it made him appear younger than he was, and wondered if they even made waders for kids. He thought he'd have a look in the Cabela's catalog later on. "Have it your way," he said, "but be careful at that headgate."

The boy turned away, waving like there was a chance he'd be gone longer than the irrigating required, and McEban watched him go down the drive kicking a rock ahead of him through the loose gravel, a shovel slung over his shoulder. At the edge of the pasture he bent through the fence and, when he was clear of the wires, slapped the blade of the shovel into the ditch, a spray of water fanning up before him, sparkling in the sunlight. For a moment McEban felt a jolt of contentment, something akin to a boy's decent happiness.

He popped a handful of ice cubes loose from a tray, filled a glass with the cubes and quartered a lime.

Then he lifted the bottle of tequila down from a cupboard, easing the glass stopper out and holding it under his nose. Roses, cinnamon, vanilla. At three hundred dollars a bottle he'd come to imagine it as the scent of an exotic perfume. The ice cracked when he filled the glass. "Herradura Seleccion Suprema." He liked to pronounce the name out loud. He'd done the same thing the first time he ordered a bottle on the Internet with Paul leaning over his shoulder, eating an apple while he studied the screen.

"Jesus Christ," Paul had said. "Are you sure?"

"I'm sure it's the right kind. I heard her say it once." He turned in the chair. "That it was the best. Can I have a bite of that?"

Paul handed him the apple, reached around to the mouse and scrolled down the screen. "Creamy to the palate," he read aloud, then stood away. "I guess it better be." And then: "It's your money. You want to spend it on my sister, that's fine by me. The rest of that apple's yours too."

He waited until Paul left the room before clicking on the BUY IT NOW button.

McEban carried the glass down the hallway, setting it on the floor to pull his boots off. He stood them to the side of the door, and when he smelled the sour odor of his socks he pulled them off too, then knocked on the door.

"Come in." She managed to make the two words sound like lyrics from a song.

He closed the door behind him and handed the glass down to her, and she held it balanced on the edge of the tub. He lowered the toilet seat and sat, watching as she pushed her feet against the foot of the tub to slide herself upright, closing her eyes as she sipped from the glass. Her shoulders and breasts were foamy with bath bubbles.

"Oh, that's perfect. Won't you try it, Barnum? Just once?"

"I'm okay."

"Just a taste. I want you to know what a sweet thing it is you're doing." She held the glass out to him, her arm dripping on the bathmat.

"All right."

He leaned over and took the glass from her and she slid back into the water, her knees folding up out of the bubbles. He took a sip, holding it in the back of his mouth, wondering if Kenneth was having trouble with the dams.

"It's wonderful, isn't it?" Her face was turned toward him, watching as he swallowed.

"It's good."

"Just good?"

"I thought it might be better."

"It's not a crime to enjoy yourself." She turned the hot-water faucet with a foot, until it started drizzling. "If you're done you can set it there on the floor."

He placed the glass on the bathmat, the sides already slick with condensation.

"The ranch looks better than I remember," she said.

"You were only gone three weeks."

"It always looks better than I remember."

"I might open this window a little," he said. The boy was probably now at the headgate. He imagined the water boiling in the chute as the slide was raised, the smell of alfalfa and clover.

"If you're hot you could always take off those heavy clothes."

She was widening and closing her knees, the movement stirring the bubbles into islands.

He pushed the bottom sash up a couple of inches, watching the steam bleed out through the opening. "I'm okay."

"I forgot," she said. "I forgot we don't do that anymore." She leaned over the side for another sip, the water sheeting and finally beading across the blues, reds and yellows of the tattoo that covered her shoulders. Then she slipped back into the water, with her head gone under and her feet up against the tiles by the faucets.

When they were new to each other, right after Kenneth was born and Paul was the age Kenneth is now, they'd settle the older boy in his bed and skid the cradle into the hallway outside the bathroom door where they could hear the baby cooing and check on him if he wasn't. She'd take him by the hand, leading him in to sit with her while she bathed, and they'd talk about how both boys might turn out, and what she imagined she'd do with her life, asking about his past but rarely speaking of her own. When they ran out of conversation, she opened her legs and let him watch as she languidly caressed herself, one hand slowly circling, the other fingers pressing against a nipple and finally squeezing the whole breast, then the other, and he unsnapped his shirt and lowered his pants and pulled at himself just as slowly, watching as she stiffened and rose against her hands, imagining them as his own.

Afterward he cleaned himself at the sink, gaping stolidly at the big, grateful, unmarried son of a bitch in the fogged mirror, still fumbling with his pants and shirt and feelings of mild indecency. He never once believed it would go on like this forever, thinking of it as a sort of prelude, but after two years it finally occurred to him that nothing more interesting was likely to happen, that their evenings together in the bathroom held no more significance for her than the occasional load of laundry she washed and dried. She was just helping out.

He still masturbates, alone at night in his bed, but not for the pleasure of it. Now he jacks off so he can sleep.

She rose up out of the water sputtering, smoothing her hair back, and drank from the glass again. "I'll bet you're wondering what the Guides are thinking," she said.

"I wasn't, but that'd be fine."

She settled and closed her eyes, pinching her nose and then inhaling through the left nostril, clamping it shut, exhaling through the right. Back and forth. It's a technique she'd spent some time trying to teach him, but it only left him feeling uncomfortably lightheaded.

She dropped her hand away, breathing in heavily. The bubbles were completely gone from the water's surface and her breasts bobbed in front of her tucked chin. "They're ready."

"I guess I could hear something about Paul," he said. "If they're willing."

Her face tightened in concentration, in seriousness, and he turned to see a raven outside the window, cawing from the branches of an apple tree.

"Family questions are the hardest," she said.

The bird shifted black and silver in a shaft of sunlight, mottled where the leaves shadowed its shoulders, and she turned the faucet off with a foot without opening her eyes. There was just the sound of the overflow draining.

"This will be his last lifetime," she said. "They say he's filled with the immutable soul of the divine."

"They actually said immutable?" He was wondering if Kenneth was done setting the dam above the knob in the east pasture, but didn't feel he could just get up and go check. "What about Griff, then?"

The strain showed in her face. She spread a hand on her belly. "She's not pregnant."

"That isn't what I was thinking about." He leaned over and took another sip of tequila and put the glass back. He wanted to see if it was better the second time around. "I was only wondering if she and Paul might get married sometime."

"They say it's not yet determined."

The steam was mostly cleared from the room.

"They say there're obstacles for the female. That she's caught in a muddied vibration. Don't you want to ask about Kenneth?"

"I don't worry about Kenneth."

"You could ask the Guides about yourself if you wanted."

"I don't worry much about me, either."

She scratched the inside of her left thigh and, bringing her leg up, her calf.

He stood from the toilet. "I need to help that boy with the water. I shouldn't have let him out there by himself."

She opened her eyes. "You used to ask about us. About you and me."

"I already know something about that."

Her hand still rested on her belly. "I always think about you, Barnum. When I'm gone I always do."

"I believe you." He was standing over her now, looking down at her hair floating in dark fans to the sides of her face.

"Our souls are entwined." Her voice was even and patient, as though she was instructing a child. "They were even before we met. Can't you feel it?"

At the window a pair of pale-blue butterflies now dipped, guttering in a slight breeze.

"No," he said, "I can't."

She crossed her ankles, turning her legs out. "If we allowed ourselves the luxury of intimacy on this physical plane"—she swept her arm through the air to indicate the room, or the house, or the whole universe—"it would shatter our sacred union."

"Is that what your Guides say?"

"It's a fact my heart knows for certain."

He looked down at his feet. They were pale and dirty and he meant to shower before he went to bed, in his small upstairs bathroom. "I just wonder sometimes why you bother to drive back here like you do."

She sat straight up in the tub, shivering. "Would you close that window?"

He did.

"I come home because I miss you and Kenneth. And the ranch." She started the hot water again, dropping some bath beads in under the stream. "It's important to me to be from somewhere."

When he didn't say anything she looked up at him. She'd worked her face into a convincing expression of contrition, the kind that gets her a day's extension on the grocery coupons she's let expire.

"A thing's always sweeter when you miss it." She reached out and took his hand, pulling him toward her, guiding the hand to a breast, holding it there. "You can't miss something if you have it all the time."

He nodded, imagining how clumsy he must appear, hunched over, his knees angled into the porcelain rim of the tub, his free hand hanging uselessly at his side.

"Can you feel my heart?"

"Yes, I can." He wasn't sure he'd spoken aloud.

"I love you in my heart." She smiled full tilt, and when he thought he might tip forward he drew his hand away, wiping it on his shirttail as he straightened. He stood watching as she finished the tequila, her head thrown back, her throat smooth as jade.

"Would you be a sweetheart and fix me another?" She extended the glass, a drift of new bubbles rolling back along her thighs. "Maybe two wedges of lime this time?"

"Sure."

"Have we got plenty?"

"I bought half a dozen."

In the hallway he poured the remaining ice out of the glass into his mouth. Hearing her shut the water off again, he swallowed a trickle of melted ice, feeling as hollow as he had when he was just nineteen and his mother had left and he'd found his father sitting dead in the barn in his only suit, the pistol in his lap, his brains blown back against the upright stanchion and along the length of weathered lumber at the side of the stall. He felt he could understand how something like that might happen.

# Seven

GRIFF ROLLED to the edge of the bed and sat blinking. She was gummy with sweat, logy, and it took a moment before she could straighten up into the half dark and reel through the clothing they'd left scattered across the floor and finally into the bathroom. She ran water in the sink until it turned icy, drawn up from the bottom of the well shaft, and held the insides of her wrists under the faucet. And then she drank.

She returned to the bedroom toweling her neck, beneath her arms and breasts, and threw the towel back into the bathroom. She'd been angry when they'd made love, grasping, careless, crying out as someone drowning might, and afterward, when she was still upset, they'd made love again. Now he slept turned on his side, his knees drawn up, with a panel of moonlight on his back, the headboard and the night table.

She slipped into a robe, knotting the sash loosely, and pulled the sheet from under his legs. She covered him, set the portable fan up on the chest at the foot of the bed and turned it on. He shivered and drew the sheet over his shoulder.

In the front room she found a cup of yogurt in the refrigerator and sat at the table next to the open windows that looked out over the porch. She bent a leg underneath to sit up higher in the chair, scooping the yogurt into her mouth with a forefinger. She hadn't turned on a light, and in this darkened room the memories of Ansel Magnuson here in the evenings with his zwieback and herring and schnapps were unavoidable. And then she thought of Mitch Bradley in the bunkhouse at Einar's. Two honest bachelors hired by these separate families, consigning their lifetimes' work as though this were part of the adoption process, finally dying with the achievement of being remembered not as trusted strangers but as blood.

She mopped her forehead with the hem of the robe, the smell of her heated body rising into her face, and she couldn't think of a single thing left in this world that held the good animal scent of Ansel or Mitch.

She'd never been comfortable in the summer's heat and wondered how people managed in Mississippi or Louisiana or Latin America, and maybe it was the heat that had sparked their argument, but it still was a variation of the same fight they'd been having for the last year, this episode peculiar only because of the application she'd found in his printer. She was sitting at the kitchen table reading through the paperwork when Paul came in from his run. She held up the top sheet.

"Uganda? You're applying for a year in *Uganda*?"

She looked back at the form, trying to find an exact date, and he peeled his T-shirt over his head.

"It's just an application."

"Were you going to mention it, or just send me a postcard?"

He took the pitcher of ice water out of the refrigerator and poured a glass, drinking it down all at once, squeezing his eyes shut against the sharp pain that spiked between his brows, then pressed the heel of his free hand against his forehead.

"Are you going to answer me?"

He nodded, dropping the hand and leaning back against the counter. "They want me to do a statistical analysis of rural HIV patients. If I get it." He poured another glass full. "My thesis advisor suggested it. He said there's no problem in finishing my master's when I get back." He wiped his mouth with the T-shirt. "Anyway, I don't see what difference it makes where I go. You weren't going to come to Chicago, so now you won't come to Africa."

"Fuck you." She stood out of the chair. "I could visit you in Chicago."

"So visit me in Africa."

"For what, a weekend? How long do you think I can leave Einar?"

He sat down at the table and she walked out onto the porch. She screamed, and again even louder, then slammed the screen door when she came back in. "Did you even stop to wonder how I might feel about it?"

"It's a chance to do something I think's important."

"And when I want to take care of my grandfather, that's what? A waste of my life?"

"Now you're just being mean."

The application was spread across the table and she snatched a page, wadded it up and pitched it hard against his chest, at the same time suffering that peculiar dislocation of having been standing to the side and watching herself react like a child. She placed her hands on the table, leaning toward him. Her voice came out choked. "I don't give a shit where you go."

He reached across the table, taking her hands, holding on to them. He was smiling. "Not even the tiniest little pinch of shit?"

Unlike her, he couldn't stay mad, and that's why arguing rarely got them anywhere.

She shifted on the chair in the darkness. Beyond the porch, McEban's house stood unlighted and vague in the distance, but a light was on in Rita's Airstream, parked along the south side of the house, and the moonlight was sparkling in sweeps across the irrigated pastures, glowing on the stones spaced along the drive.

She tried to envision her father's face because she found it comforting to imagine that the dead might care for her. She pictured them waiting—thousands of years' worth of souls—with their arms outstretched, welcoming.

When she drives the two-lanes that wind through the Bighorns she often stops to sit beside the *descansos* erected in the borrow ditches. Simple crosses, some hung with wreaths of plastic flowers, once a teddy bear, once a baseball glove, almost always a message of loss: *Look homeward, Angel. If tears could build a stairway to Heaven. Your memory is my treasure.* She wonders what she might write to mark the place where her father died. Something to let him know she does not mourn.

She stood and started toward the kitchen, stopping abruptly when she heard the porchboards grind, and when a dark figure rose at the window her heart spiked and her legs jerked her backward.

"Did I scare you?" Just a whisper through the screening.

She leaned into the table, her right leg still pumping, cocked up on the ball of her foot. She'd nearly fallen.

"Hell yes, you scared me." She bent the leg up, digging at a cramp in her calf. "What are you doing out there?"

"Nothing." He bobbed up higher, spreading his arms and moaning like a cartoon ghost.

"Goddamnit, Kenneth, get in here."

The front door screeched on its hinges when he stepped into the room. "Were you thinking about something scary?" He was giggling.

"I was thinking about my dad."

She opened the refrigerator, and they squinted against the light.

"You want to go riding?"

"I'll bet you sneak down here all the time, don't you?"

"Sometimes I do." He looked toward the bedroom. "Uncle Paul never notices. I didn't mean to scare you."

She set the yogurt back in the refrigerator and closed the door.

"Do you?" he asked.

"Do I what?"

"Want to go riding?"

"Now?"

"It's too hot to sleep," he said.

He waited while she dressed, and they walked through the dappled shadows the moon cast through the cottonwoods along the creek bottom, then over a plank footbridge to the barn, the chirring of crickets and the rush of water loud in the darkness, their footfalls muffled in the duff.

He had a brown-and-white pinto bridled, the reins looped over a corral pole, and as they approached he chanted, "There now, there now," so the horse wouldn't shy, but his voice was so childishly shrill it sounded like the call of a night bird.

"We can both ride Spencer," he told her.

The horse nuzzled his broad forehead into the boy's chest, pushing him back a step, and he turned the animal against the side of the corral.

"Are you sure?" she asked.

"McEban says our dog could ride Spencer."

"You don't have a dog."

"He meant if we did."

She stepped to the horse's flank, resting an arm across his hips. "It'll just take a minute to saddle him."

"He's good to go the way he is," he said, and the horse nickered softly, as if to vouch for him.

She stood up onto the second rail, sidestepping to the horse's withers and swinging a leg over. Kenneth still stood on the ground, reaching out to her, and she gripped his wrist, pulling him up behind her. He was light as a cat, all bone and sinew and eagerness, and the horse hadn't even raised his head, standing like he'd gone to sleep.

"I told you he was okay," the boy said.

They wove through the trees on the north side of the creek, the old horse plodding, occasionally grunting in complaint, and Kenneth sat pressed against her, his arms encircling her waist.

"How far do you want to go?" she asked, but he was right, she felt refreshed, contented, her arms and face cooling, as though her body's heat was wicking out into the mottled night. She felt him shift, looking past her to get his bearings.

"Not much farther." He pressed a cheek against her shoulder blade. "I'm a little bit afraid of the dark," he admitted, and then: "Do you think my mom's crazy?"

The horse snorted at a downfall and balked before stepping over. They gripped tighter with their knees.

"What do you think?"

"If she is crazy it's probably okay."

"Then I guess it doesn't matter."

"That's what I think." He looked around her again. "Once, in a book I read, it said a kid would be okay if there was just one person to watch out for him." He was whispering. "The book was in the counselor's office at school."

"What were you doing there?" She raked her heels along the horse's ribs, and he quickened his pace.

"It was because I hit Ricky Wheeler in the neck. He's the one who said my mom was crazy, but I didn't tell the counselor that was why and Ricky didn't either. I had to apologize to the whole class." He unclasped his hands, pointing ahead to a clearing. "Up there," he said.

Then they were out of the trees and the air grew warmer, their shadows falling away to the right, lumped together and following them through the tall meadow grass.

"Can you keep a secret?"

"Sure I can." She felt him leaning into her.

"Rodney isn't just my mom's friend. He's my real dad."

He'd made the statement as plainly as if reading from a book in a counselor's office. "Who told you that?"

"Nobody did. I figured it out by myself, but I don't want you to tell McEban."

"I won't tell anybody."

There was the hollow drumming of a sage grouse beating its wings against a downed cottonwood.

"I know there's you and Uncle Paul and my mom, but if I'm going to turn out okay it's mostly because McEban's watching out for me." He dropped his hands away from her. "Right here's perfect."

She reined the horse in and he slid to the ground, pulling his T-shirt over his head, stumbling, waving an arm to right his balance, still gripping the white shirt as though it were the limp body of something he'd snatched out of the dark.

"You truly are a little shithead," she said.

"It'll be fun."

His smile flashed in the moonlight, and he sat down in the graveled apron at the edge of the creek, tugging at his boots.

"You told me we were just going riding."

"And it's not a secret." He was peeling his socks off. "You can tell anybody you know how much fun it is."

She looked at the creek, where it deepened into a long pool of flat water, edging the southern crescent of the meadow. "Who do you think I'm going to tell I went swimming in the middle of the night?"

He was on his feet again, unbuckling his belt. "Spencer likes it too," he said. "Uncle Paul and I swam him last summer."

"At night?"

He nodded. "You can ask him."

She looked to the water once more and then slid down beside him and they piled their clothes on the smooth stones, and when all he said about her nakedness was, "You're really, really white" she swung back onto the horse, pulling him up after her.

He was wriggling, twisting left and right to look past her, his knees thumping the backs of her thighs. "Put him in there." He pointed at the headwater of the pool.

"You're sure about this?"

"It's easy." He turned, shaking his hand toward the broad flash of rapids where the pool emptied. "That's where we come out. It's only cold the first time."

By the third trip through she felt as if she were shining, lit from within, and Kenneth hung on tight as the horse fell from under them, swimming, and they floated behind and above him in the sound of churning water and their laughter, his arms encircling her, their legs paddling away.

"Can we go again?" he asked.

The horse was standing in the tailwaters, blowing hard, water streaming into the shallows, and the pull of gravity had fallen upon them both again, feeling newly invented.

"Just once?" she asked. He was slippery against her. "How about as many times as you want?"

His smile went wild and he dropped his hands to her hips as she reined the old horse around toward the head of the pool.

She was cool and relaxed as she slipped into bed, and Paul woke, smiling as the boy had smiled. He swept his hair away from his eyes, listening while she told him where she'd been.

"You're still an asshole," she said.

He lay back against the pillow. "I know I am." He yawned. "Did he get a little boner?"

"Yeah, he did." She turned and settled back in against him.

"He got one with me too." She could feel his breath on her shoulder, on the back of her neck. "He's too little for it to mean anything," he said. "It just feels good."

"I know," she whispered, and pulled his arm around her and held his hand open against her belly, her eyes shut, slipping away into sleep as though adrift in clear water.

# Eight

WHEN HE WAS UP to speed, with the windows down and the swirl of summer air plucking at his shirt, he cracked open a Bud. He let a car pass, and when there wasn't another in the rearview mirror he drank down half the beer, wedging the bottle between his legs. He radioed Starla.

"Isn't it your day off?" she asked.

She sounded annoyed, as though he'd interrupted her during the last episode of *The Sopranos*.

"Just checking in. In case something comes up."

"I thought you and Jean'd be at the parade, or the rodeo or somewhere."

"I'm not feeling that festive," he said, "and anyway, there'll be a better parade tomorrow."

When there was only the sound of Starla snapping her gum he broke the connection, and ramped up onto the interstate heading south toward Sheridan, propping his elbow in the window so it wouldn't ache as much. He sipped the beer, watching the clouds mass over the Bighorns to the west. In the foreground the prairie grass stood dried and blanching, bowed heavy with hardened seed-heads, but the creek bottoms were still lush.

He stopped at a rest area just north of town and snapped open his cell phone and dialed *67 and the telephone number and sat watching a heavy woman lift a dachshund out of her RV. She tucked the dog under her arm and started for a mown patch of prairie behind the toilets.

On the third ring a woman's voice announced: "Merrick, Russell, Marcus and King."

"Is Larry there?"

The woman couldn't bend clear to the ground but she got over far enough to drop the dog, and it bounced just once and stood wagging its tail. Then it ran in a tight circle around her.

"Do you mean Mr. Russell, sir?"

"I mean Larry."

A man who looked like the woman might if she cut her hair came down the RV's steps sideways, one step at a time, and opened an aluminum lawn chair on the asphalt, easing himself into it, apparently for the simple pleasure of watching his wife and dog.

"Mr. Russell is unavailable at the moment. May I take a message?"

"What about tomorrow?"

"Tomorrow's the Fourth of July, sir."

"I'm aware of that," he said.

The dog still raced in a circle, just out of reach, as though it'd been bred to bring obese women to bay on open ground.

"I'm afraid Mr. Russell will be gone through the end of the week. Who may I say's calling?"

"I've seen the man naked. You can tell him that's who called."

"I guess I know why you blocked your number."

The receptionist's voice was strained but now also curious.

"I guess you do," he said.

In Sheridan he pulled through the drive-up window at the Dairy Queen and ordered two Butterfinger Blizzards, then parked at the curb across the street from Helen's split-level. He was halfway through the first one when she opened the gate from the sideyard, walking out wrapped in a lime-green beach towel. She bent to pull a garden hose farther away from the house, and a muscled-up Rottweiler straddled the sprinkler, biting at the water until she told him to quit. When she was satisfied the spray wasn't soaking the fencing she called the dog back through the gate.

He carried the untouched Blizzard in his good hand, staying out of the flowerbeds, standing finally up against the chin-high board fence, staring into the backyard. "Hello," he called, and heard the dog growling but couldn't see it. A voice he didn't recognize was repeating something in Spanish.

"Is that you?" Helen called.

"It's Crane."

"That's who I meant by 'you.'"

He eased the gate open. The Mexican said something about would she mind if he used the bathroom.

"Is your dog friendly?"

"Why don't you come ahead and we'll see."

Around the corner of the house he found her on a redwood chaise. The top half of her swimsuit lay in a little heap on the ground, and she'd pulled the towel up under her chin. Both she and the dog were staring at him. He held up the Blizzard. "I brought you something."

She punched the off button on a boom box, where it sat unevenly on the flagstones, and the voice stopped asking for directions to the airport. "Larry's taking me to Acapulco in September."

He nodded, sitting on the edge of a second lounger.

"What's in the cup?" she asked, and then more pointedly, "You know it's been twelve years? You do know that, don't you?"

He'd been staring at the dog and didn't realize he wasn't listening. He scooted forward, offering the Blizzard.

"Something sweet," he said.

She popped the lid, stared inside, then laid the cup on its side in front of the dog, who immediately pinned it between its front paws and buried its nose in the ice cream, its dark eyes still on Crane.

"I had to check," she said. "A large dose of chocolate can kill a dog."

"I didn't know that. I didn't even know you had a dog." He looked around the patio, at each piece of lawn furniture. "I was surprised to see you come out and change the sprinkler."

"And you were just driving by?"

"I was across the street."

"How often does that happen?"

"This is the first time. I had to look up your address in the phone book." His mind kept drifting, and he stared down between his boots to focus. There were ants at work in the cracks between the stones. "I would've thought Larry could afford an underground system," he said.

"One of the zones sprung a leak. There's supposed to be someone out later today."

"You look good." He was still staring down.

"I'm a vegan now," she said.

He looked up when he heard the dog tearing the cup to get at the last of the Blizzard. "Larry going without steak and eggs and milk and whatever else too?"

"The man needs his red meat," she said.

When there were only a few shreds of paper left the dog started a low, threatening growl, and Helen slapped him on the head with the flat of her hand.

"Hush, now," is what she said when she slapped him a second time. "I'm guessing you already know Larry's not home, or you would've brought him a milkshake too."

"I called his office."

"Did you really?"

"I told his secretary I'd seen him naked. It seemed kind of funny at the time."

"Does it still seem funny?"

He shrugged. "Not as much."

She stroked the dog's head, and it settled its chin on its front paws. "Did you tell Kathy that the time you saw her boss naked he was on top of your wife?"

"I didn't realize it had been twelve years already."

"What's wrong with your arm?"

He brought it into his lap, holding it there, wondering if its uselessness was obvious to everyone. "It sort of buzzes."

"Like what? Like a bee?"

"I haven't been feeling very well."

"Not just your arm?"

"Generally, I guess."

"So you thought after twelve years you'd check in to tell me you're sick?"

"I was just driving around."

"Did you think it would cheer me up?"

"I wasn't thinking about it one way or the other. I was driving around and then I called Larry, and then you changed your sprinkler."

"Are you dying?"

The question surprised him. "We're all dying."

"But are you over here to tell me you're going faster than the rest of us?"

She was wearing sunglasses, but it didn't matter, he'd never been very good at reading her expressions. "That's a pretty big leap," he said.

"Not really. You look like hell."

"I've ended up with what my granddad had."

She stared at him. Long enough that he looked away, and then back to see if she was still staring at him.

"That's absolutely fucked." She pushed the glasses to the top of her head.

"I guess I just needed to hear somebody say that out loud."

He stood up, and the dog growled and got slapped again.

She gathered the pieces of the cup and scrunched them together. "If you want to know, I divorced you because I was afraid," she said. "We've never talked about that."

He watched her squeeze the paper even tighter. "When we were married? You were afraid of me?"

"Yes, I was."

"I never laid a hand on you." He was massaging the bad arm, watching her place the scraps precisely on top of the boom box, still holding the towel across her breasts.

"But it felt like you wanted to. Like you had to remind yourself not to."

They heard a truck pull to the curb in front of the house.

"That must be your sprinkler guy," he said.

"Can you turn around?"

"What?"

"I need to get dressed."

He stared at the mountains. "Maybe what you felt was something I brought home with me? From being a cop?"

"Maybe that's all it was," she said. "It was a long time ago. We were very, very young."

The sound of a truckdoor closing, the drop of a tailgate.

"You never felt like that with Larry? I mean uneasy."

"I guess living with Larry's kind of like a diet without meat."

She stepped to his side. She had her top on now and the towel wrapped around her waist. They could see the cab of a white truck over the fence.

"I must've been feeling homesick or something," he said.

Her smile had a certain ease, a coziness that reminded him of an apartment they'd rented in their twenties.

"Will you turn off the hose on your way out?"

"Sure I will."

"It was good to see you."

"You too."

"Tell the sprinkler guy I'll be out in a minute."

"All right."

She turned, circling his neck with her bare arms, and pulled him against her. Her chin just cleared his shoulder, the wind catching in her hair, fanning it into his face. It smelled like he remembered, like when they were just kids, in high school.

"I'm sorry," she whispered. "Truly I am."

He raised his arms like he might embrace her, then let them drop to his sides. "Thank you," he said.

She stepped back and the dog got to its feet, its lips bunched in a soundless snarl.

"At least you didn't get bitten."

She had her sunglasses on again, and he could see his reflection in their lenses. He looked worn out.

# Nine

GRIFF HAD PROMISED to help stack the first cutting of alfalfa at the Rocking M and got up in the dark, and when Einar heard her in the kitchen he dressed and went out and sat under the overhead light at the table. He could feel the warmth of it on his head, the muffled agitation of the miller moths circling against the bright globe.

They listened to the weather and the ranch report on the radio, having a breakfast of toast and jam and coffee, and then he became anxious she might leave without speaking to him.

"I like it that McEban still square-bales his hay," he said.

"What?"

"I said, I like it that—"

"You mean, that he didn't go to those big round bales like everybody else?"

"That's exactly what I mean."

"Me too," she said. "I like how the square bales look when they're stacked."

"The shadows they throw." He felt better now that they'd spoken. "In the winter."

She fixed him a plate of leftover ham and green beans for his supper, stretching plastic wrap over the plate, then sliced a tomato, a cucumber and onion into a shallow Tupperware container, drizzling olive oil and vinegar over the raw vegetables. She showed him where she'd grouped it all together in the refrigerator.

"I've still got time to make you something for lunch." She turned the radio off. "In case you change your mind."

"You'd better not," he said. "If I eat in the middle of the day I'll need to lie down." He hadn't moved from the table.

"I'm not going to be home until late." She was in the mudroom getting her jacket and workgloves and cap.

"You can stay all night if you like."

"I might."

"I think you should," he said.

She came back, kissed him and looked around the kitchen, and when there was nothing left to do she kissed him again. He thought she smelled like wet coins, like stripped copper wiring mixed with something sweet, and wondered if she ate candy in bed. If it helped her sleep.

She stopped at the door. "You won't forget to smoke your cigarette?"

"Not hardly," he said.

He heard her on the porch and then the truck starting up in the workyard. Her kiss had tasted fruity from the lip balm she used, and now he had the whole day to himself. An old man with a single task he expected to accomplish before she returned, every part of which he'd rehearsed a dozen times in his imagination.

He washed his face and shaved, working his tongue over his bottom lip to see if he could still taste her, and he could.

Before it got any hotter he started up through the sage and the paintbrush and yarrow, turning back and forth on the ascending grades of the switchbacks, keeping to the trail his nearly forty years of diligence has worn into the hillside just opposite the house.

When he became short of breath he stopped until he regained it, and when a cloud passed before the sun he didn't move at all, allowing the breeze to cool him thoroughly. He was in no hurry.

He simply meant to gain the top of the rise one deliberate step at a time, stabbing a shovel into the earth as a staff, with Griff's high-school backpack slung over his shoulder and a long, iron tamping bar balanced atop that same shoulder, a bulging plastic garbage bag dangling like something an old hobo might invent. A pair of fluorescent dice hung from a carabiner clicked through a webbed loop on the side of the backpack, and underneath it the patch of a frowning yellow bee with the stitched caption *Bee-otch*.

It took the better part of an hour, but when he topped out under the big cottonwood he felt all right. Not great, but not worn down to the nub. It surprised him. He leaned the shovel and tamping bar against the tree and shrugged off the backpack, setting it by the garbage bag. He eased down onto the single cane chair that stood next to the trunk, tipping his hat off and hanging it on a knee so the wind could work at his hair. When his scalp prickled he dabbed at his head with a bandanna.

He'd watched the pastures and buildings that lay below him, the prairie stretching eastward toward the curved horizon, the comforting press of the Bighorns at his back, his whole life and didn't need to see it all now to know what was there.

He shut his eyes and the memories of summer colors and the sense of expanse brightened in his mind. And as always there were the quick, familiar flashes from the lives of his wife and son and Mitch, and when he opened his eyes the sun caught on the black marble gravestones before him, flaring up like portals to a separate world.

A leaf brushed his cheek and he pulled the branch down to snap one lengthwise under his nose, enjoying the sweet, clean scent. Then he seated his hat and stood from the chair.

Just south of Ella's marker he stepped off a six-by-three-foot plot, dragging the heel of his boot to describe its perimeter. Then he took up the tamping bar.

Two hours later he'd broken through the hardpan with the beveled end of the bar and shoveled out a foot of the dry, caked earth. After that he found more rocks, but the soil was looser, just like he knew it would be. He retrieved one of the old quart bottles he'd filled at the tap and packed in the knapsack and drank most of it. He thought if he had to take a leak, he'd piss in the hole and make the digging easier. Though his shirt was damp under his arms and across his back, he still felt fine, thinking he might get out and dig a hole once a week, that it would be a real improvement in his life. Then he wished he could see well enough to drive into town so the tourists could have a look at him. A couple of times in the past year a woman in city clothes had asked to take his picture, and he'd enjoyed the experience. It made him feel he hadn't faded away altogether, that he was still somehow worthy of notice, even if only as a sort of rural oddity.

He dug a while longer and then sat in the chair to rest and eat a plum, waking sometime later with his chin on his chest. He wasn't sure how long he'd slept and squinted at the sky until he found where it brightened, satisfied that he still had most of the afternoon.

He remembered the two weeks they'd spent trenching out a new leach field for Mitch's septic tank. Griffin had been a boy then, just nine or ten, and they could have had old Dan Hanson over with his backhoe and finished the job in an afternoon, but Einar wanted to give his son a bone-wearying chore and let him own the satisfaction of having completed it.

When he was down deep enough that it was just a little bit of a struggle to climb out, he stopped and threw the bar and shovel back toward the tree, then took his hat off and lay down with his heels against one end and his head just short of the other with his arms folded across his chest. His hat was turned up on his stomach. He felt relaxed, comfortable, but got worried that if he died right then and there it might look like a suicide, so he climbed out, pleased with the extravagance of the hole. He could have dug something smaller, but what he intended was in fact a kind of burial, and beyond that he'd wanted to see what it was like lying down in the cool, dry ground. So he'd have an idea of what was coming next.

He dragged the garbage bag to the soft mound of earth he'd shoveled up out of the hole, working his butt back into the loose soil and lifting the bag by its bottom. He gave it a shake and it emptied in an instant: all the letters he'd written Ella from Korea, most of the family photographs, wedding rings, birth and death certificates, marriage licenses, everything he could put his hands on that authenticated his eighty years of using up a body. Now it all lay three feet down in the earth and hadn't made more of a sound than a curtain lifting in the breeze. He dropped the bag on top and rummaged through the backpack for the can of lighter fluid and the box of matches.

He stood listening to the crackle of it burning, and when there was just the faint odor of smoke he shoveled the hole full and sat in the chair. The day had gone exactly as he'd planned.

He'd kept back a cigar box of mementos for Griff, to provide some offering, because he doesn't imagine she'll understand what he's done. He expects her to be pissed off.

He kept a single wedding picture of Griffin and Jean, so she could always know what her young parents looked like, as well as one of himself and Ella. Two photographs of Mitch: one taken when he was twenty, wearing his Army uniform, the other of him middle-aged and riding a dappled gray gelding they called Ford. The first trophy buckle her dad won on a saddle bronc at a little show in Greybull. A brooch of Ella's she's long favored and the Silver Star he never felt he deserved, but it's how he wants to be held in her heart, as a man who performed his life's duties with at least some gallantry. And the Norsk Bibel, which he thinks of as a poorly rendered novel, but he hadn't burned his other books either. He sat up straighter in the chair, reviewing his decisions.

He's dug the hole and made the fire because when he dies he doesn't want her to have to deal with anything but the disposal of his body. That's fair, he thinks. There's no getting around a dead body, and he's already spoken to Sid Farnsworth, the undertaker down in Sheridan, about the arrangements. He's already paid. She'll have to dial 911, and that's it, maybe drive a box or two of his clothes in to the Goodwill, and they agreed a year ago that the Nature Conservancy gets the land just as soon as there isn't a Gilkyson to care for it. So she'll have the ranch without it going to taxes, and if she has a kid it'll have a place to live. He wants her to move forward, and wants it to be easy for her. He doesn't want her history to limit her, as he believes his history has limited him. And if Marin's here he wants it to be easy for her too.

"I'm not crazy," he said, remembering how he'd searched her room for an hour, finding her diary, her school pictures and some papers, almost packing it all up here with the rest. But he hadn't. He'd caught himself in time, and that was getting harder to do. No, he'd put her things aside, sitting there with his eyes closed and waiting until he was able to distinguish what was reasonable and what wasn't, and the fact that he'd succeeded was reassuring. He didn't think a crazy man could have.

"A crazy man would have burned it all," he said aloud, then he napped again, and when he woke the heat was gone from the day. He gathered up the tools and the backpack and started back down to the house to eat his cold supper.

# Ten

THE BISQUE KILN was still warmer than her body, but just barely, and Griff was leaning over into its barrel with a small whiskbroom, sweeping the powdery grit from the last firing into the slightly flattened mouth of a tomato-sauce can. In spite of her cotton mask the dust made her sneeze, and when she swallowed her mouth tasted of baked alkali. She pinched the mask away, sliding it up over her forehead, whispering, "A rose is a rose is a rose" because she liked the velvety resonance of the phrase against the coarse firebrick lining the interior.

He'd been waiting for her when she returned home from Paul's this morning. He was sitting at the kitchen table in the same clothes he'd worn the day before, his sweat-stiffened hair standing in tufts, his dirty hands worrying the corner of a laminated place-mat. He smelled of smoke.

She asked if there'd been an accident and he slammed the flat of a hand on the tabletop, knocking the saltshaker over.

"This is my goddamn house," he shouted. Her diary and a dozen photographs were stacked by his arm, and now fanned toward the table's edge.

"Why don't I fix us some breakfast?" she said, and he smacked the table again, but this time recoiling from the sound as though he'd just regained his hearing.

She'd seen him like this once before, in the garden this summer, pawing at the soft earth and pushing her away when she tried to help him to his feet, his eyes gone wild and blind to her.

He slumped in the chair. "I believe I've had all the breakfast I'll ever want." His mouth gaped, his jaw quivering.

When she turned her head as though she might be looking at her diary, he opened his hands and reached toward her as if he meant to accept some object she was handing to him.

"I didn't read it," he said, folding his arms on the table, resting his forehead against them, weeping with the abandon of a child. When he was able to sit up again, he choked out through the sobs what he'd done, what he'd burned. He offered to walk her up the hill and show her the newly mounded grave he'd made of his life.

Now the afternoon seemed hollow and she turned on the radio so the jazz on NPR would keep her company. She settled on a stool at the work island in the middle of the room.

Arced across the table before her was a ceramic spinal column, its ribs arranged alongside by length and, nearest to her, a pelvis that appeared to have belonged to a woman or a small bear. Each piece was a chalky white, the surfaces pitted, in places roughened.

Behind her was a bank of windows, the panes small and unwashed, and below them the tiered plywood shelving where she's racked the raw-fired pieces and arranged her shaping tools, the buffed-steel rods and dowels she uses for her assemblages, the colored bottles of glaze, the spools of copper wire. Her slab roller was pushed up tightly in a corner, and next to it the big trough where she reconstituted the dried clay. It was the clay that possessed her, the feel of it, from the very first time. When she's kneeling at the trough, up to her elbows in the wet and slick and seemingly torsional muck, it is as though she has reached down the shaft of a muddied well and gripped the body of some ancient creature—a feeling at once horrible and intimate and thrilling.

She held her hands up in the yellow afternoon light and closed them into fists, dropping them finally onto the table and sitting there quietly, trying to summon the conviction that she would be able to care for him if his mind collapsed completely. Feed, bathe and dress him, reason with him. Keep them both safe from these episodes of sulking infancy.

The door stood propped open and a magpie strutted through the glare of the workyard, stopping at the edge of the studio's porch with its head cocked and turned, neck feathers ruffed, the black bead of an eye glistening. Then light flashed off the glass of a car turning into the drive, and the bird stepped back and rose into flight.

She untied her utility apron, lifted it over her head and hung it on a hook by the door.

A dog ran to the edge of the yard, cocking a leg up to pee, and when she crossed the porch he came toward her wagging his tail. His chest and legs were white, his body brindled in overlapping swatches of blue merle and liver. She squatted at the hose bib to wash her hands, standing when she heard the car door shut. She shaded her eyes, watching a tall woman in tan shorts and a navy-blue T-shirt approach, stopping to stretch her arms above her head, her curly gray hair cut to match the sharp line of her jaw, and Griff thought, *Please, don't let me fuck this up.*

"He's friendly." The silver Volvo parked behind her was the same color as her hair.

Griff squatted again at the bib, running her cupped hands full, and the dog stepped forward to lap at the water, watching her, one eye hazel, the other pale blue. When he'd had enough he backed away and sat in the border of dampened earth.

"His eyes are different colors," Griff said.

"Don't you wish yours were?"

The woman bent at the waist to drink from the spigot and the dog darted in, snapping at her hair, his back end wiggling as though attached to a separate axis. She pushed him away, laughing, and shut the water off, turning toward the house. She raked her wet hands back through her hair.

"He's inside," Griff said.

"In the middle of the day?"

"Yes, ma'am."

She wiped at her chin with the back of a hand. "What about Mitch? He stay indoors all day too?"

"Mitch died."

"I'm sorry to hear that." She moved into the shade the building cast. "Did he go hard?"

"Yes, he did. He suffered a lot." The woman nodded, asking nothing more, so Griff added, "He died when I was eleven."

"How old are you now?"

"Nineteen."

"Can we step in out of this heat?" She was staring up into the hot, pale sky.

"We can go in the house if you want. I made up the guest room for you."

"I can't just yet. I'll let you know when I'm ready."

"Yes, ma'am."

She extended her hand. "This is going to work out a lot better if you call me Marin." She indicated the dog. "His name's Sammy."

Griff took her hand. "Everybody calls me Griff."

"Like your dad?"

She nodded and turned and Marin followed her up onto the porch and into the studio, where Griff turned off the radio.

Marin leaned back against the work island, scuffing a heel against the worn floorboards, rutted and stained in patterns of neat's-foot, diesel and two-cycle oils, turpentine and creosote. She inhaled deeply. "It still smells like my daddy's shop."

"It's mine now," Griff said, hating how that sounded, adding that it was Einar who allowed her to use it. "We moved the tools over to the granary," she said.

Marin picked up one of the ceramic ribs, pressing it against her side as though comparing the size, then placing it back on the worktable. She looked at the raw pieces heaped on the shelving. "Do you mostly make bones?"

Griff stepped to a steel rod held upright in the jaws of a vise at the table's edge. It was curved gracefully, like a girl's spine, the five lumbar vertebrae held in place by a variegated and grooved coccyx that was tucked in stiffly, like some docked vestigial tail. "I use the rods and wire to piece them together."

"You make skeletons, then?"

"Sort of."

"Are you nervous?"

Griff took her hands out of her front pockets and, not knowing what to do with them, tucked them into her back pockets. "More than I thought."

Marin smiled. "I knew I would be." She lifted the pelvis up, sighting out the window through its cradle. "Mitch was a sweetheart. I always hoped he'd get lucky and have something quick like a heart attack."

"I need you to put that down."

Marin lowered the curved bone as she might a chalice. "I'm not going to drop it."

"You might."

"I guess I might." She placed it carefully back on the table and Griff stepped forward, squaring it with the arrangement of ribs.

"It took me a long time to get it right," she said.

They listened to the dog circling and finally settling on the porch.

"How sick is he?"

"I don't know for sure. He won't go to the doctor, but Paul doesn't think he's going crazy. He thinks it's something else."

"Paul's not a doctor, then?"

"He's my boyfriend."

Marin stared vacantly out the window. "I always thought it was sad here. Even when everyone was alive."

"I like it better than anywhere I've ever been."

Marin turned to her. "You look a lot like I used to. When I was a girl."

"Thank you."

"I'm not sure it's a compliment."

"I think it is."

"I'm ready now. Now I think we can go in."

He'd bathed and dressed in clean clothes and was lying on top of the bedcovers, napping. They came in without trying to be quiet and stared down at him.

"He had a bad night." Griff stepped back toward the doorway, leaning into a dresser.

Marin remained by the bed. "He comes from a long line of people who've had bad nights." She took his hand and he opened his eyes, blinking up at her. "It's your sister," she whispered.

She sat on the edge of the bed, against his hip, and he pulled his hand away, groping at the nightstand until he felt his glasses. When he got them on he thrust his head forward, squinting, and when he still wasn't satisfied he swung the magnifying glass around. Marin held her face up close to the lens.

"Oh, my," he said.

He lightly touched her face and hair while he studied her, then folded the glass back against the wall.

"I've gotten a little older," she said.

His eyes appeared bluer to Griff than they had in some time.

"You look just about the same to me. About right, anyway." He relaxed back against the pillows, holding her hand in both of his. "I'm sorry about your friend."

"You mean Alice."

"Yes, that's it exactly," he said, "Alice Clark. McEban read about her passing on his Internet. He's a wizard when he gets up and rolling on his computer. Sells his cows on it. Did you come out on 80?"

"I don't understand."

"On that interstate through Nebraska."

"No, I drove through South Dakota."

"That's how I thought you'd come. I told him so." He looked pleased. "McEban thought 80, but that's because he likes those sandhills. I believe that prejudiced his thinking. He said if it was him he'd have driven north on the two lanes out of North Platte." He was speaking rapidly, as though he had a good deal to relate and not much time. "Did you stop and have a look at that Crazy Horse mountain in the Black Hills?"

"I missed it," she said. "I only stopped for a night, and to call your granddaughter. To tell her I was on my way."

"I've always wanted to get up there to South Dakota and see how they're coming along with that Crazy Horse sculpture. Sometimes you don't pay attention to what you've got in your own backyard. I'm guilty of that. I mean putting your head down like I have. Just looking for your enjoyment in work. Sometimes I think that might've been a mistake."

"I always thought I'd like to go sailing on Lake Michigan," she said, "and I never did."

"Well, there you are."

"Yes," she said, "there I was, for sixty years. And I never once even swam in the lake."

Einar nodded, fixing his gaze on the foot of the bed as though someone had settled there. Some other visitor. "I imagine she was easy to get along with. Your Alice," he said. "I can't see you staying with someone all those years and her not being easy to live with." He looked back up at her.

"It was very easy."

"That's what I thought. I thought it must have been."

They were quiet for a moment. He still held her hand.

"Do you think she would have liked it here?" he asked.

"I think so."

"I think she could've gotten used to it. Maybe walking in the mountains. Maybe if the wind wasn't blowing." He turned her hand, smoothing it as though intending to read the lines in her palm. "McEban printed up a copy of her obituary for me. I read where she taught Eastern studies. That you both had."

"Yes," she said. "I retired, but Alice was still teaching."

"That's it. That's what it said."

"I didn't imagine you'd know about all this. I thought I might have to explain everything about my life, and that you might not care."

"Why wouldn't I care?"

"I've been gone a long time, and I never called or wrote to tell you anything."

He'd taken his glasses off, tapping them against his leg, and she slipped them out of his hand, setting them on the nightstand.

"I didn't lift a finger to stay in touch," she said. "It didn't have to be like that."

"It was both of us."

She nodded in a remote sort of agreement, staring out the window so intently that Griff thought there must be something standing just past the glass, looking in at them, but there was only the bright, empty light of the afternoon.

"I thought you might not care for me because of Alice. Because of us being women."

"I wouldn't know anything about that." His face was pinched, his breathing short and ragged. "What I wish is that Griff, or McEban or somebody, would've heard me say that your Alice would have fit in here just fine. That she might have liked a walk in the mountains now and then. I wish I would've said something like that out loud."

She was crying now, not sobbing but crying steadily, and she leaned over to pull him away from his pillows, hugging him up against her. She cupped his head to her shoulder, rocking them, shushing like a mother would. Just an old woman holding an old man, maybe both of them remembering when they'd been young together in this very house, clinging to each other because they were frightened by something just beyond what they could express.

# Eleven

HE WAS UP on his knees in the truckseat, turned sideways, with the seatbelt slanting down under his arm and across his ribcage. "When the Boogeyman peeks in his closet," he said, his voice chattering because the roadbed had deteriorated to a dry washboard, then he started giggling and couldn't stop.

They jounced down through the cattleguard and he pivoted around facing forward, straining against the seatbelt like he'd fallen upon a guitar string, singing out, *"Boing, boing, boing."*

"Goddamnit, Kenneth."

"You don't know, do you?" He was still giggling. "You don't know what the Boogeyman was checking for?"

"Sit down like you should."

McEban hunched forward over the steering wheel to let the air get at his back, and Kenneth sat down, crossing his arms over his chest. The dust they'd raised stood so thickly in the cab they appeared blurred to each other.

The boy announced: "You owe me a quarter for cussing."

His feet didn't quite reach the floormat and the dashboard was heaped up with catalogs and receipts, a single workglove, a pair of vise grips and an antenna cable McEban bought at the NAPA auto-parts in Sheridan, still shrink-wrapped because they decided they liked the radio better when it didn't work, all of it coated with the reddish talc. The Sunday funnies from a *Billings Gazette* fluttered and snapped on the seat between them.

"The Boogeyman was checking to see if it was Chuck Norris who was in there." His voice a shrill vibrato.

"I was going to say Chuck Norris."

"I'll bet you weren't." He pinched a quarter out of the coins in the ashtray, slipping it into his front pocket. "I can't see where we're going."

"You know where we're going. Look out the side window if you need something to see."

"You were going to say Superman."

"No, I wasn't. If you'd have given me a minute I would've said Chuck Norris."

Kenneth turned toward the window, opening his mouth, sticking his tongue out. The air tasted sweet, of red clover and sage, of the flowering cress that bordered the sloughs.

After breakfast McEban had perched him on a kitchen stool with a bath towel safety-pinned around his neck and given him a buzz cut. He'd used the Oster Turbo Clippers he'd bought at the Wal-Mart in Billings, and they were both anxious to see how it would turn out. Now the boy sat rubbing the bristle at the crown of his head.

"I like how it feels," he said.

"I could freshen it every couple weeks if you want."

"That'd be okay in the summer." He still had his hands up, dabbing. "Could you make a pie out of clover?"

"I couldn't."

"Could somebody?"

"Maybe Chuck Norris could."

The boy smiled, poking through the clutter on the dash until he found a pair of sunglasses. He wiped the lenses on his shirttail and put them on. "I don't know why I can't get up on my knees.

You said if we ever got in a wreck the airbag would squish me no matter how I was sitting."

"When did I say that?"

"When I was littler."

"Well, you're bigger now. You won't squish if you're sitting down like you are."

Curtis Hanson was whipping weeds in the borrow ditch behind their row of mailboxes, his two stocky blue heelers jackknifing in the air at his sides, snapping at the flying weedstalks. Curtis waved and McEban waved back, turning onto the county road. It was hot enough that the macadam felt greasy under the tires and the truck slewed and caught.

"You know why Chuck Norris's dogs pick up their own poop?"

"I think that's probably something I knew last week."

"I've told you this one before," the boy said, staring right at him.

"You look like some kind of bug in those glasses."

He lowered the glasses, narrowing his eyes, speaking each word distinctly: "Because Chuck Norris doesn't take shit from anybody."

"I think you better put that quarter back in the ashtray."


They stopped in the alley behind the Ace Hardware and McEban backed around to the end of a rusted Quonset hut. The double doors were slid fully open on their tracks, below a faded sign reading JOEY'S WELDING. They dropped the tailgate, and Joey came out and shook McEban's hand and then the boy's and stood with them.

He wore a leather apron over a stained sweatshirt that was baggy in the elbows, the sleeves dotted with burn holes. They all stared at the broken sickle bar in the bed of the truck.

"You find the same rock you did last year?" Joey coughed productively and turned and spat against the side of the building.

"It was a different rock this time."

"You think about buying new?" He wiped his mouth with the back of his hand.

"I would if you told me I had to. I'm not sure I can afford new."

Joey nodded, leaning over the sidewall. His welding helmet, hinged back on his head, was skull-shaped and bright red with yellow flames painted on the sides to represent ears. He ran the pad of a thumb over a jagged end of the sickle bar. "I guess you won't have to just yet."

They carried in each half, going wide around the other men at work with their torches, and set the pieces up on an angle-iron-and-sheet-metal worktable. Kenneth stared up into the banks of fluorescent lights overhead, shading his eyes, searching the corrugated walls for a window. There weren't any.

"I forgot how hot it gets in here." McEban's face was flushed, and he tipped his hat off and cocked an arm up, digging his forehead into the angle his elbow offered.

"It's not as hot as working over a grill in Mississippi." Joey peeled away the yellow customer copy from the work order and handed it to him. "I did that once, and it was hotter."

They started back toward the truck.

"Or unloading boxcars, or running the press at a dry cleaners. Not everybody gets to work outdoors."

They stopped on the cement apron in the sun.

"A bakery's no fun in the summer, either."

"How long do you figure?" McEban asked.

"How about Friday?"

"Morning?"

When Joey nodded, the welding mask came down, its dark lens flashing in the sunlight. He pushed it back up. "Late morning, to be on the safe side."

Kenneth looked at McEban to see what he thought of the helmet, but if he was thinking anything at all it didn't show. His mother always said, "McEban wouldn't say shit if he had a mouth full of it." If she was right, he thought, it worked in her favor.

They dropped off a pair of boots at Burke's to have them resoled and -heeled, and stayed longer in the bank than was necessary, enjoying the central air. When they felt refreshed, they walked across Bighorn Avenue to the Carnegie Library and stood on the plastic runners that covered the carpet between the bookshelves to argue over their list, whispering about which books might provide the most enjoyment.

Kenneth liked the building's musty odor, how the sunlight fell in through the high louvered windows, the general effort made for quietude and solemnity. When he was too young to have figured out how the world worked yet, he thought the place an actual annex of heaven. He believed, when he tilted a book down from the shelf, sat cross-legged in the aisle and held it open reverently against his thighs, that he was holding the soul of the man or woman who had written it. He wept when Mr. Simmler, the librarian, told him, "Young sir, your head is in a place where the sun will not shine." He called all the boys in town "young sir" and the girls "young madam."

They settled finally on *Smoky, The Adventures of Robin Hood* and *Artemis Fowl.* Kenneth carried the books up to the circulation desk and stood waiting for Mr. Simmler to finish his game of solitaire, raising up on his toes so he could see the cards. "You can play the red four on the black five," he said.

Mr. Simmler tilted his head, studying the layout. "So I can." He played the four over, but now his concentration was broken and he laid the deck aside. "What have you got there?"

Kenneth slid the books up on the counter, and Mr. Simmler took up *The Adventures of Robin Hood.* "All good choices, young sir." He slipped the date-due cards from the pockets inside the front covers and stamped them. He was wearing a green visor and a bolo tie with four silver aces fanned at his throat, and when he looked over to where they racked the magazines, Kenneth looked too.

McEban was leaned against the metal shelving and leafing through a *Popular Mechanics*. "Indeed," Mr. Simmler said.

When they left the Carnegie it wasn't late enough to drive home and fix supper, and still hot as the welding shop, so they parked where the Fourth Street Bridge used to be. Bikes were tilted over among the cottonwoods, and they could hear the screams of boys, a dog barking, the laughter of older children. McEban stepped out of the truck and Kenneth worked his swimming trunks out from behind the seat.

"Anybody watching?" he called, and when McEban shook his head he peeled down to his underwear and pulled the trunks on, kneeling on the seat to tie the cord at the waistband. "Mr. Simmler looks like he wishes he was dealing cards in a Western movie."

McEban smiled from where he stood with a boot up on the front bumper. "As far as I know he's never worked anywhere but the library."

Kenneth jumped out, turning his left foot up to get at the bottle cap stuck to his heel. He pried it off and wound up like a big leaguer, pitching it into the trees.

They started slowly toward the creek, Kenneth being careful about the scatter of brown glass, stopping to watch an astonishingly pale fat boy climb to the top of the concrete abutment and launch himself, shrieking, out into the air over the creek. A heartbeat passed and the noise was abruptly choked off, and then a spray of water rose into the sunlight.

"Was that Clyde or Claude?" McEban asked.

"Clyde."

"How can you tell?"

"Claude's fatter."

Across the creek on the far abutment, two high-school girls in bikinis were lounging on towels with a tall boy standing between them drinking a bottle of beer. One girl was smoking, and all of them were watching a black Labrador swimming hard after a floating yellow tennis ball.

"I'm going to do it today," Kenneth said.

"I thought you already had."

"I could have, but I wanted to wait till you could see me."

"I'm glad you did."

They walked out across the backfill to the top of the broken concrete and looked down. Below them the water was green and deep and flat, and downstream the fat twins had wedged themselves among the rocks where the stream turned white and foamy, churning against their shoulders, and they called out again and again as though something unexpected and mildly obscene was happening. "I'm getting a massage. Oh my God, I'm getting the very best massage."

"It looks farther down when you're up here," Kenneth said.

"Yeah, it does."

"I think I better see how cold the water is first."

"That's what I'd do."

The boy climbed down the side of the abutment, where the retaining wall had fallen away in ruin, the rusted rebar showing through, and waded out into the pool. He stood waist-deep, shivering, and McEban tried to imagine what had happened to the bridge and why he'd never wondered about it before. It was already gone when he was a boy, to fire or flood or poor design, and suddenly it occurred to him that he'd taken this, like most of his life, as a matter of course.

The black dog climbed out of the creek, sheeting water and lunging up the slope between the girls, bracing to shake mightily, and they screamed, turning away and throwing their hands up to shield their faces. All three of them were laughing, and the boy set his beer down and worked the ball out of the dog's mouth, bounced it once and then threw it in a high arc upstream. The dog leapt without looking, and they all shaded their eyes against the glare to watch him hit the water, go under and come up as the ball smacked down at the head of the pool, everybody applauding and hooting, feeling lighthearted and forgetful of any lesser afternoon.

Kenneth climbed back up, hugging his sides, then sucking in a deep breath and nodding while McEban stood off to the side. He ran right past him, his face stiff in concentration, and out into the air, his legs still cycling as he dropped, and came up gasping, beating at the surface with both arms. Then he went slack, letting the current take him.

McEban climbed down to the water's edge, pulled off his boots and socks, rolled up his pants and walked in up to his knees. The fat boys were jumping in holding hands when his cell phone rang, and he worked it out of his pocket and said hello.

Kenneth was at the top again, waiting for him to look, but McEban was wading downstream talking angrily into his phone, so he jumped again right away, howling so the other kids couldn't eavesdrop. After he jumped a third and fourth time and got to the shore, McEban was sitting in the sand pulling his boots on over his dampened socks.

"We have to go," he said.

"Now?"

"Right away."

Someone threw the ball again and they heard the dog hit the water.

McEban stood up, stomping his feet harder into the boots. "You think this is something you'll remember?"

"Sure," Kenneth said. Then, "What?"

"Today." McEban swept a hand toward the abutments. "All the times we've come down here. When you're older you think this is something you'll remember?"

"Why wouldn't I?" the boy asked, but he felt scared. Like he hadn't jumped. Like he'd chickened out and they both had agreed it was a feat he would never accomplish.

They'd been mostly quiet on the drive home. McEban said something about the weather, how he preferred the longer days of summer in spite of the heat, and he'd nodded in numbed agreement. His face felt heated, and something seemed to be fluttering behind his breastbone. The only thing that felt fine was his new haircut, beaded with creekwater, the breeze providing a welcome coolness. That was the best part of the trip.

But here they were home and he'd changed out of his wet swimming trunks, standing on the porch with his backpack leaned against his leg, waiting for McEban to be done talking with Rodney. He shifted his stance, adjusting the basketball against his hip. He'd thought about packing his baseball and glove, but didn't know how a game of catch would go over in Laramie. He knew he could shoot baskets by himself. He watched the men at the pickup, thinking he might be getting sick, and then he was sure of it.

"I need to see you for a minute," he called. His voice sounded frail and he cleared his throat.

They turned, staring at him, and he knew for a fact he was the last person he could think of to figure out that this friend of his mother's was his real dad, and that McEban had always known it.

"I'm sorry," he said when McEban stepped up beside him.

"For what? Did you set fire to something?" He was trying to make a joke, but it didn't come out funny.

"I'm getting sick," the boy told him.

"You were fine a while ago."

"Now I feel like puking."

They heard the pickup door open and watched Rodney pull the keys out of the ignition to make the dinging sound stop, then lean back into the shade of the cab.

"I don't like it either, Kenneth, but this isn't something we can get away from. He showed me the papers. He showed me where your mother signed."

The boy looked at where she parked her trailer beside the house, the spot rutted from the tires, the bunchgrass broken and discolored. "You would've told me if you knew this was going to happen, right?"

McEban knelt down on a knee in front of him. "I guess maybe not," he said. "I guess I always thought it might, I just didn't know when. But I'll bet this turns out to be fine."

"Is that what you really think?"

"It's only for three weeks. I think you can have a good time if you'll let yourself."

Kenneth bounced the ball once, then settled it on a porch chair. "I need you to look at something."

"All right."

"Inside, I mean."

McEban followed him into the kitchen and he bent over at the counter, wedging his hands up against the edge like some rough cop had just ordered him to. When they heard the truckdoor slam, Kenneth laid his face against his arm and looked out the screen door. "I hurt my back."

McEban stared down at his thin back, the T-shirt stained off-center on the right side near his waist. The blood was bright and fresh, dried only at the edges. "Well, Jesus Christ," he said, carefully pinching the shirt up.

"Is it bad?" the boy asked.

"You sound like you wouldn't mind if we had to go in to the doctor's."

"I wouldn't."

"It's not that bad."

Kenneth nodded, his cheek still pressed against his arm. "I didn't think it was. I could sort of see it with the hand mirror in the bathroom."

The skin was scraped away behind his right kidney, but it didn't appear to go deeper. "I'll bet this hurt like a son of a bitch when you did it."

"I didn't feel anything till I got out of the water. That's two quarters you owe me."

"I'm going to have to put something on it."

"You sure?"

"I'll find something that won't sting too much."

McEban went into the bathroom and came back with a bottle of hydrogen peroxide, a bag of cotton balls, a tube of antibiotic salve, a package of square gauze bandages and tape, all of it cradled up against his chest. When he dabbed at the wound with a peroxide-soaked cotton ball, the boy widened his stance and hung his head between his shoulders. McEban could hear him breathing through his mouth.

"That's not too bad, is it?"

"It's okay."

"When did this happen?"

"Last time I jumped, I came down too close to the concrete. I was showing off."

"How come you didn't say anything?" He was peeling the packaging away from the gauze.

"I didn't think it was a good time to say something."

"And when did you think a good time would be?" McEban smoothed the tape around the edges of the bandage and pulled the T-shirt down. "Did you think it'd heal up on the drive home?"

They heard footfalls on the porch, the scrape of a chair being moved.

"I didn't want you saying anything to my mom when you were on the phone. I didn't want her to know." He pointed his chin toward the porch, looking like he might finally cry. "Or him."

"How'd you figure out who I was talking to?"

"It wasn't that hard."

McEban got a brown paper lunch sack from under the sink and put the gauze and antibiotic and tape in and folded the top back, and when Kenneth turned around he handed it to him. "I want you to put some salve on every day. And wash your hands first."

"Okay."

"If you don't it'll get worse."

"I'll do it."

"I know you will."

They were stalling, like nothing had changed and they were just standing around throwing out possibilities about what they might fix for dinner. They heard Rodney get up out of the chair. He passed in front of the screen door and they watched him walk back to the truck.

"My library books will be overdue before I come home."

"I'll take them back for you. If you want, you can check out the same books at the library in Laramie."

"I don't have a card for the Laramie library."

"They'll give you one."

"Are you sure?"

"I'll say something to him."

The boy nodded. "What if I can't think of anything to talk about? On the drive. What if he doesn't say anything either?"

"Well, I bet his radio works."

Kenneth was looking down at his feet. They both watched the tears fall at the toes of his boots. There weren't many.

"You know why Chuck Norris doesn't read books?" McEban asked.

The boy shook his head, still looking down.

"I can't believe you don't know this one."

He pulled the bottom of his T-shirt up and wiped his eyes. "How come you do?"

"I looked it up on the computer the other day. When you were over at Bobby Martens'."

McEban waited until he was done wiping his face, shaking his head like there was water in his ears. He waited for him to stand up straight and take a deep breath. "He doesn't read them because he doesn't have to. He just stares them down until he gets the information he wants."

The boy's eyes were still full but he smiled, like he was giving a gift, and they both knew that's what it was.

# Twelve

CRANE KNOCKED on the door again and waited. To the east a weedy lot, the sage grubbed out around a swing set, the pipe-metal uprights peeling and rusted, a plastic seat hanging by a single chain, paddling in the wind, the slide broken loose from its base and twisted Möbius-wise, and beyond a sagging barbed wire fence and an overgrazed stretch of prairie. He wondered briefly if he would have been any good at a trade that didn't require a uniform and confrontation. To the west, three other weathered duplexes described the arc of the cul-de-sac.

Lately, his calves and thighs have felt as though corn kernels were popping endlessly through the muscles and tendons, and he bounced on the balls of his feet, squatting twice, and then bent at the waist to touch the toes of his boots. It helped a little. He knew it soon wouldn't.

He straightened up, meaning to knock once more, and the filmy curtain in the window to his right hooked back and released but he couldn't see who was behind it. Then a woman's voice, harsh and impatient: "Why don't you come on in, for Christ's sake. It's unlocked."

He stepped inside, blinking in the dimly lit front room, and when the woman asked if he was done with his calisthenics he saw where she was sitting, in an overstuffed chair by the window.

"Yes, ma'am," he said. "I am."

"Can't do 'em myself. Got a gone-to-hell disc in my back. Ruptured is what they say, but then, as you can clearly see I didn't injure myself jogging." She tucked her chin into the swell of her neck, stuck her tongue out and squinted down over her cheeks, trying to locate the fleck of tobacco at the very tip of her tongue, then flicked it off with a fingernail. "I ought to buy filtered."

"Looks like it."

"Benton's parking tickets finally catch up with him?"

"No, ma'am. I don't know anything about any tickets."

"When I seen you come in the drive I thought that's what it must be about."

"I'm here about your daughter."

"You say you're here about Janey?"

"Yes, ma'am."

"Why don't you see if you can find you a place to sit." She had a canker sore in the corner of her mouth and dabbed at it with a yellowed forefinger. "I get nervous with somebody standing over me."

He sat down in the middle of the couch across from her, the cheap cushions bobbing at his sides. On the coffee table there was a canister of black powder, an electric melting pot, a dipper, bullet mold, a cereal bowl heaped with newly formed lead balls.

"Don't knock that stuff over," she said.

He moved to the end of the couch where he could stretch out his legs.

"Benton's queer as a three-dollar bill for all that mountain-man bullshit."

She leaned over and stubbed out her cigarette in a plate beside the chair, then pulled the cannula prongs from her nostrils, biting down on them to suck in the air. She sat gathering herself. "It's the shits bein' sick," she said.

"It's no fun, that's for sure."

"Tell me about it. I ain't even forty-five yet."

They waited for her breathing to calm, then she wiped the cannula on the sleeve of her robe and arranged it back in her nose.

"I cried like a little child when them heartless bitches come over here and took her away from me."

"Excuse me?"

He'd been thinking he should have gone to a better college. Somewhere out of Wyoming. One that would've broadened his take on the world. He heard the toilet flush, and a man walked into the kitchen tucking his shirttails in.

"Goddamn," he said. "I didn't know we had company."

He was angular and gaunt as an undernourished farm animal, wore buckskin pants and a rough cotton shirt, a necklace made of bearclaws and, on his belt, a beaded bag and a long sheathed knife that looked like he could chop kindling with it. His dirty hair was drawn back and tied with a leather thong, but he was clean-shaven.

"We was just talkin' about the day they come and took Janey from us," she said.

"You mean them dykes from the Social Services." He was getting a coffee cup down from the cupboard.

"There wasn't a goddamn social thing about either one of 'em." She pinched off the oxygen tube and lit another cigarette.

Her husband chuckled. "She thinks that shit's going to light up like propane."

"You don't know it won't."

"I know more than you think."

Sitting up straighter seemed to ease her breathing. "You're more full of crap than the Christmas goose," she said, and then, "This here's Benton."

"You want coffee?" he offered.

"If it's already made, black's fine."

"It's always made," he said. "So, what do you need Janey for? She get crosswise of the law?"

"I've just got some questions that need answers. I think she could help me out."

The woman started to laugh and then coughed for a while, which put her out of breath again. She pulled a little plastic garbage can closer, spat in it, straightened up and sat there with her eyes closed, settling. "They must teach you that sorry line in cop school," she said, smiling with her eyes still closed. " 'I just got some questions to ask.' Christ, they even got them numbnut pretend cops on the TV sayin' it."

Benton handed Crane a cup of coffee and sat down on the other end of the couch. He plucked a lead ball out of the bowl, holding it up in the weak sunlight, rolling it between the pads of his thumb and forefinger. "You ever been to that Mountain Man Rendezvous they got up in Red Lodge?" he asked.

Crane balanced the cup on a knee. There was a shimmering slick on top of the coffee like it had been sweetened with motor oil. "No, I never have."

The man sat back in the couch. "Janey always said she thought I resembled Jeremiah Johnson. In the movie. I guess you saw that."

"Some years ago."

"And I'd look like Angelina-fuckin'-Jolie," she said, "if I shed about two hundred and fifty pounds. You goin' to tell me what you want my Janey for?"

He was staring at an unframed Charlie Russell print thumbtacked to the wall, fly-spotted and stained, the edges curling.

"Hello?" She made it sound like a cuss word, and when he focused on her she was glaring at him.

"I'm sorry. I was thinking about my leg." He stretched his right leg out, flexing the toe back, and the pain that shot through his calf made him gasp. He felt the sweat standing across his forehead.

"Well, Jesus Christ," she said. "If you're going to have some kind of attack maybe you better leave."

"I'm fine now."

"You goin' tell me or aren't you?"

"I just have a few questions for her about her boyfriend." He set the cup on a blue plastic milk crate beside the couch. "He got in some trouble, and Janey's name was in his cell phone. I called for a couple days but she never did answer, so I decided to come over in case you might know where she was."

"She ain't here," the woman said. "And she hasn't been since they took her. She was only fourteen and that was three years ago." She took a drag from her cigarette, holding in the smoke as long as she could, then exhaled through her nose and made the cannula whistle. "Her name the only one you got out of that phone?"

"No, I spoke with all his friends. They seemed like good kids. They said Janey was his girl, and I imagine she's a good kid too."

"How you doing on your coffee?" the husband asked.

"I'm fine with what I've got." He turned back to the woman. "So you haven't heard from her, is what you're saying?"

She struggled up to the edge of her easy chair again. "We seen her once in the grocery store but she was already checked out, and you know how kids is once the glands kick in. Revs 'em up. You can't hardly get 'em to stay put."

"I know what you mean."

"You have a daughter, do you?"

"Stepdaughter."

"Same goddamn thing."

"I always thought so."

"What's the boyfriend done?"

"He was killed."

"Like in an accident."

"No, that's not it. He was murdered."

She nodded, using the hand towel draped on her knee to swab her neck, front and back. "Benton, I need this air changed out," she said, and he got up from the couch and dragged an oxygen bottle out from behind it, and jostled the green cylinder into place beside her chair.

She lit a fresh cigarette from the one she was done with, reaching a framed photo down from a shelf at her shoulder. She wiped the glass with the towel at her neck, then leaned over her knees to offer Crane the picture. "Right there's what she looked like." She eased back in the chair, watching her husband change the regulator over to the fresh bottle. "I seen that photo in the Wal-Mart and thought it was Janey herself, but it ain't. I mean, I got no idea who that girl is there. They take them photos just to sell you the frame, but that one there I bought for the picture. If that ain't a likeness of Janey you can kiss my fat ass."

Crane squared the frame in his hands. The picture was of a blonde girl, her hair done into curls at the top of her head, and she wore a shiny white dress and a strand of pearls. She looked like a bridesmaid for a friend who'd gotten pregnant in high school and probably wouldn't be going to college. "That's a beautiful girl," he said.

"You got that right," the woman said.

Benton walked the empty bottle to the door and came back, bending over to squint at the oxygen gauge. He tapped it with a fingernail. "You need me to fetch you your nebulizer, sweety pie?"

"I'm fine without it for now." She stubbed her cigarette in the plate, then pitched forward again coughing. Her scalp showed through her thin hair, reddening.

"I wish she'd give them things up," Benton said. "Throw 'em in the goddamn ditch. You ever smoke?"

"No. I never liked the taste of them."

"Me neither."

"Well, good for you healthy sons a bitches." She was sitting up sucking on her cannula. "You can give that picture back now if you're done with it."

He handed the picture over to her. "I knew a girl who looked something like that when I was in high school," he said.

"I guess Benton here's up shit's creek now," she said. "I been tellin' the simple son of a bitch he can't just park where he likes without gettin' one of them license plates with a wheelchair on it."

Crane stood from the couch. "I really don't care where you park, Mrs. Grasslie. Neither one of you."

"Well, you goddamn for sure should. What if I wasn't handi-capped? What about that?"

"If you hear from your daughter, would you ask her to get in touch with me?"

She rolled her head back, staring at the ceiling. "We ain't gonna hear from her."

"But if you do."

She leveled her head. "Can I get you to leave on out of here if I say I will?"

"I guess I'm done anyway." He had his hand on the doorknob, thinking about the young, nervous kids he'd interviewed, most of them just smoking pot on the weekends, a few of them tweaking, pale and reckless and empty. He was looking out through the thin curtain at his cruiser. "I didn't have to come back here," he said. "I had the GI Bill after Bush One's war. I could've gone lots of places."

"I wish I'd have fought in a war." The skinny husband looked up from where he knelt at the coffee table, carefully placing little bars of lead into the melting pot.

Crane stared at him. "I guess I just couldn't think of anyplace else to go."

"I hear that," the woman said. She tried to turn toward him but it was a hard position to hold and the effort shortened her breath. "Before you get out of here I need you to understand that we grew her up good. Got her started out right," she said. "There wasn't nothin' wrong with what we done."

"Yes, ma'am. If you say so."

"Maybe Kayla knows where she is," Benton said, and they both looked at him. He appeared excited by the thought.

"Kayla don't know word one about her sister," she said. "Or us neither."

"You don't know what she knows."

"She don't know shit from Shinola. That's what I know."

"I might like to ask her," Crane said.

She slumped back in the chair, puffed out her cheeks and lit another cigarette. "Well, I hope you have a good goddamn time in Denver, then. That's what I hope."

"Colorado?"

"There ain't no Denver anything else as far as I know." She turned to Benton, flicking the lighted cigarette at him like he was a bothersome dog. "You sure got a lot to say about girls you didn't father," she said.

He picked the cigarette off the carpet, keeping his head down, rubbing at a spot in the shag that had been singed.

# Thirteen

Eınar and griff had gone to bed early and Marin had tried to sleep. But her head was pounding, the room too warm, close, even with the windows thrown open. Then the first wave of nausea hit.

She stumbled out into the hallway, drawing a robe across her shoulders, and stood clinging to the beading in the rough wooden wallboards. Her body was now soaked with sweat, but it felt better to be up and moving. She thought a cool glass of water might help.

In the kitchen she tipped a chair over, the sound of it striking the floor tearing through her like a gunshot, and her legs gave out. She sat down hard, more shocked than hurt, a collage of disjointed images from the drive west snapping through her mind as unexpected as a camera's flash. The dank motel room in Sioux Falls, asleep for an hour in its shallow tub, the whine of traffic, the bitter coffee she brewed on the counter beside the television. There were fragments of phone poles ticking by, wires sagging with blackbirds, a ball thrown for Sammy.

She crawled to the door, leaning into the jamb, finally dragging herself out onto the porch. The air was cooler but it didn't comfort her, as the optimism she and Alice had tried to maintain after the surgeries hadn't comforted, and when the remembered odors of body wastes and antiseptics and salves swept through her, she vomited over the edge. She had no idea what she thought she was going to do.

She slept in ragged bouts through the night, visions cycling of Alice's graying face, her thinning neck and hands, her hair brittle and then gone completely after the first rounds of chemo. At one point she heard the hospital's simpleminded pastor refer to "God in His wisdom," and recalled that she too had prayed, bargaining for her lover's life. She felt the hollowing disappointment of the loss all over again, the wretchedness of an ineffective mendicant.

Griff found her in the morning and got her into bed. She cleaned her great-aunt's face and hands, feeding her spoonfuls of warm sugar water, and in the afternoon she was able to sip a half cup of tea. She fell back to sleep, not waking until the next afternoon. She lay motionless in her bed, counting the knots in the ceilingboards to stay focused, feeling fragile as glassware.

That evening she had the strength to shower and dress in a clean nightgown, and Griff brought her a tray with coffee, a soft-boiled egg and toast.

She sipped the coffee, tapped the egg with the edge of a spoon. "How's Einar taking all of this?"

"He's been sitting on a chair in the hallway."

"Is he out there now?" Marin turned toward the door. "Are you there?" she called.

They heard the chairlegs scrape.

"I'm right here." He was standing in the doorway.

"Have you lost your mind, sitting out there like that?"

"I probably have."

She shook her head and took a bite of toast. "That's the most pathetic thing I've ever heard."

He moved to the bed, reaching out gently to find her, and she patted his hand.

"I just let myself get rundown. That's all it was."

"Yes," he said with some surety, as though the problem had now been resolved to his satisfaction. "That's exactly what happened."

.  .  .

In the afternoons they sat together on the porch, just the two of
them, speaking easily of the habits of songbirds, the rising cost
of groceries and gasoline, how the warming of the planet was re-
ported vacuously—as though it were no more than the wear and
tear of an ordinary garment—and how sugar inevitably destroyed
a person's vitality, and toward the end of that first week, having
grown more accustomed to each other, they launched into stories
from their childhood. The brandings, dances, weddings, broken
bones, rodeos, storms, arguments. At times pulling their chairs
around, each facing the other, reaching across their laps to hold
hands.

Griff busied herself in the kitchen, keeping the front windows
open so she could eavesdrop, listening for bursts of Marin's laughter that she thought she would have recognized anywhere and
known as the sound of family.

"Dance with me," Marin suggested one afternoon, standing up,
pulling him to his feet, and they waltzed clumsily down the porch
and back while she hummed the rhythm of a slow-moving melody,
the side of her face at rest against his chest.

The last cool hours of each evening were reserved for her walk. It
was a sixty-year-old habit, and she could name the succession of
good dogs she'd kept to provide their silent company.

She explored the treeline above the pastures and downstream
as far as the county road, Sammy racing ahead as she came along
steadily. She would stop at times, calling him back, and he sat
patiently listening to her warnings about porcupines and skunks
and mountain lions, her reminders that he was new to this country. He yawned, stretching, nosing her hand before striking out
again.

On the third evening out he managed to get sprayed by a

skunk, and Griff helped her scrub him with a mixture of hydrogen peroxide, baking powder and liquid soap. He braced up under the garden hose, allowing it, and just yesterday they'd seen a skunk again, a mother with three kits, and he'd lain flat, whining softly until they passed. So now he knew about skunks, she thought, good for him.

This evening she was searching for morels. She carried a plastic grocery bag and a paring knife, weaving deliberately through the trees a half mile upstream from the barn when Sammy started to bark and she looked up expecting another skunk, and her heart revved and she dropped the knife. She was standing at the edge of a clearing grown up in native grass and lupine, a place where she'd played as a girl. She lowered her hand from where she'd raised it against her chest and bent down to retrieve the knife. In the middle of the meadow was a heap of antlers, gathered bones and horns five feet high and ten feet across. But it was the figures that made her hold her breath.

They stood apart from the mound of bones, a dozen feet or so out from its edges, spaced evenly around the perimeter as though circling. She stood searching each figure for motion; they were that distinct and lifelike in their postures. There were six of them. She could not look away, and when there was only the movement of the wind in the trees she struck out through the waist-high grass and flowers, Sammy staying at her side. "It's all right," she whispered. They were still twenty feet away.

The figures were human-sized, five adults—a wolf-headed man, his mouth wide in triumph, she-bear, moose, long-horned bull and bighorn ram—and a single child, its skull reptilian, fragile and snake-fanged. Their knees were cocked, arms extended heavenward, backs arched, one offering up a nugget of agate in its raised hands. On another, a tail curved away in an S, the last of its vertebrae no bigger than a snail's body. It was as though the earth had thrown up an accumulation of its dead, regathering the parts into this resurrection of creatures.

She stopped at every one of them, fingering a hip, a shoulder, a cage of ribs, discovering how each ceramic bone had been attached to its armature of steel rods with copper wires and rawhide ligatures. The bones were colored ochre, caramel and cinnamon, the figures mostly unadorned. Here, a necklace of raven feathers. There, a bracelet woven of moss and flowers, an anklet of green beads, some figures rendered with more artistry.

She lifted an antler from the pile, then set it back in place. It was real, and the bones of cattle and horses and wild things mixed in with the mound of antlers were real. She imagined Griff carrying them in from the surrounding countryside. The years it must have taken.

On the northmost edge of the meadow she found a split-log bench and sat, her eyes welling with a sense of unexpected peace, her arms and legs gone weak. When her vision blurred the figures seemed to rock and leap, dancing around the heaped-up antlers as though the pile were a kind of shrine. She imagined she could hear the joyful hymns they sang.

She sat until it was too dark to see, and when Sammy whined she stood and shook her head, stomping her feet in the damp night air, feeling the episodes of her life edging back in increments: anger, jealousy, disappointment, pride. The belief of having been in love. It had all been bled away somehow, and she'd been reduced to just a simpler, and quieted, animal. She looked up into the spray of stars.

"No one can know for sure," she said.

# Fourteen

HE WOKE AT FIVE-THIRTY, the time he always got up in the summer, and swung his legs over the edge of the bed. He sat listening. No one was moving in the house. He was used to the racket of McEban in the kitchen, noisy and impatient with the coffeepot, the smell of frying bacon. He walked to the door, cracking it open to listen. Still nothing. He tiptoed to the bathroom at the end of the hall, easing the door shut behind him. He peed against the porcelain above the waterline to avoid the sound of splashing. When he was done he lowered the seat and sat. He worried it would be too loud if he flushed, deciding not to chance it. He hadn't been here long enough to know the rules.

In his bedroom again he dressed and sat in the desk chair by the window looking out at the empty street below. A boy on a bicycle rode past throwing rolled newspapers from the canvas saddlebags at the back of his bike. Each paper was wrapped in clear plastic, and the boy gripped it by the excess part of the sleeve, swinging it around his head before letting it fly. Like David was supposed to have done with his slingshot. He wanted to rush out of the house, introduce himself, offer to help, but he didn't. The rules again.

He thought the room must be someone's office when they

didn't have a guest. There was a computer on the desk, a Mac like McEban's, but he didn't turn it on. Beside the desk were stacks of papers, books and boxes, and he peeked around in one and found a hole-punch, a stapler and padded envelopes, but the snooping just made him more nervous and he left the others untouched. He didn't want to be caught going through someone's belongings. There was still no one up in the house.

He put his shoes on to go downstairs, careful to place his feet where each step butted up against the wallboard, because he'd seen stairs built, knowing the boards were nailed solidly at the edges and wouldn't squeak. In the living room he sat on the couch, then moved to a chair because he didn't want to hog a big piece of furniture all to himself.

He was chilly and rubbed his arms. At first, he couldn't figure out why Laramie was so much cooler than the ranch. It was August here too. And then he'd spotted the vent in the ceiling of his room and, holding his hand underneath, felt the rush of air. They kept their whole house colder than the bank in Ishawooa.

In the kitchen he poured a glass of milk. He thought this would be all right, that it might even be expected. It had been late when he and his father arrived the night before, but his father's wife had waited up for them. Her name was Claire, and she was so pretty he forgot about being tired. She'd given him a glass of milk without asking if he wanted one, and made a sandwich with plenty of mayonnaise when he said that's how he liked it. He thought about making a sandwich this morning but didn't want to risk the disturbance. When he finished the milk he placed the glass in the sink, running it full of water, as McEban had taught him to, so a crust wouldn't form in the bottom.

He thought about going outside, but what if Rodney got up and couldn't find him? He counted the squares in the linoleum. Twenty-five across and twenty the other direction. He did the math.

When he couldn't sit anymore, he searched very quietly under the sink and in the pantry, finding an all-purpose cleaner and a brush, a bucket and rubber gloves, and got down on his knees cleaning one square thoroughly, and then the next, subtracting against the total. That's where he was when Claire came in wearing a pink-and-lavender robe, staring at him openmouthed as if she'd discovered a thief. She wasn't wearing slippers, her feet so white he could see the blue veins beneath the skin.

He said he was sorry, that he hoped he hadn't woken her.

"Oh, my God," she said. She hugged him. She called him a sweet boy, and he stayed as still as he could, breathing shallowly, enjoying every bit of it. He didn't think about pulling away. His mother was good at lots of things, like telling stories, but she wasn't much of a toucher. McEban hugged him sometimes, but not like this. He couldn't remember any similar experience in his life.

Later that morning his father loaded everyone in the car, Claire, and his new brother and sister, Kurt and Corley, and they bought a paper bucket of chicken, mashed potatoes, rolls, gravy and cole-slaw at the Colonel's, and drove east out of town up a long grade until they topped out in the National Forest. Vedauwoo. That's what the place was called and it was cool as the house up there, though the sun was hot on their faces. Big, pale stones were standing everywhere, like a herd of elephants, and when he stood in the glare reflecting off a stone it felt as if he was onstage at the high school in Sheridan, which he'd done once in a play, with all the spotlights on him, unable to see the audience, even with his hand raised over his eyes.

Claire spread a blanket out in the shade of one of the stones, holding little Corley on her lap, and they had their picnic. The gravy and potatoes were barely warm, but it didn't matter. Every-one was relaxed and quick to laugh, and then he and his father threw a football back and forth, letting Kurt try when he wanted, but he was only a year older than his sister, only three and a half, and wasn't any good. When Kenneth lobbed the ball softly toward his little outstretched arms, it bounced into his face and he cried until Claire took him by the wrists and swung him around in circles.

On the ride back to Laramie he tried to keep every episode of the day linked together in his mind, like a highway with each separate memory represented by the yellow dashes in the middle, so he could tell McEban. But he already knew that Claire's hair in the sunlight was what he'd remember most. Above anything else. It was a deep red color, and he'd always liked red hair and thought Rodney must too. That it was a preference he'd gotten from his father. And she had freckles on her forehead and arms that had darkened in the sun as the afternoon wore on, and he liked those too.

On Monday his father went back to work at the university. He was teaching summer school but said he didn't mind, that he liked to stay busy and they could use the extra money.

Kenneth got up with him and when they were eating their cereal—because that's what you had for breakfast in Laramie—he asked his father to make a list of chores. Rodney just laughed at first, reminding him he was on vacation, and then Kenneth brought him the pad and pen by the phone. Rodney's list said:

> *Play basketball in the driveway.*
> *Sweep the driveway with the broom in the garage if you feel like it.*
> *Take a nap after lunch.*
> *Read a book.*
> *There's a shelf of DVDs, but don't watch the ones rated R.*
> *Enjoy yourself.*

After his father left, and before Claire and the little kids got up, he swept the driveway. He thought about calling McEban to see how he was, but he had no idea what a long-distance phone call cost. Besides, he'd almost cried when Claire hugged him, so he wasn't sure what hearing McEban's voice would make him do.

He took his wallet from his back pocket and slipped out the credit-card-size calendar he'd gotten at the feed store in Ishawooa, counting out how many days were left. Eighteen. He counted twice to make sure, then put his wallet back.

He left a note on the counter for Claire and walked a couple of blocks down Baker, stopping where it dead-ended into Ninth. He could see a park across the street with a lake in the middle. He waited for a break in the traffic and sprinted across, walking around the lake twice before sitting on the curb watching for license plates from different states. There weren't as many as he'd hoped, and then Claire was coming down Baker. She had Corley up against her hip, Kurt by the hand, and his little brother was sucking the thumb of his other hand. He crossed back to where she stood waiting for him.

"I left a note," he said.

"That's how I knew where you were. And I saw the list your father made." She set the little girl down, holding the back of her collar so she couldn't go anywhere. Kurt stood gripping the crotch of his pants. "Do you have to go to the bathroom?"

He shook his head.

"Are you sure?"

Kurt shook his head again.

"Can you swim in that lake?" Kenneth asked.

"I wouldn't," she said, and then, "You're used to a good deal more, aren't you?"

He shrugged. "McEban and I, and my Uncle Paul, we don't sit around a lot."

"What do you do all day when you're home? I mean in Ishawooa."

They both acted as if she hadn't said "home" like that.

"I've got a horse," he told her. He thought about all the chores during a day, from start to finish, and couldn't decide where to begin. "A ranch doesn't run itself," he said. It was something he'd heard McEban say.

Corley began to cry, and Kurt said, "I can ride a horse better than anyone. Better than you. Or, better than anybody."

"Well, you can help me today." She spun around toward the house. "That'll be something to do."

They all drove to the store together. His job was to keep his brother from touching anything, which wasn't especially hard after Claire let the kids pick out their candy. She asked him what his favorite was and he said a box of brownie mix. That made her laugh, so he was glad that's what he'd chosen. He'd also been thinking about a bag of Skittles. The small one.

When they got home and unloaded the groceries, she pointed out what cupboards and drawers he should look in for the things he needed to mix his brownies. His brother and sister painted on tablets of paper laid out on the kitchen floor, and they ate lunch while the oven was heating.

"Did your mother teach you to cook?" she asked.

"McEban did."

She wiped Corley's mouth, the little girl fighting away from her. "I hear your mother's writing a book."

He set the pan in the oven, squaring it in the middle of the top rack. It made him uneasy to talk about his mother's talents, because he knew how much she relied on the advice of ghosts. Ghosts made him nervous. "It's about how to live a spiritual life." He sat back down at the table. "She says everybody needs to heal their relationship with the world." He was proud of his memory. "She says we have to break free from our trances of unworthiness and fear."

"Really?"

Kurt said, "Spiritual life, spiritual life, spiritual life," like he was a parrot showing off. Then he lowered his voice, repeating the same phrase again, pretending to be a frog.

"She hasn't let me read it yet. She says it's a work in progress and if anybody reads it before it's done it might break her confidence." He carried his plate to the sink, then the other plates. "She teaches too." He didn't want Claire to think his mother wasn't a hard worker.

"I'm going back to teaching when the kids are older." She was drinking out of Kurt's glass and the rim was all slimy with his spit, but she acted like she didn't notice. "That's where I met your father. At the university here. Do you like school?"

He knew the next question would be about which class was his favorite. "Science is my best subject," he said, picturing Rodney in a classroom with a chalkboard behind.

"Are any of your teachers mean?"

"Mrs. Kazepa smiles a lot but she's not ever happy."

"It seems like there's always one."

"My mom teaches all over the place. In different towns, and in every one somebody likes her so much they ask her to stay with them. So she never has to get a room in a motel." He thought about his mother's brochures. "She's real good at showing people how to live in their bodies." It sounded important, worthwhile, when he said it out loud.

"I think your father told me something about that." She drank from the slimy glass again, and he thought he might puke if she kept it up. "Does Mr. McEban just make desserts?"

"He makes everything."

"Kurtie, look at me," she said. "We aren't going to have an accident today, are we?"

The little boy shook his head.

Kenneth opened the oven, stabbing at the brownies with a toothpick, and they were almost done. He helped her gather the art supplies, stacking the tablets and crayons and colored markers in the pantry, then slipped on the oven mitts and set the pan up on the stove. He was trying to remember what McEban had said about his mother's teaching when his brother dragged a chair to the stove.

"They're too hot, honey," Claire said. "We'll all have some of Kenneth's treat after our naps."

Kurt climbed up onto the chair, staring down into the pan. "I only like the swirly ones." His voice was choked with horror, his brows knitting, his eyes filled with tears. "These ones are just brown. I hate them. I hate the brown ones."

He stomped his foot and she lifted him out of the chair, standing him on the floor by the table. She knelt in front of him, holding his head between her hands so he couldn't look anyplace else. He was starting to sob.

"Boys who whine don't get treats." She spoke evenly, calmly. "They don't get anything at all."

He was sucking at the air like a fish wishing she'd drop him back in the water.

Kenneth finally remembered the exact phrase. "McEban thinks we fit in our bodies just fine."

She looked at him, smiling, and then back at her son: "You get what you get, and you don't have a fit. Do you understand?"

He nodded, tears dripping from his chin. "I have to go to the bathroom," he said.


After the kids had taken their naps and eaten a square of brownie, she led him into the laundry room and started explaining how to operate the washer and dryer, but when he said he knew about darks and whites and water temperature she let him do it himself.

And then there wasn't anything else she could think of, so he went out in the driveway and shot baskets for an hour until she called him back in.

"I have a present for you," she said.

She held out an iPod and he stared down at it in the palm of her hand, putting his hands in his pockets.

"Do you already have one?"

"They're too expensive."

She looked to the hallway where Kurt was pushing a red plastic truck against his sister's leg. She told him to stop and turned back to Kenneth. "This one's old, and whether you want it or not I'm going to get a new one."

"Maybe Rodney would like it."

"He has his own."

The iPod didn't look all that used. "What would you do with it if I didn't take it?"

She smiled. "You, sir, are one seriously unfun little dude."

"I just like to get things done." He was thinking he had about as much fun as anybody else. "McEban said I couldn't listen to one on the tractor, or when I'm riding a horse, because you can't hear if something bad's happening."

"Well, we don't have a tractor. Or horses, either. It's yours or it gets trashed."

He stared down at his feet, turning them so his toes were pointing straight. McEban had told him that if you learn to walk correctly when you're a kid, your hips and everything else would last a lot longer.

"I guess," he said, "if you're going to throw it away."

"I'm having an accident now." Kurt stood in the hallway, his face full of surprise.


Rodney was tired when he got home but felt better after dinner, sprawling on the living-room floor and wrestling with the little kids, and Kenneth followed Claire up to his room and she turned the computer on.

"What kind of music do you like?" she asked.

"I don't listen to music that much."

"When you do."

He thought about the music in band class, and on the radio,

and that his mother played in her trailer when she was home. "Whatever you like would be fine," he said.

He stood at her shoulder, watching her load songs on the iPod, and when she was done she showed him how to operate it. It was easy. He thought it would be. He knew really stupid kids who had one.

# Fifteen

CRANE DROVE DOWN through Ranchester and across to Dayton, continuing west on Highway 14 up the long incline that rose in ascending plateaus through the native grass and sage foothills, finally parking the cruiser in a gravel turnout in a border of pine, the evergreens draping down over the rounded crest of the Bighorns like a throw of darker, greener fabric. He'd gained fifteen hundred feet off the prairie floor and could look back east thirty miles to Sheridan and the sweep of drier, flatter land beyond.

The traffic was light. Mostly out-of-state vans and motor homes easing down off the mountain in single-line convoys, the drivers unnerved by the steep grade, geared down and traveling twenty miles under the speed limit. Occasionally a local whistled past, raising a forefinger off the steering wheel to wave. He radioed Starla.

"I'm going to catch some lunch," he told her. "Log me out for an hour."

"Roger that," she said. "BBFN."

He could hear her unwrapping a fresh stick of gum.

"I don't know what that means."

"It stands for bye-bye for now. It's text-message shorthand."

"We aren't texting, we're talking."

"That doesn't mean the rest of us can't intermingle our disciplines. Are you going to run for sheriff again?"

"I hadn't thought about it."

"Seems to me you're losing interest in law enforcement."

He pulled a Ziploc bag from the glovebox and slipped the sandwich out. "Why don't you run against me?"

"LOL."

"Laughing out loud, right?"

"You truly are the hippest of bossmen, boss."

"Just route any calls through to Hank."

"Word that."

He turned the volume down on the radio. A fence ran along the south edge of the turnout, and knotted in the top strand of wire were four pairs of panties, candy-striped, flowered, white and yellow, lifting and quivering in the wind. He finished his sandwich, checked for cell reception, and she answered on the second ring.

"It's me," he said. She'd told him when it was likely she'd be home and Larry wouldn't.

"Hey."

"You doing all right?"

"I'm just fine. What about you?"

"Better now," he said.

"I thought we agreed we weren't going to do the sweet stuff."

"That's your rule, not mine."

"If I remember correctly you said you wanted a friend. We've both got someone to sleep with."

"Have you told Larry we're friends?"

He heard her let the dog out, walk back across what sounded like a tiled floor, pull a chair back, the last raising the hair on his arm. "Where are you?" he asked.

"Did you forget the number you dialed? I'm at home."

"I mean what room."

"I'm in the kitchen."

A tremor started again in his left hand, so he switched the phone to the other. That whole side was worsening faster than the rest of him.

"I haven't told Larry anything about us."

"If we ever get around to phone sex," he said, "do you think Larry would be better than me because his vocabulary's bigger?"

"You must not be calling from the office."

"I'm parked up out of Dayton. On the road that goes over the Bighorns."

"You remember what we used to drink up there?"

"Hamm's."

"It still means a shitty beer was responsible for me losing my virginity and thinking that marrying you was a good idea. Hold on, someone's buzzing through."

The line went dead, to that flat purr he thought of as the sound wiring produced. He looked down at where his hand twitched rhythmically in his lap, then slid it under his thigh, but it wouldn't stop.

"I'm back."

"Do you really think our marriage was that shitty?"

"It's easier to remember it that way."

"It's not how I remember things."

"That's because I'm the one who filed. You, sir, were the dumpee."

"Was that Larry who buzzed through?"

"No, it was somebody else."

"Do you remember the first time we did it?" he asked.

"Did it?"

"That's what we used to call it. That's what everybody called it."

"Now I know where you're parked."

"About ten feet from the exact spot."

"That's really creepy."

"I thought maybe you'd think it was sweet," he said. "But that's no doubt how dumpees view the world."

He heard her open the refrigerator, and a semi passed. He could smell the brake pads burning.

"We shouldn't have waited twelve years," she said. "We didn't have to wait until you got sick to be able to talk."

"I needed to wait." He heard her bite into something. It made a snapping sound. "What was that?"

"It's a carrot, and that was Larry who beeped through. I don't know why I said it wasn't."

"Does he call to say he loves you?"

"He said he was going straight to Don Clayton's after work. A bunch of them play cards on Thursday night. He said he'd eat something there."

"They play even in the summer?"

"All year."

"How late?"

"Late enough," she said. "I've got to go now."

He snapped his phone shut and got out and opened the trunk. He'd been to the drugstore for shaving cream, toothpaste and the extra-strength Advil that helped take the edge off the headaches he got now in the afternoons. He shook it all out of the plastic bag and walked over to the fenceline. The ground was strewn with beer cans, the singed cardboard tubing from bottle rockets, the torn paper and plastic debris from an assortment of fireworks, condoms and their wrappers, several dozen spent shotgun shell casings. He filled the bag and emptied it in a trashcan chained to a post set back in the trees, then filled it again. When he'd picked up all the litter he cut the panties loose and trashed them too. He couldn't remember any party he'd ever attended as a kid that had this kind of variety.

He sat against the open trunk of the cruiser watching cars pass on the highway, thinking that if he were younger, or maybe healthier, this whole scene wouldn't seem so goddamn sad.

. . .

After dinner he showered and dressed in jeans and a clean shirt and told Jean he had to go back in to work.

"Is there a crime wave I haven't noticed?" She was tearing open a red Netflix envelope, pulling the DVD out.

"Paperwork," he said. "What'd you get?"

*"Rome,"* she said. "I missed some episodes." She finished her bourbon and poured another at the kitchen counter. Her neck was reddened from the sun.

"How'd it go in your garden today?"

"It grew," she said.

He kissed her on the cheek.

"You could stay. We could watch some TV, and you wouldn't have to say a thing to me. It'd be like you weren't even here."

"Duty calls," he said.

She turned toward the living room with her drink and the DVD, and he figured she must've started on the bourbon around four, four-thirty. That was the stage she was in, this quiet, distracted mood. She'd be ready for a fight in an hour and ready for bed an hour after that, and if she remembered what they'd fought about the next morning she never mentioned it. Mornings were her best time. He stopped on the sunporch and called back into the house, "I love you," but heard no reply.

He drove his '92 Dodge pickup out north on Highway 345 with the windows down and when he cleared the last little subdivision of pricey new five-acre ranchettes he turned the lights off, continuing in the waxing twilight and faint starlight. The pale roadway seemed to rise up out of the landscape, gripping him with the sensation of not having to steer at all, as though he were effortlessly lifting off a runway, but his right front tire bit into the gravel off the shoulder and he overcorrected across the center line, then straightened and switched the headlights back on. For the first time it occurred to him that maybe killing himself would be just the ticket, just not tonight.

He turned onto a graded ranch road by the Montana line and drove west for a mile before pulling over. He shut off the lights and killed the engine, the night sounds swelling, and with them an expectation of disappointment. She wasn't here and he now doubted she'd come. He looked at the lighted dial of his wrist-watch—not yet ten-thirty—and laid his head back against the headrest, shutting his eyes, focusing lightly on the low, rounded whistling of a screech owl, and then there was the sound of something collapsing around him and he snapped his head up as she cranked her SUV in a U-turn through the gravel and parked in front of him, bumper to bumper. He looked at his watch again, slowly understanding he'd been asleep for half an hour.

She climbed in, closing the door and exhaling as though she'd run the whole distance from Sheridan. She held a brown paper sack on her lap, the top folded down.

"I about gave up on you," he said.

She was staring straight ahead out the windshield. "The first time I got about a mile out of town and lost my nerve. I turned around and drove right back home. The second time I just slowed down when I thought about turning around."

He reached over to take her hand but she hunched forward, staring in the side mirror.

"Isn't this kind of public?"

He glanced in the rearview mirror. There weren't any lights, nothing but the weak, cloud-cast shadows. "I guess it would be if somebody came by."

He drove another mile before finding a two-track heading south. He opened and closed the barbed-wire gate behind them, idling out across a pasture of a dozen sections or more. They parked on a rise with a view across the foothills to the south, and up toward Montana in the other direction, sitting for a moment listening to the engine tick as it cooled.

"I'm not unhappy."

"I am," he said.

She looked at him. "Can we get out?"

They walked toward the mountains until they came to a sandstone outcropping and scooted out on their butts to the weathered edge, sitting there with their feet dangling. There was enough light so that the sage still appeared to have some color to it, a kind of blanched moss, and the sky held a band of royal blue around the horizon.

She unrolled the top of the sack and pulled out a six-pack of Miller Lite, popping the tab on one and then another. "I couldn't find any Hamm's," she said. "I don't know whether they even make it anymore."

There was a muted scraping to their right, nothing more than hearing your neck scratch against a corduroy collar, and they both turned toward the sound.

"Are there rattlesnakes out here?"

"I don't know. Yeah, there probably are."

She slid around behind him, settling again on his other side. "Are you very frightened?"

"Mostly I'm worried about the end of it. About what it'll do to Jean if I last a long time."

"Maybe she'll surprise you."

"Maybe she will. I've been surprised by lots of things."

They put the empty cans in the sack and opened new ones.

"I don't think I would have wanted a divorce if we'd been older," she said. "If we were as old as we are now."

He could make out the rise of her cheeks, the bridge of her nose, but not the color of her hair or eyes. She was staring straight at him.

"I was still young enough then to think my life could change," she said. "I'm over that now."

"I thought you said you weren't unhappy."

"There's a difference."

She leaned into him and he draped an arm across her shoulders, holding her tight. It was his better arm.

"I guess I've never expected anything to change," he said. "But then I'll eat the same goddamn thing for lunch every day, and never once think about ordering something different."

She laughed softly, and he stroked her hair.

"I'm not going to leave Larry. I know better. That's where I'm going with this."

"I never thought you would."

She looked away, sipping her beer. "When I think about you dying, I get that same feeling of wanting to run. Like when I was young." The slight palsy in his arm set up a vibration in her shoulders and neck, enough to make her voice quaver, and he brought it back into his lap.

"That's about how I feel too," he said.

She set her beer down and pressed against him, wrapping herself around the arm as a girl might cling to a vine, as a woman might if she thought the warmth of her body could heal.

# Sixteen

A BANK OF COTTONWOOD fluff had drifted in against the river-rock foundation, and when Paul parked beside the cabin it huffed up in the headlights, skittering away into a brake of wild roses. He cut the engine, sitting quietly in the darkness, the sawing of crickets, the gentle exhale of the night winds feeling like an embrace.

He flipped his cell phone open, the face and number pad glowing amber in his hand. He'd turned the ringer off while he and Griff were at the drive-in, and there still weren't any messages. He dialed and she answered on the first ring.

"Hey, baby." It was her half-phony, half-seductive voice.

"This is Paul."

"Well then, hey, baby brother."

She laughed, and he could hear others laughing around her, the click of glassware against a faint background of conversation.

"Don't you check your messages? I've been calling since this morning."

"I sure wish I would've looked at my caller ID. Right now, for instance."

"Most people wouldn't admit that."

"I've never for a minute thought I was like anybody else." The background noise dimmed.

"Where are you?"

"I'm enjoying a cocktail."

"Where?"

"At a lovely home in Seattle."

"How lovely?"

"Very," she said. "The poor can't afford enlightenment."

"You want to tell me why you shipped Kenneth south?"

"He wasn't *shipped* anywhere. He's with his father."

"I know where he is, and as far as fathering goes, Rodney's just a guy you met at a powwow in Lodge Grass twelve years ago." He heard the sizzle and buzz of rainfall. "You drinking outside?"

"I am now. How did dear McEban take it? When Rodney showed up with the papers, I mean?"

"He absorbed the blow."

"The Guides thought it was best."

"It's me, Rita. You don't have to act like you believe your own bullshit."

"I believe if you were more in touch with your higher self, this is something you'd understand."

"What I understand is that Rodney got a wild hair up his ass and decided he wanted to play father for a month."

"The man has his own children."

"So, this was your idea?"

"Mrs. Rodney thought it was a good idea too. After I explained the situation to her."

"Jesus Christ, Rita."

"Her name's Claire. Unlike you she's a person of deep compassion."

He could hear the hiss of a car passing in the street. "I can't believe you did this to your own kid."

"Mostly it's important for Rodney. Growth-wise, that is."

"Why don't you just say you wanted to punish him for knocking you up."

"I was never meant to bear a child. I don't have the hips for it, or the temperament."

"Really?"

"Bye now," she said.

He snapped the phone shut, tossing it on the dash and sliding the seat back. He thought he'd sit just long enough to allow the sound of her voice to drain out of his mind, but he didn't want to be out here all night, and the kitchen lights were still on at McEban's.

He stepped up onto the porch and looked in through the window. The aluminum shelving from the refrigerator was tilting out of the sink, the countertops stacked with dishes. He let the door slam coming in and stood in the mudroom. McEban was on his knees on the floor. He'd stripped off his T-shirt, his pale torso as thickly muscled as an ape's.

He sat back on his heels. "How was the village?"

"Hopping."

"Were they showing anything good at the movies?" There was a bucket of soapy water at his side.

*"The Man Who Shot Liberty Valance."*

"Jimmy Stewart was in that, wasn't he?"

"Yeah, he was. They're going to play an old Western one day every week all summer long. Mostly for the tourists, I guess. Will you go to bed if I help you?"

McEban looked around as though gauging the amount of work left. "I think I would."

"You wouldn't sneak back down and start another project?"

"I believe I'd be satisfied along those lines."

He bent to the floor again, and Paul slipped his shoes off, tiptoed across the worn linoleum and pulled a rag from a box full of them underneath the sink. His eyes watered from the stink of the cleaning solution.

"I'm going to Africa," he said.

McEban quit scrubbing, still hunched forward on his hands and knees, his back wet as the floor, sweat dripping from his nose.

He sat back again, drawing an arm across his face. "Where to in Africa?"

"Uganda. For an NGO."

"Good for you."

"You know what NGO stands for?"

"Nongovernmental organization." He reached out to wipe a spot he'd missed. "I don't know why I know that, but I do. You going to be gone for the rest of your life?"

"For a year."

McEban slipped a can of Copenhagen from a back pocket, pinched out a dab and settled it in his lip. "Do you think the boy's all right?"

"I think he'd have called if he wasn't."

"I'm worried he'll feel miserable and just hang on until he can't stand it anymore."

"Like you would."

"Yeah, like that." He took a cloth out of the bucket, wrung it out and wiped off his face and chest, then dropped it back in the bucket.

"I miss him too," Paul said.

McEban got up and stepped to the sink, pulled the shelving out and emptied the bucket. "Maybe Kenneth and I'll go see a movie when he gets home. I guess he'd like anything with horses in it." He was rinsing the bucket with the spray nozzle.

"I hope you're not taking it personally, but she doesn't give a fuck about anybody."

McEban shut the water off, turning the bucket upside down in the basin. "If you mean Rita you ought to say her name."

"Who else would I mean?"

McEban was watching a miller moth circling the light over the sink. His hands and face were so darkly tanned it looked like those parts of him came from another race.

"Is Griff going with you?"

"I don't think so. What'll you do if Kenneth grows up like me? Takes off for some other continent?"

He was remembering nights as a boy, waking from a bad dream, and McEban coming in and lying down next to him, holding him until he got back to sleep. He used to wonder if the man sat up at night just waiting to help.

"He told me the other day he'd like to keep on here."

"Isn't that what I said when I was his age?"

"I guess, when I've thought about it, I thought he might stick around. Maybe until I died." He started stacking the plates back into the cupboard.

"You know that's fucked up, don't you?"

"Not entirely I don't. You ought to take the digital camera with you, send back some pictures." He smiled, the tendons standing out in his neck, his ears lifting slightly. "Maybe one of Lake Victoria if you got down there."

He lifted the bucket out of the sink and the strainer basket out of the drain, spitting a stream of tobacco juice against the porcelain and then running water over it. "You think you're going to be okay without Griff?"

"I don't know."

The moth fluttered against McEban's neck and he snatched it out of the air, held it for a moment loosely in his fist and then threw it hard against a cupboard door, and it fell quivering on the countertop. "I hate those little sons of bitches."

"Especially when they fly around your ears."

They could hear the horses moving in the pasture outside the window.

"I'm scared shitless." Paul pinched the moth up by a wing and dropped it in the disposal side of the sink. "I guess I came up here tonight to say something about that."

"You mean generally?"

"No, I mean when Griff and I start fighting about something."

McEban wet a paper towel, wiping the gray smudge off the cupboard. "I used to feel like that sometimes."

"Should you have said 'Rita'?"

"Before her. There was a woman I cared about who lives in Nebraska now."

A horse snorted, and then another, and they could hear them pounding away toward the far end of the pasture.

"Then it goes away? Feeling like this?"

"Yeah, it does. But you miss it."

# Seventeen

Jean had been thinking about winter. Not winter in Wyoming, but in a casita in Santa Fe or Albuquerque. Maybe Tucson. Red tiled roof, doors and shutters painted the color of blue ink. Walled patio. An arbor of thatched ocotillo, borders of cholla and yucca. She was staring out at her garden, thinking what a relief it would be to live in a place where she wouldn't be tempted to grow a single goddamn vegetable. Drought-resistant, is what she's after. She'd started a new life once in Florida and just let that yard go to a weedy sandlot. She'd liked it there.

Last night she Googled the exact times of the mid-December dawns and dusks in each city, and at the very least she was going to gain forty-plus minutes of daylight. Almost fifty-five in Tucson. It was easier to start over in warm weather. A piece of cake to get up and get on with your life when you don't have to plug your car in so the engine block won't freeze.

Her friend Sally once said living through a Wyoming winter was evidence of low self-esteem. Thanksgiving, she thought, would be a good time to leave.

She tore the foil back on the Marlboro Lights, tapping the pack against her wrist while watching Griff drive in and park.

She held the water bottle up in the light and shook it hard, the ice rattling against the dark plastic sides. It was one of those new bottles with a soft plastic nipple you could bite into to suck the liquid up, so you could drink and drive without having to tip your head back. She'd filled this one with Smirnoff.

"Hey," the girl said. She set a small wooden box on the table, *House of Windsor* in red lettering on top.

"Hey yourself. Can I have one of your cigars?"

"There's just pictures inside."

Jean was thinking of Crane at breakfast this morning. How he'd stared at her, the sadness in his face so palpable it had made her want to scream. "You still ride around with your stepdaddy in his copmobile?"

"Not for awhile."

"But you're fine with each other?"

"Sure." She preferred her mother like this. Sweetly buzzed. "That's not the kind of plastic bottle that gives you cancer, is it?"

"No, it's the safe kind." Jean shook the ice again. "I checked."

"I might make a drink myself."

"There's orange juice inside if you want a mixer." She blew a plume of smoke toward the kitchen door.

When Griff came back out her mother had opened the cigar box and taken out the wedding picture of herself and Griffin.

"Isn't this a peach?" She tossed the picture down on the table. "God, I didn't know shit then, except that your dad was a catch."

"Can I leave this stuff over here?"

Jean slumped back in her chair. "Worst mistake I ever made in my life was letting you stay out there with that old man after Crane and I got married." The sweet buzz was souring. "I know damn well it's why you gave up on me. Us not living together."

"Einar burned a bunch of stuff." There were kids in the yard next door running through a sprinkler, laughing. "Some of it was mine."

"No shit." The good mood returned. "What you ought to do is move out now. You get stuck there after he turns into a total nutcase, it'll look worse. If you leave then, I mean."

Griff stirred her drink with a finger and Jean straightened her legs, pulling her summer dress up mid-thigh.

"At least I've still got good calves." She looked up smiling, boxing her hands in front of her face like she was holding a camera, making a clicking sound. "Wyoming snapshot. Mother and daughter getting hammered in the middle of the day. It doesn't get any better than that."

"Einar's sister came out from Chicago."

"Marin?"

"Yes."

Jean reached over to pat her daughter's hand. "I think it's wonderful you're taking in new patients for your nursing home, dear. Makes me proud, being a dropout nurse's assistant myself."

"I didn't know you quit."

"It's the shit and piss they don't tell you about when you sign up. Bodily fluids. That's what it comes down to." She sucked from her bottle.

"She came out to help with Einar."

"The prodigal lesbian leading the blind." Jean stubbed the cigarette out, using the butt to rake the ash up against the sides. "I'm thinking of moving. Maybe the southwest this time."

"You and Crane?"

"I'm afraid your step-buddy has been out screwing another pooch."

Griff was staring at the caragana at the border of the yard, grown up thick with yellow blossoms. "I don't think he's the type." She was trying to count the times she'd moved with her mother. She could remember the house in Florida. The one in Iowa.

"Well, he sure as hell ain't fucking me."

A magpie dove at the bird feeder and a vireo hit the screen, bouncing to the ground.

Griff stood up to watch the little olive-gray bird right itself, shaking its head. "Do you have a cat?"

"We're out of cats." Jean leaned forward with her elbows on the table. "Is this too much information for you all at once?"

"I just think you're wrong."

"Oh, God, it's you, isn't it?"

"Not funny, Mother."

Jean sat up straighter. "What if he's fucking somebody *older* than me? Wouldn't that suck shit?"

The stunned bird took a step, falling onto its side again.

"Can I ask you something?"

"As long as it doesn't have anything to do with what's wrong with me."

"Do you think my work's any good?"

"You mean your skeleton thingies?"

"Yes."

Jean stared at the raw wood in the ceiling, considering. "Well, they're a lot more interesting than gnomes, or jockeys, or Greek goddesses. Did I tell you I saw a five-foot-high angel at the tree farm in Sheridan?"

"Lawn ornaments?"

"Which one am I supposed to be?"

"I don't have anyone in particular in mind when I make them."

"You know I don't know how to talk about art." She leaned forward, staring down again at her wedding photograph. "But I do know what this is." She was tapping a finger on the table. "What you've got right there is a picture of the last time your mother was feeling lucky."

# Eighteen

HELEN PARKED by the office and the only person in the lobby was a stocky boy, maybe twenty-five, with a bad complexion. He was watching a Rockies game on the plasma TV in the breakfast nook and, when he noticed her, hurried around behind the counter.

"I'm Mrs. Johnson," she said. "I think my husband already checked us in."

The gold-colored nametag over his shirt pocket read *Tyler.*

"Yes, ma'am," he said. "He said you'd be coming in separately."

He coded a key card, slid it across the counter and smoothed out a map of the complex, bending over it with a red pen and drawing a line around to the back of the westernmost wing. "If you park around here, it'll be hard to see your car from the highway." He was smiling—leering, really—and staring unguardedly at her breasts.

She folded the map. "Is your manager on duty?"

The smile dropped away, along with the color from his face. "Yes, ma'am. She's in the back."

"You want me to have a talk with her about this attitude you've got going on?"

"No, ma'am."

"Then try not being such a smutty little shithead. Okay?"

He lowered his voice. "Yes, ma'am."

She drove around to the back of the Spring Hill Suites, spotted Crane's pickup and parked beside it. When she let herself in, the drapes were drawn and she stood there blinking.

"What did you tell him?" He was sitting in a chair by the table in the little efficiency kitchen.

"I said I was going to spend the afternoon at the Sanctuary. It's a spa up on Twenty-fourth. I said I was going to get a massage and something called a Vichy Shower Body Polish."

"They have a pool here."

"What did you tell Jean?"

"We needed a Costco run. I already went."

There was the sharp bleating of a car alarm, then just the grind of traffic.

"Did you bring anything to drink?" she asked.

"There's a bottle of wine in the refrigerator."

She dropped her purse by the door and walked to the refrigerator, taking the bottle out. It was open.

"There's some glasses in the cupboard right there, and some mugs." He lifted up his juice glass.

She set a coffee mug down from the cupboard, pouring it half full. "I'm glad we're doing this."

"Me too."

She snapped on the light in the hood over the stove and stepped out of her sandals and unbuttoned her blouse, taking her time, stopping to sip the wine. She dropped the blouse on the floor, then her shorts, her bra and panties on top. She smiled, taking up the mug, and turned toward the bedroom, the light from the stove glinting in the single gold chain around her neck.

He finished his wine and pulled his boots off and walked to the bedroom doorway. She was sitting with the covers folded to her waist, the lamp on beside the bed. He looked toward the window, but the curtains were drawn. He pulled his shirttails loose. "I'm not going to be a lot of good to you." He shrugged. "I should've said something about it the other night." He watched her set her wine on the night table.

"The ALS take this away from you too?"

"I guess that's what it was."

"Didn't you go to a doctor? I mean, don't you want to find out?"

"I didn't see the point."

"Jean might've."

"I think she's relieved."

There was the rattling drone of the air conditioner, the cadence of the traffic beyond, constant as a dog chewing a bone.

"It's going to be a long afternoon with you just standing there," she said.

He nodded, snapping the front of his shirt open, stepping out of his jeans and underpants. He stood for a moment holding his clothes, and she laughed.

"What?"

"Nothing."

"Tell me."

"It's kind of like going back to the house where you were raised."

"You mean everything looks smaller than you remember?"

"I meant familiar."

He set his jeans and underwear on the seat of a chair and pulled his shirt off.

"Your socks too," she said.

She turned onto her side, and he pressed in against her, his knees bent against the backs of her thighs. She reached up and turned off the lamp.

"You upset?" he asked.

"I'll get over it in a minute."

He put an arm around her, across her breasts. "I guess I really didn't think what this would be like. I thought I did, but I hadn't."

"You remember Sarah Meeks?"

"From high school?"

"Yeah." She turned and lay facing him. "I saw her in Denver. At a gallery. She had three little girls with her."

"I didn't know her very well."

"Neither did I, but I recognized her right away. Her husband was with her. I think he said he sold something, I don't remember what, but I've been thinking about those kids." He could smell the wine on her breath. "Do you regret not having any?"

"I've had Griff. Sort of. We've gotten along all right."

"I regret it," she said.

He pulled away, looking down at her. "You still could."

"With Larry?"

"Yeah."

She tucked her head, pressing her forehead against his chest. She'd always liked the sour-spicy scent of his body. "It's too late for that." She touched his chest lightly, with just the tips of her fingers, then looked up at him. "Did you ever think about what you'd be when you grew up?"

"I never thought I'd be a cop."

"What about when you were a kid?"

"You'll laugh."

"I promise I won't."

He rolled onto his back. "I thought I was going to be special."

"Like a movie star?"

"More like a heart surgeon, or an architect. I thought I'd be a man people would admire."

"Women, you mean."

"I mean both. I thought maybe I'd invent something useful. It really wasn't so much about money."

She got up on an elbow, looking down at him. "But you never had something you were crazy to do? Something you thought you might die if you never did?"

"There wasn't anything like that."

She lay down against him. "You're lucky," she said.

"You think so?"

"Yes, I do. I think it would be hard to die knowing you never took a shot at something you felt like you needed to do."

"Is that how you feel?"

"I was wild to get married to you." She held her hand flat against his chest. "I wasn't worth a damn at it, but it's what I used to dream about when I was a girl."

"Shit."

"I know. You should've married a woman with higher aspirations."

He looked toward the window again. There still wasn't anything to see. "Not much turns out like you think it might."

# Nineteen

It had been eight years and all they'd done was box up his clothes and strip the sheets from the bed after the funeral home took the body away. Einar had also taken the framed photograph of the 9th Cavalry buffalo soldier. He'd cleaned the glass, hanging it over his bed as others might a crucifix. It kept the memory of Mitch present in his mind.

The man in the photo was dressed in uniform, standing his horse in a field of snow, a grouping of storm-obscured buildings in the background. On the back, a simple X in the lower right corner, dated 1884. Had the rider been able to cipher out the letters he would have written his name as Abraham Bradley.

He'd come west out of Georgia in 1883 with Mitch's father just old enough not to slow him down, and a consumptive wife who would weaken and die a year later. As a widower he'd leased his son to the owner of a freight wagon for a dollar a year, and the man had fed and housed the boy, working him hard as a rented animal but not so brutally as to break him down.

If Abraham was self-conscious about his decision to abandon the boy it didn't show in the photograph. He sat that thin-necked cavalry mount as though he'd been granted ownership of the world and all that roamed across it. He died nine months later of the bloody flux, shitting himself down to under a hundred pounds.

Marin got Paul to haul Mitch's used-up old mattress to the dump, along with the worn and canvas-patched easy chairs and a dresser with the laminate splintered off. And Griff found a newly-wed couple who were thankful for the nightstand and steamer trunk, the Formica dining table and mismatched chairs. They unbolted the vise and dental drill from Mitch's workbench, disassembling the scarred planking they'd been mounted on and stacking the boards out of the weather behind the granary.

That left only a single carved elk antler mounted on the north wall with an eight-year-old calendar hanging next to it. Griff leaned the antler out on the porch, and Marin hired a handyman from town to take up the linoleum in the bathroom and replace it with slate-colored tiles. After he was finished they went back in and scrubbed the logs, chinking and floorboards.

Now Griff and Marin stood together just inside the door. The brass urn that held Alice's ashes was centered on a windowsill, the single object Marin had moved in. She unclipped a tape measure from her belt, running the tape out, Griff holding its end in the far corner under the front windows. Marin recorded the distance, letting the tape rewind. She held a pad of engineering paper, segmented into a grid of quarter-inch squares, up against her forearm, finishing the rough diagram as she walked out onto the porch.

They sat at the shaded table, taking turns petting Sammy.

"Did she want you to scatter her ashes somewhere?"

"I think I'm just going to keep them around." Marin smiled. "Like she did with me." She tore the top sheet away from the pad and slipped a credit card out of her wallet, using it as a straight-edge to copy the interior measurements of the cabin onto an unmarked sheet of paper.

"If you and Einar can wait until next week to do your shopping I can come up to Billings with you."

"We'll be fine," Marin said. "I don't want you to change your plans." She was bent over her diagram. "Anyway, I already asked

Marlene Silas if she'd take care of Sammy." A mosquito landed on her arm, and she slapped it.

"I didn't know Buddhists went around smacking bugs."

"Maybe he'll come back as something that doesn't suck blood." She tapped at the pad with her pen. "I'm sorry for what I said in your studio when we first met."

"I don't remember what you said."

"It was something dismissive about you only making bones."

Griff shrugged. "I didn't take it wrong."

"You should've. I wasn't trying to be flattering." She pushed her glasses up on the bridge of her nose. "I saw your sculptures," she said. "You ought to show them somewhere. In a gallery."

"Paul says that all the time."

"Well, he's right."

"I can make better ones now."

"Maybe you can, but the ones up in the meadow kicked my old butt around the block."

Griff tilted Mitch's antler away from the wall and held it in her lap. "Are you going to have any of your furniture shipped out from Chicago?" She worked the pad of a thumb against the heads and shoulders of the horses carved into the antler's base, streaming out along the bottom tines.

"You don't take compliments very well, do you?"

"I was just wondering."

"I'm going to keep it all in Chicago. In case someone needs to live there."

"Like Paul?"

"We talked about him using the place when he goes back to school."

Griff stared down at the antler. She remembered others into which Mitch had carved the bodies of wolves, bears and mountain lions, all of them given away to friends.

"I'm glad I didn't have to see him get old." Marin slotted the pen behind her ear. "Sitting in there all alone carving those things with that old drill."

"You can have this one if you want."

Marin shook her head. "It's a little too Western for me."

They sat watching the nighthawks feeding in the dusk, falling like shards of gray stone, the air coming alive with the breathy sighs their wings made as they pulled out of their dives.

"My bone people," she said. "They're what I see when I close my eyes."

"Would they be there now? If you shut your eyes?"

"Yes."

A pair of bats steered through the nighthawks, seeming to stagger in their jolting flight. Behind them, the tops of the Bighorns, soft and darkening.

Marin sang, " 'Now that the day has reached its close, the sun doth shine no more.' " Her voice was flat on the higher notes.

"What's that from?"

She sang: " 'In sleep the toil-worn find repose and all who wept before.' " A light went on in the kitchen of the main house. "It's a hymn my mother and Einar used to sing in the evenings. I haven't thought of it for years. They were the ones with the good voices."

"I've never heard him sing anything," Griff said.

They heard him searching through cupboards, the chatter of silverware taken from a drawer.

"Just before I left for Chicago, which seems like another lifetime ago. Einar was only twenty then, maybe twenty-one, I always forget his birthday, and Mitch was about the same. You should've seen them." Her hand went to her throat. "You almost had to look at them out of the corner of your eye. To bear it, I mean." She was still watching the hawks flying in arcs above the cottonwood. "Sometimes I think they were too beautiful to have lived anywhere but here. They'd have looked out of place." She pushed her chair back. "I thought that even though it was girls I liked best."

She stood up, and Sammy scrambled ahead down the porchsteps. "The figures you made, they made me feel like I was ready to pass on."

"You mean die?"

"Yes. That's what I mean," she said. "They made me feel satisfied with my life."

# Twenty

THE NIGHT AFTER Claire gave him the iPod he fell asleep listening to the Red Hot Chili Peppers, waking in the middle of the night with a headache, the buzzing in his chest so acute that he lifted his T-shirt to see what was going on. After that, he let it charge while he slept.

He wore the earbuds during the day when they couldn't find enough for him to do or he got bored shooting baskets, and when he'd heard all the songs three times and they started cycling through again, he pushed the double dash to make it stop. On the evening of his fourteenth day in Laramie, he wrapped the earbud wires in a neat coil around the body of the iPod, laid it out in plain sight beside the computer, then waited.

Once everyone was in bed, he turned the computer on and printed out maps of Laramie, Cheyenne and the interstate to the north. There were windows on the maps, like the little clouds above a comic-book character with what they're saying or thinking printed inside, except these had the addresses and telephone numbers of the bus stations in each town.

He'd checked it all out on the computer the week before, and he had to be at the bus station in Laramie by three-thirty in the morning to buy his ticket. He'd ride the bus to Denver and change to another to come back up through Wyoming to Gillette, where he had to change again, not getting to Sheridan until almost ten o'clock that night. Almost eighteen hours, and it had only taken Rodney six hours to drive from Ishawooa to Laramie, but there weren't any alternatives he could think of. He guessed it was because most people had cars of their own, and only really, really poor people, or kids who wanted to get home, took the bus. He'd never been to Denver and was excited to see it, if a little afraid he'd mess up somehow, having no firsthand experience with public transportation. He wasn't worried about the change in Gillette. He'd been there before and thought a monkey could change buses in Gillette. He thought he'd figure out how to get to the ranch after that.

He turned the computer off, dusting it and the printer and the tables and shelves with a sock. Then he stripped the bed and wadded the sheets on the floor by the door and folded the blanket into a perfect square, centering it at the foot of the mattress. He placed the pillow on top, then packed.

He cracked the door open, listening until his legs started to quiver, and when he was sure they were all asleep he crept downstairs with his backpack, the dirty sheets under his arm. He put them in the hamper and tiptoed into the kitchen, where he didn't need to turn on a light with the yellow glow from the streetlamp pouring in through the window over the sink.

He made two sandwiches with the lunchmeat and cheese he found in the refrigerator, stuffing them both into a single Ziploc baggy and slipping that into an outside pocket of his backpack. He got an apple and put that in too. Then he found the pad and pen by the phone and sat at the kitchen table, thinking about what to write. He wanted them to know he appreciated everything they'd done for him. He thought writing it longhand in pen was better than printing it out on the computer—more personal, like they were friends.

*Thank you, very much,* he wrote. *I had a wonderful time. It is a good thing to know I have a brother and sister, and a spare father and mother.*

*Your house is nice and quiet even though you live in a city. I will have lots of stories to tell from this adventure, and good times to remember. Don't worry because I know how to get home. I paid attention on the trip here. Good-bye, Kenneth.*

He left the note on the kitchen table, where it would be the first thing they saw when they came down for breakfast. He checked the LCD display on the microwave and it was only just after midnight. He was too excited to know if he was sleepy.

He emptied his pockets and counted out the money on the counter by the sink. This was the third time, but he wanted to make sure he hadn't made a mistake. McEban had given him two fifty-dollar bills, and he'd saved seventy-three dollars from his allowance, all in ones, a thick roll held tight with a rubber band. The computer had said the bus ticket would cost a hundred and four dollars, and he laid out the two fifties and four ones, stacking twenty singles for expenses beside it. He folded the last forty-nine dollars, doubling the rubber band around it, lifted up his pants leg and stuffed it down the top of his boot. He put the money for the ticket in his shirt pocket, the traveling money in his jeans.

He thought leaving cash for the food he was taking might be insulting, so he dug in the bottom of his backpack for the empty Copenhagen can McEban had let him have. He popped the lid off and pinched the top layer of Kleenex away and lifted the arrowhead out, a long, tapering point made of moss agate that he held up to the light over the sink. Then he set it on top of the note and added a postscript.

*This is mine and I'd like you to have it. I found it when I was six and one half on top of the Bighorns, but I can't tell you exactly where. It is a secret. I made two sandwiches. Kenneth again.*

After taking a hard look at everything in the kitchen so he could recreate the room for McEban, he slipped out the door, and stood under a shade tree by the garage, watching the street. It was empty. He whispered the full content of the lies he thought he might have to use to get home, to reassure himself he had them firmly in his memory. His mother had told him once that it wasn't lying if you told people what they wanted to hear, so he'd lain in bed at night thinking about every problem a ten-year-old boy might encounter on an eighteen-hour bus trip, all the questions he might be asked, making lists of the answers he thought people would want to hear. He didn't kid himself about them not being lies.

Then he picked up his basketball from where he'd left it on the edge of the driveway.

# Twenty-one

JEAN WASN'T THERE when he got home, and he looked for a note but couldn't find one. He showered and shaved and stretched out on the bed and fell asleep with the windows open and a breeze coming through. He slept undisturbed for an hour and a half, and when he woke she still wasn't home. He remembered vivid fragments of a dream in which he was flying, or falling, but couldn't piece together any sort of narrative, wondering if the ALS was affecting his subconscious as well.

He pulled on a pair of sweatpants and a T-shirt and went out to the kitchen to find something to make for supper, taking a Tupperware container of cooked rice from the refrigerator and layering the bottom of a bowl with it, then browning a package of hamburger and spooning it over the rice. He grated a hard cheese onto the hamburger and nuked it for a minute, then diced part of an onion and a red pepper, and dumped them on top. It was his favorite meal, something he'd made after school when he was a kid.

He carried the bowl to the couch in the living room, surfing through the channels while he ate. He ended up watching an episode of *CSI: Miami*, jeering at the story line as he imagined a lot of cops did.

After he'd cleaned up the kitchen and she still wasn't home, he found her stash in the back of her underwear drawer and rolled a joint that he took out to the sunporch so he wouldn't stink up the house. Having smoked dope only a couple of times in college, and never since, he couldn't remember what was supposed to happen to him, but it was a relief, even briefly, to be focused on something other than his body's deterioration. He sat back, waiting for it to kick in, and imagined Jean driving up and catching him, and when this scenario just made him laugh he assumed he was stoned.

He stayed out on the porch through the evening. When it was dark, he turned on the bug zapper hanging under the eaves and sat listening to the intermittent buzz of bugs frying and the sounds of the neighborhood winding down. The phone rang once and he let the machine get it, but the caller didn't leave a message.

It was after midnight when he stripped out of his clothes and went to bed, and he wasn't quite asleep when she came in, making no effort to be quiet. He heard her mix a drink in the kitchen, and when he opened his eyes she was standing in the bedroom doorway staring at him.

"Don't pretend you're asleep," she said.

He folded an arm behind his head. The light was on in the hallway behind her, and he could see the outline of her legs through the thin material of her skirt. "You drunk?"

"Drunk enough to come home." She walked into the room, set her drink on the dresser, pulled her blouse over her head and stepped out of her skirt. She threw her clothes toward the closet and took a sip from the glass, then put it back.

"What does that mean, exactly?" he asked.

"What does what mean?" She slid her panties down, kicking them toward the closet too, and stood at the foot of the bed, winging her elbows out to unhook her bra, tossing it after the rest. She cupped her breasts up and ducked her chin to blow back and forth across them. "Jesus, that feels good," she said.

"What does it mean, saying you're drunk enough to come home?"

She snorted a short laugh and walked to the window and sat on the sill staring at him, holding the cool glass of ice and whiskey and water against her forehead, her legs crossed at her ankles.

The light from the streetlamp turned the hair at the crown of her head amber and lipped just over her shoulders, falling in scallops on her left hip and thigh. He thought she still looked good but knew it really didn't matter anymore. That part was over. "You going to answer me?"

She finished her drink, set the glass on the windowsill and stood away from the window. "You know damn well what it means."

She was rotating her head in a circle like he'd seen pro basketball players do to loosen up before going back onto the court. She pulled the sheet away and stepped across him, straddling his hips, settling down on his limp cock. She paused as though she couldn't remember what came next, then leaned forward and kissed him, her hips fidgeting. He could feel her breasts pressed against his chest.

"I know you can do this," she said. "I need you to."

She reached down between her legs, gripping his cock and working her thumb at the base of the glans, smiling like she would at a joke that wasn't funny. She kissed him again, grinding her hips in punishing little circles and digging at his chest with her fingernails. When she checked again and his cock was still limp, she rolled off and lay staring at the ceiling. "That makes what?" she asked. "The last three times?"

"I don't know what's wrong with me."

She got up on an elbow. "Really?"

"I probably ought to try something. Viagra, maybe."

"Maybe you should."

She got up and pulled a black T-shirt from under her pillow. Stenciled on the front, under a white horse head with an orange mane, was *Denver Broncos*. The shoulder seams reached almost to her elbows and the hem hung mid-thigh. She retrieved her glass from the sill and went back to the kitchen, and he heard her making another drink.

Then she was standing again in the doorway. "You know what pisses me off?"

"I guess not the whole list." He folded his pillow behind his head.

She was leaning into the jamb with one leg bent up, pressing the sole of that foot against the opposite knee. It made for an odd silhouette, he thought, birdlike.

"You know what Viagra's good for?" she asked.

"I think so."

"Yeah, well I do too. It's a real lifesaver for the assholes who are getting it someplace else. Every Tom, Dick and Crane can come trotting home with their limp dicks, whining about the heartache of ED. ED, my ass. Your only dysfunction is you'd rather fuck stray pussy more than me."

"Funny, they don't say anything about that in the ads."

She sipped her drink. "I need to know something," she said. "So I can keep everything in perspective."

"All right."

"I'd like to know when you think you might have the balls to tell me what's going on."

"That's something we can talk about tomorrow."

"You mean when I'm not drunk?"

"Yes."

"Fuck you."

She straightened her leg, leaning over into the opposite jamb, and he stood up and found where he'd dropped his clothes on the floor and stepped into the sweatpants and sat back down on the bed.

"You want to know the worst thing I ever did?" she asked.

"Tell me."

"I really hate that tone of voice."

"Go ahead. I want to know."

She walked away, and he pulled the T-shirt on. She was sitting on the counter beside the sink when he came into the kitchen, the bottle of Jim Beam next to her. He sat at the table, and she leaned back against the cupboards.

"So, the worst thing I ever did?"

"I'm ready," he said.

She parted her legs and, when he looked away, turned to spit in the sink, pulling the T-shirt down over her knees. She lit a cigarette from the pack by the bottle and dropped the paper match in the drain. "I wished you were dead. That's the worst thing I ever did."

He stared at her.

"I don't mean fuck you, fuck me, I wish you were dead. I mean the whole nine yards, front to back. Smell the blood, watch the light go out of your eyes, appear appropriately heartbroken at the funeral, answer the condolence cards promptly and pack your shit off to the landfill." She took a long drag from her cigarette, tilting her head back to exhale, staring at him down over her cheeks. "So how does that sit with you, Mr. Maybe-Viagra-Might-Let-Me-Fake-Fuck-My-Wife-Now-and-Then?"

His left arm and both calves were buzzing, and he tried to swallow and coughed. "Not great." He cleared his throat, careful not to gag. That's what frightened him most, the choking. He'd watched it happen to his grandfather.

"Good," she said, "because I didn't even get to the part about burning sage in every room of the house to run your fucking stink out."

He wiped the spittle from the corners of his mouth. "Have you thought about me dying today?"

"Today's not over with yet." She drained her glass and poured it half full of whiskey, holding it under the tap for a splash of cold water.

"You've been drinking a lot, even for you."

"Have I?"

"Yes, you have."

She sipped the drink. "Why don't you tell me what you expect me to do?"

"I guess I don't know what to expect."

"Jesus, you must fucking think I'm made out of iron or something."

"I think you're the most beautiful woman I've ever seen. I still think that."

"You've got a twisted way of showing it."

"I haven't been feeling well."

"But well enough to fuck your ex-wife. That's something, isn't it? I'm sorry you haven't been up to handling us both."

"That's not what's happening."

"Bullshit." She drank down half her drink.

"It's not like that with Helen."

"Give it the fuck up, Crane. Janice Obermueller already told me she saw you two having dinner at the Olive Garden in Billings."

They heard a car pull into the drive, then a door slamming shut.

Jean slid off the counter, staggering sideways toward the refrigerator before catching herself. "You want to know something? I really do wish you were dead. It would've been easier for you." She stubbed her cigarette out in the sink, looking at him over her shoulder. "Because right now you've got to hate yourself even more than I do."

They could hear a light knock at the screen door, and Jean pushed away from the counter.

"I didn't make love to her."

"Couldn't, or wouldn't?"

"I just didn't."

The knock again, still light.

"Come on in and join the party," Jean called.

She was gripping the backladder of a chair, bracing herself, when the girl stepped into the doorway, the kitchen light reflecting off her eyebrow stud and the ring in her lower lip.

"I need to see the sheriff," she said, nearly whispering.

Jean stared at her, weaving, then shrugged and dropped her hands from the chair. "I'm going to bed."

She turned and lurched toward the bedroom, holding a palm out against the wall to steady herself, and he heard a picture fall in the hallway.

"I'm Janey Schilling," the girl said. "My sister said you wanted to talk to me."


They walked out around her car and he held the door open to the cruiser and she ducked in.

"I'm sorry it's so late," she said. "I saw your lights on, so I thought it would be okay."

"I'm glad you did."

She turned in the seat and pressed a hand up against the wire mesh separating the front seat from the back, then looked at him.

"This your first ride in one of these?"

She nodded.

"Go on ahead and put your seatbelt on," he said, backing them around and thinking about driving out north with the windows down, through the troughs of cool air holding tight against the sloughs along the roadway, thinking that might put her at ease. But he didn't know if she was crazy, in which case it'd be better to have her in the office, even if it scared her a little.

"I almost didn't come over tonight. I almost just went back to Denver."

"You're doing the right thing," he said.

"Anyway, I don't sleep hardly ever. I'm up all the time."

"Yeah, that's me too."

When he crossed the bridge east of town, a night hatch came up out of the willows along the river and the insects pocked the windshield like puffs of ash.

"I guess the fish'll be biting on those bugs tomorrow." She tried to make it sound conversational, like they knew each other.

"I don't know the first thing about fishing," he said. "Sometimes I act like I do, but I don't."

"My stepdad took me."

"I met him."

"Benton?" She turned to look at him in the dashlights. She was fingering the ring in her lip.

"Your mother too."

"Kayla just said you called and were looking for me."

He turned onto the main drag and hit the switch to spray washing fluid over the windshield, the wiperblades streaking the insects across the glass. When he noticed the car idling in front of the office, he pulled into the lot next to the drugstore.

They sat staring across the street at the building, a bleak institutional green except for the northwest corner, now weathered down to the gray cinderblock. A raised "R" had fallen off the sign above the door: ISHAWOOA CO. SHE IFF OFFICE. Then Starla reeled out onto the front stoop with two younger women, all hanging onto and shushing one another between bursts of laughter. They loaded into her '93 Pontiac, and she backed out and drove off. Crane pulled across the street and parked and got out, but the girl didn't even open her door.

"It's all right," he said. "We're just going in here to talk. I'm not going to lock you up."

She walked with him past the lighted cubicle where the night dispatch sat.

"Evening, Pearl," he said.

She looked up from her crossword-puzzle book, pink plastic barrettes in her gray hair, her hands thin and liver-spotted. "I had nothing to do with it," she said.

"Never entered my mind." He continued down the hallway, the girl following just a step behind.

"Did you know those people?" She was whispering.

"The tall one works dispatch during the day." He threw the keys on his desk and dropped into his chair. "Every once in a while she and her buddies get shitfaced and come in to fire up the Breathalyzer and see what they blow. Like a competition."

"Nice." She stepped to the window beside the door and put up the blind, staring at the jail cells across the hall. "I'm not tweaking anymore." She turned, hugging herself. "I been in rehab. That's where I was when you were trying to find me."

"I'm going to need to know what happened to your boyfriend," he said, motioning toward the chair across from him.

She sat down, sucking on her lip ring. "If I start crying you shouldn't worry about it," she said. "I cry more than I used to."

"That won't bother me."

She was knitting and releasing her fingers now, over and over, and when she saw him watching she laid her hands out on her thighs. "I didn't have to come up here. Nobody made me. I was doing real good in rehab."

"I understand that."

"It was an accident."

"All right."

She looked over her shoulder.

"You want me to close the door?"

She nodded, so he got up and swung the door shut and returned to his desk.

She started to cry quietly. "I swear I didn't know Brady had a gun." She was staring at the floor. "I don't think JC knew either."

"You mean Brady Croonquist?" He tried to keep his voice natural, as she had when talking about what bugs a fish might rise to. "Jake Croonquist's son?"

"I don't know what his daddy's name is." She pulled her sleeve down over her hand and wiped her eyes with it. "Brady owns a ranch. I know that."

"Was it his trailer?"

"He said it was safe, that nobody could come on his place without permission. But his house isn't anywhere near the trailer. It's way back up the creek from there."

"I know where it is."

"I was only there once. At his house."

She held her hands up over her eyes and started to sob, rocking out over her knees. He walked a box of Kleenex around to her, setting it on the floor beside her chair and sitting back against the desk.

"You're saying Brady's the one cooking the stuff?"

She blew her nose, holding the used tissue in her lap. "It was JC and me, but Brady showed us how."

"He set you up?"

"Yeah, but for a long time Brady just bought whatever anybody stole. So they'd have money if they needed to get high. Like he'd buy stereos or guns or computers, whatever. He's got a barn full. JC used to help him take loads of it up to Billings to sell. One time they drove a truckload down to Denver." She blew her nose again. "Brady used to always say he didn't make nothing but profit, then a couple months ago he said he might as well make *all* the profit. That's when JC and me started cooking for him."

"I can't help you if you're going to lie to me."

"I'm not lying." Her eyes sparked, and then she remembered where she was. She looked to make sure the door was still shut. "I swear I'm not."

"And nobody else was out there?"

"Just JC and me, and when Brady drove up I even waved to him through the window. Then there was this explosion and JC was on the floor, on fire and screaming. It knocked me down too, but I didn't catch fire." She was crying hard again.

He walked back around his desk and sat down. "It counts for something that you came all the way up here," he said. "You're sure you weren't the one with the gun?"

She was sniffling and shaking her head. She wiped at her eyes. "Brady'll kill me if he finds out I told you."

"Nobody's going to find out."

She pushed her hair away from her face. "I just came up for my stuff. When I left I didn't take nothing, not my clothes or anything. I left it all with my girlfriend." She was trembling. "I don't know why we even done it," she said. "Mostly they cook it over on the reservation." She was standing now, and he stood up too. "I don't mean the Indians. They don't. It's other people from someplace else, and they sell it to the Indians and everywhere off the reservation, and Brady could've just bought it from them." She pointed to the jail cells through the window across the hallway. "Can I go in there?"

"If you want."

He stood outside the bars while she went in and sat down on a cot, hugging herself again like she was cold.

"You think you're done with meth?"

"I'm trying to be," she said. "You only got these four cells?"

"That's it."

Under the fluorescent lighting her face appeared hollowed, ghostly.

"I guess that's all you need." She tried to smile. "Unless you have to lock up your dispatcher and her friends."

"Harley weekend's a bonanza," he said. "And the Fourth of July Rodeo." He felt a wave of nausea rise and looked away, waiting for it to pass. He was careful when he swallowed. "You got any place to go?" he asked.

"I'm going back to Denver if you let me. My sister got me a job washing dishes at the restaurant where she works. She's helping me study for my GED."

"Come on out of there."

She followed him back to his office. "Will I have to come back up here? To testify or something?"

"We'll have to wait and see what you need to do. I'll talk to the county attorney."

"What time is it?"

He pointed at the clock on the wall. It was one-thirty.

"That was my girlfriend's car I was driving," she said. "She'll need it for work in the morning."

He took a form out of the file cabinet and handed it to her with a pen. "I want you to write out a statement," he said. "Just what you told me about JC and Brady, and your sister's address if that's where you're staying."

She scooted the chair up to the corner of the desk. "Do you have a dictionary?"

"Just do the best you can."

"My bus leaves out of Sheridan at three-fifteen."

They both looked at the clock again.

"I'll take you down there," he said. "We'll swing by and get your girlfriend's car and drop that off, then I'll run you down to Sheridan. We can get something to eat if you want. If you're hungry."

"Doesn't your wife mind you working all night?"

"Not so much." He pointed at the form. "Make sure everything's printed out clear. So I can read it real easy."

She bent over the lined, white paper, her tongue working at the ring in her lip.

# Twenty-two

HE WAS GOOD at paying attention. McEban only had to show him how to do something once and that was it, and he'd gone over the Google map twice and it really wasn't that far. Most of the dogs had been brought in for the night or were tied up in their yards, so he didn't have to worry about mean dogs that might bite, and for the first few blocks he was having fun.

He made believe all his warriors were holding steady behind him, relying on his superior scouting abilities. He listened for enemy movement, creeping along on his belly, on his hands and knees where the cover was better. All the hedges and bushes were grown up, and he nudged the basketball forward, butting it with the top of his head. He wished he'd thought to draw a friendly face on it before he left the house, like Tom Hanks had on his volleyball in *Cast Away*.

He made it undiscovered through the park and around the lake and into a yard on the corner of Shield and North Fourth. He was surprised how many streetlamps were burned out, and a lot of the ones still working cast a weak, fuzzy yellow light. The big thing to watch out for was headlights. Mainly cops' headlights, but also people who were good citizens and might call the cops. He didn't think drunks and college students posed the same kind of threat. If they spotted him they might just shake their heads, not believing an Indian scout had flashed in front of their car in the middle of the night, and anyway, he was small for his age, which was good, because white people didn't get as tense and worried around kids as they did around grownup Indians. Sort of like you were just the cub of an animal that was going to grow up and be dangerous, but you were still more cuddly than vicious, and then he thought about something stalking *him* in the dark. Some bloodthirsty demon prowling around looking for kids to grab and rip their hearts out before they could even scream. He got so revved up he couldn't shut his mind down, like he'd had three Mountain Dews in a row.

When he got to Third, which was the main street downtown, there were a few people out on the sidewalks and a lot more cars, so he wasn't as worried about the demon realm. Then he remembered the story he'd heard about a college student who got beaten to death here because he was gay, and he wasn't completely sure he wasn't. He'd asked McEban, who said it was all wiring and he'd know soon enough, and when he asked how he'd know, McEban said if he was gay he'd get a hard-on when he looked at boys, and if not, then girls would do the trick. He was under the one-ton changing out the universal joint, and Kenneth was afraid to say that almost everything gave him a hard-on, but then McEban must have thought of it by himself, or remembered what it was like when he was a kid. He scooted out from underneath the truck and lay there looking up. "You're just fine," he said, "either way."

He snuck along, crouching from car to car where they were parked at the curb, finally crossing Third on Sully, still north of most of the bars that were open this late. When he reached the far curb he heard a siren and stuffed his basketball up under his T-shirt, tucking it into his jeans, and ran as fast as he could for a block and a half, across a big vacant lot and out through a stretch of gravel and over some railroad tracks. He knelt under a parked train of flatbeds and stockcars, looking back across the empty lot and finally realizing the siren must have been for someone else. He was sucking at the air.

The odors of creosote and diesel and something he didn't recognize were so strong they made his eyes burn. When he crawled out the other side, looking up at the boxcar he'd been hiding under, he counted four tiers of pigs packed in tight. They were all grunting and shifting, slobbering and shitting, and he remembered Westerns he'd seen on television where the good guys stampeded hundreds of cattle to cover their escape, and pigs would be just as good if he could climb up and pry away the locks and slide the gates open. Then the empty tracks filled with the rumble of an approaching train, and a yellow Union Pacific engine was chugging toward him. He trotted along the shoulder of Railroad Street until he hit Lyons and turned west. The basketball bouncing under his shirt made him think of Curtis Hanson's beer belly. He kept running until he was across the street from an auto-parts store, and pressed the button on the side of his wristwatch to make the face glow. McEban had given him the watch and now it was only two in the morning, and the Greyhound station was supposed to be in the office of the auto-parts store, and here he was without anything having ripped his heart out.

When he looked in the window, there was only the man standing behind the counter and a woman sitting in a chair, nobody else, and he knew he needed to get lucky. He sat down between two cars at the edge of the parking lot to wait. He was still so keyed up that he wasn't worried about falling asleep. He took one of the sandwiches out of his backpack and tore it in half, saving the rest for later. Then a car pulled through and a long-haired guy got out, saying thanks to whoever dropped him off, and went into the office. About fifteen minutes after that a pickup parked and the driver stood leaning against the sidewall smoking and finally slid a suitcase out of the bed and went inside. Kenneth followed right behind, slipping into a chair by the door, watching as he bought his ticket.

The woman and the long-haired guy were trying to doze, and when the man at the counter turned around Kenneth nodded at him. He nodded back like any good neighbor would and didn't look like a demon or anything, just maybe like he had a job that didn't pay very well. He was about as old as McEban and dressed pretty much like McEban would have if he was going somewhere on a bus. Kenneth waited until he went back outside to smoke, squeezing through the door before it closed to stand with him.

"Nice night, isn't it," the man said, and Kenneth agreed with him. Along the horizon, the stars were brighter.

"I'm not going to give you a cigarette if that's what you're after. You're too young for 'em."

Kenneth thought the man probably needed glasses because of how he was holding his head. "No, sir. I'm never going to smoke."

"Good for you. I hope you're right about that."

"I'm just waiting for my mom. She got real sick and then she had to go home to get her medicine." He looked at his wristwatch for effect. "She was hoping it would make her feel better."

The man dropped the butt on the ground, rubbed it out with the toe of his boot and shook another cigarette out of the pack, then tapped the filter against the edge of the pack. "I'm not about to go looking for your mother, either," he said. "I don't believe I've got the time for it, and I don't want you standing there thinking I'll make the time."

"No, sir."

The man lit the cigarette, cupping his hands around the match. They were scarred and thick and plenty used. "Maybe you ought to call her." He pointed toward the building. "I imagine they've got a phone indoors there."

Kenneth nodded and walked a few steps toward the door, trying to think of what to say next. He looked up and down the street. "I called her one time already and she said she was too sick to get out of bed." He tried to remember something that might make his eyes well with tears. Something sad. "She said I probably shouldn't call her back." He was thinking of when a colt kicked him in the knee, but it just made his leg ache.

"Well, I guess it's up to you," the man said. "If it was me I'd try her again."

His mother had told him that specific lies were better than general ones, that people felt more comfortable if you gave them little bits of information. "I'm supposed to meet my cousins in Sheridan," he said. "They'll be waiting for me."

"How many cousins have you got?"

"I've got three. They're all younger, but we get along okay." He pulled the money out of his shirt pocket and held it toward the man, who bit down on the filter and reached out to take it.

He thumbed his hat back, turning so the light from the window fell across his hands as he riffled through the bills. "This here's a hundred and four dollars."

"Yes, sir. That's how much she said it was. She said it was the price of my ticket."

The man took the cigarette out of his mouth. "So what you're asking me to do is walk back in there and buy you a ticket for Sheridan, Wyoming? Is that right?"

"They won't sell one to a kid."

The man nodded. He still held the money. "What'd you say was wrong with your mom?"

"She had a migraine headache. She gets them sometimes."

"And you're how old?"

"I'm ten."

He flicked the ash off his cigarette with the nail of his little finger. "I wouldn't be helping you run away, would I?"

"No, sir."

He took a drag, looking away from the town lights toward where the night sky ground down against the darker horizon. "I used to get them damn migraines," he said. "I haven't for some time."

"My mom says it's like she's been kicked in the head." He was still thinking about the colt.

"Well, she's right about that."

"She said on the phone if she was too sick to come back I should just walk up and ask somebody to buy me the ticket."

"And you picked me?"

"You look like a man I met once."

"I do, do I?"

"Yes, sir."

The man was staring back through the window of the office like he was concerned they were being watched. Then he dropped the butt and ground it out too. "If I'm helping you run off, I don't want to know a thing about it. Not one thing, you understand?"

"Yes, sir."

"If that's what I'm doing, you just keep lying to me."

Kenneth bounced the basketball and caught it, holding it against his hip again.

"Is that what I'm doing?"

"No, sir."

"All right." He nodded toward the basketball. "You any good with that thing?"

"Not so far."

"I never was neither."

He put the money in his shirt pocket, and took out a handkerchief and tipped off his hat, staring down at the boy as he wiped the sweatband clean.

He waited until the woman passenger was getting on and stepped up close behind her, and when she turned down the aisle he handed the driver his ticket.

The man just stared at him, then looked at the ticket again. "This kid with you?" he asked.

The woman turned in the aisle. She looked sleepy and stood shaking her head.

"I can't let you ride," the driver said, and handed the ticket back.

"What's the holdup here?"

Kenneth turned and the driver rocked forward in his seat to look past him.

"This boy yours?" he asked.

It was the man who'd been smoking. He was standing with a foot up on the first step. He said, "You're probably thinking he's too good looking to be related to me."

"That ain't it," the driver said. He smiled but wasn't friendly, more like a mean cop. "What I was thinking is this boy's a little dark to be yours."

The man stepped up into the front of the bus, and Kenneth wondered why he hadn't looked so big when they were standing out in the lot. It was like the bus was suddenly too small for him. The driver noticed too.

"I probably didn't hear you say what I thought you did," the man said.

"I don't want any trouble," the driver said.

"Then I guess you ought to take your hand away from my boy's shoulder." He was whispering, but it was like he was yelling his lungs out.

The driver brought his hand back into his lap, staring out the windshield like he was watching something in front of the bus. Kenneth looked too, but there was nothing to see.

"Why don't you go find yourself a seat," the big man said, and Kenneth turned away and walked halfway to the back and took one by the window.

The man stopped in the aisle and bent down over him. "I didn't know your name or I'd have used it."

"It's Kenneth."

"Well, get some sleep if you can, Kenneth. Mine's Jerry." Then he moved a couple rows back, lifting his bag up into the overhead rack.

When the bus pulled out he lay over against his backpack, drawing his legs onto the empty seat beside him, and when he woke it was still dark and more people were getting on, and when he woke up again Jerry was shaking his shoulder. He didn't really remember walking off the bus, but they were standing on the street, the buildings rising up around them.

"Is this Denver?"

"Mile-high," Jerry said, handing him his backpack and basketball, dropping his own bag to the sidewalk and lighting a cigarette. "Your next ride leaves from the Amtrak station, but that ain't for two hours."

"Where are we now?" He turned in a circle, searching the faces of the tall buildings.

"You're at the Greyhound terminal. I guess they're trying to make this as hard as they can, bringing you all the way down here before starting you back north again. You hungry?"

"My mom packed me a sandwich."

"That must've been before she got her headache."

"She packed two, but I ate half of one already."

"You like eggs?"

"Yes, sir."

They walked up Twentieth so the boy could see the outside of Coors Field, then turned down Wazee to a restaurant Jerry said he'd always wanted to try. It was still early, so they were almost the only ones there. They took a booth by the window, and their waitress brought coffee and a glass of milk for Kenneth while they studied the menus.

"It's expensive here," the boy said.

"You get what you want. This one's on me."

"I got my own money."

"I'm sure you do, but I wouldn't mind hearing you say thank you."

Kenneth looked at him over the top of the menu. "Thank you," he said.

"You ever had an omelet?"

"I don't know what that is."

"It's eggs. They got a Denver omelet advertised, and here we are. You game?"

Kenneth nodded, folding the menu and setting it to the side.

Jerry scooted out of the booth. "Order me one too. And more coffee, and rye toast if they've got it."

"Where are you going?"

"I'm just going outside for a smoke. You'll see me standing there through that window."

When the waitress came back, Kenneth ordered their omelets and finished his milk, watching Jerry smoke and pace back and forth. He ordered a second glass to drink with his meal, and they ate with their heads down, not speaking until the waitress asked if they wanted anything else.

"No, thank you," Jerry said, "that should do it." Then he turned to Kenneth. "What do you think you'd have done if I hadn't bought you that ticket?" He sat back, working a toothpick in his mouth.

"My mom said I could offer some extra money. For the trouble, I mean."

"Like a bribe."

"I guess so."

"Your mom thinks of everything, doesn't she?"

"She's real smart."

"What kind of bribe did I miss out on?"

"Ten dollars."

"Is that all you got?"

"I've got more than that down in my boot."

Jerry smiled, dragging his suitcase from under the table. "You ready?"

"How far is it?" Kenneth said, slipping his backpack over his shoulders. "I have to go to the bathroom."

"It's only a block but you ought to go now. The restrooms will be nicer here. I'll just be waiting outside when you're done."

They walked over to the Amtrak station on Wynkoop and found the bus they needed.

"You say howdy to your cousins for me."

"Aren't you coming?"

Jerry was leaning against a concrete pillar holding his pack of cigarettes, but he hadn't shaken one out. "Not me," he said. "I thought I'd walk over here just so I could see you get on this bus." He stuck a cigarette in his mouth and put the pack away. "And for Christ's sake don't go telling everybody you meet about that money you got stuck down your boots."

"I won't."

"All right, then." Jerry extended his hand. "It was nice to meet you, Mr. Kenneth."

He felt a little bit like crying and kept his head down when they shook hands and then walked right on the bus, taking another seat by the window. Jerry stood watching by the pillar until they pulled away.

He was so tired his eyes felt scratchy and he nodded asleep on the short stretches between stops in Longmont and Greeley and Fort Collins, and then they were in Cheyenne, with the bus driver staring in the rearview mirror and calling, "Twenty minutes."

He used the bathroom on the bus, and when he came out he could see the driver through the window talking to another man dressed in a Greyhound uniform. He took his backpack and basketball with him when he got off. Having read the pamphlet in the seat about unaccompanied children, he knew he wouldn't be allowed to ride up to Wheatland, to Douglas, to Casper, to anywhere, and he could see it in their faces. He smiled at them, hooking up his backpack and walking out into the street. He'd already planned what to do next.

He stood at the pop machine on the sidewalk until the driver looked away, then ducked around the corner into the parking lot. He found a two-gallon gas can in the bed of the second pickup he looked in and climbed over the tailgate, dropping the can out by the side of the truck, counting out five one-dollar bills and pulling the head of a sledgehammer on top of them so they wouldn't blow away.

He walked quickly along Deming with the empty can, squatting up under the overpass to check his Google maps. When he got to Central he turned north for four blocks to the Sinclair on the corner, just where it was supposed to be. He filled the can and went in and bought a small bag of chips and a Dr Pepper, then sat around the corner from the station eating the other half of his sandwich and all of the chips, washing it down with the Dr Pepper.

The food made him so tired that his legs felt rubbery, but he kept north on Central until the street ended at a black-and-yellow barrier. He ducked under and crossed several railroad tracks, crawling under the couplings of the parked boxcars and watching to make sure none of them were going to move away and cut him in half. Then he was out in a huge dirt workyard, where there were maintenance buildings and cars and trucks and a man yelling what the hell did he think he was doing here. He dropped the basketball when he started to run and didn't dare go back for it, and the gas can had gotten so heavy that he ran holding it up against his chest. When he crossed over more tracks he stopped to catch his breath, the guard behind him still standing there with his ball but too far away for Kenneth to hear his screams.

He crossed three more sets of tracks and found a regular street again, walking backwards with his arm out and his thumb sticking up like he'd seen in old movies. He'd only gone two blocks when a woman pulled to the curb, waving him forward and rolling the window down on the passenger side.

It was hot and he set the gas can down, pulling up the front of his T-shirt to wipe his face.

The woman was leaning across the seat. "Are you lost?" she asked.

"No, ma'am. My mom just sent me for gas." He brought the can up to window-level for her to see. "We ran out, and she was afraid to leave me with the car." The woman tilted her head like dogs do when they hear a noise they don't understand, so he added: "She hurt her leg real bad and couldn't come with me."

The woman pushed the door open. "Get in here right now." She sounded mad.

He slid his backpack onto the backseat, setting the gas can on the floor there, and got in the front.

"How come you're all sweaty?"

"A man was chasing me."

The woman looked in the rearview mirror. "Where was he chasing you?"

"By the railroad cars."

She was pulling away from the curb, glancing in the side mirror. She still looked mad.

"A man gave me a ride to the gas station, but then I couldn't get a ride back, so I was walking."

"Where'd you say your mom ran out of gas?"

"Iron Mountain Road."

She looked at him like he'd cussed, and he thought maybe he'd remembered it wrong from the map.

"That's clear north of the city."

"Yes, ma'am."

"Then how come you're all the way down here for gas?" She looked at the gas can again, checking her wristwatch.

"This is where the man dropped me off. He said he didn't want to stop before he got home."

"What man?"

"The man who picked me up."

"I wish that son of a bitch had told you his name," she said. "I'm sorry I cussed, but I'm upset about this."

"He never did."

"Of course he didn't." She was settling now, starting to forget about being late for whatever else she had to do. "He wouldn't dare, running you down here and dropping you off like he did." She was watching the side mirror as she merged with the northbound traffic on I-25. She looked at the gas can again. "You don't think that's going to explode, do you?"

"No, ma'am. I'm sure we're all right if we leave the windows down."

She looked at him, studying him. "You're a cute one. I'll give you that," she said.

"My mom thinks I am."

"I'll bet she does. You have a crush on somebody?"

He felt like it was going to be okay. She was just being a lady now. "On two girls," he said.

When they got to Iron Mountain Road and couldn't find where his mother's car had run out of gas, she drove back to the interstate, and parked and took her cell phone out of her purse.

"I can just get out here," he said.

He watched her dialing 911 and stepped out of the car. He felt dizzy and then he was sitting on the pavement.

He heard her say "I'm at Iron Mountain and 25" and thought he should get up and run. It was like he was just waking up and didn't know if it was a school day or the weekend. He heard her coming around the car. "I've got a lost boy here," she said. She was standing with the phone to her ear, looking down at him. She looked mad again.

# Twenty-three

THEY CAME UP from the toolshed with their tongues thick in their mouths, the blood throbbing in their temples. McEban stopped twice, bending over with his hands braced against his knees, hacking up a yellowish slime. They drank from the garden hose at the side of the house, dousing their heads before stepping up on the porch to heel their boots off. Paul went in and mixed a pitcher of iced tea, stirring in three tablespoons of sugar. He brought the glasses out, set them on the edge of the porchboards and waded down into the overgrowth of mint that skirted the porch, picking a handful of leaves and rubbing them between his palms until they were just a damp, green pulp. He cupped his hands over his nose, inhaling, then pinched some mint for their tea. They sprawled on the steps sipping from their glasses, satisfied to be still at the end of the day.

All summer they'd pulled the noxious weeds from around the buildings and along the creek, piling the stalks with their blossoms in the workyard to dry. This morning they burned the pile, spending the rest of the day out spraying an herbicide on the patches of spurge and thistle, the hound's-tongue and bindweed, idling along on the ATV, a portable, thirty-four-gallon tank mounted on the rack behind the seat. Paul's joints ached like he had the flu, and he felt uneasy about spreading this poison, but there weren't enough hours in the summer to kill it all by hand. When they heard the phone ringing McEban went in for it.

"I'm driving down right now," he said, stepping back out on the porch with the cordless. "I know what time of day it is," he said, then tossed the phone onto a chair and stripped his shirt over his head.

"Is he hurt?" Paul asked.

"No, he's fine, but he got put in jail."

Paul tossed what was left of his tea out into the yard. "I can go with you if you want."

"You can make me a thermos of coffee and some sandwiches." McEban stood in the doorway. When he noticed his boots standing to the side he picked them up by their tops. "I need to shower this shit off and then I'm gone."

Paul brewed the coffee and packed a little cooler with sandwiches, fruit and a handful of the protein bars McEban favored for snacks. He gassed up the truck at the bulk tank by the shop and was pulling alongside the porch when McEban came out carrying a small duffel.

"Just keep it running," he shouted, and Paul stepped out of the truck.

"Anything special you want me to take care of while you're gone?"

McEban threw the duffel across the seat. "Just keep an eye on things." He patted his breast pocket. "I've got the cell if you need me."

Paul had time to tack new shoes on the boy's horse before dinner, afterward backing the stock truck around to the ricks of cordwood stacked against the side of the barn.

When he'd come home for Christmas holiday McEban had borrowed a Belgian mare broken to harness from an old bachelor who raised draft horses out by Ucross. They felled the dead-standing lodgepole off a quarter section of beetle-killed pine, limbing the trunks, cutting them to eight-foot lengths and skidding them through the snow to a loading ramp. The last week of December they sawed it all down to fit in the woodstove in the shop, splitting and stacking it there out of the weather.

He threw two cords up onto the bed of the truck, one stick at a time, then showered and changed, idling out in compound to the paved road.

They'd built this kiln when she was fifteen and he was in his last year of high school. Einar had hired Curtis Hanson to grade a track up the creek from the buildings, graveling it just enough that the cement truck wouldn't get stuck, then they poured and leveled the pad in an afternoon.

Her high-school art teacher knew a potter from the Archie Bray outfit in Helena and convinced him to come down and oversee the construction. Hermann was a large man, thick through the gut and ass and arms, and they lined up the cinderblock for the base and stacked the firebrick, McEban welding the angle-iron armature, the hinges and hardware. Then they set the arch, layering two inches of insulating fiber over the top with a half inch of Portland cement, a fireclay-and-slurry coating over that. When they were done Griff was left with this small, cross-draft kiln, the chimneystack built back against the sidehill. She named it Prometheus.

Lastly, they set posts at the corners and midway down each side of the pad to support the beams and a corrugated tin roof, so they could fire in any sort of weather. The sides stood open.

This evening she was almost finished loading the bisque and greenware into the firing chamber when Paul backed in and started stacking the wood off close to the firedoor. She already had half a cord of kindling split and arranged by the stokeholes, and a hammock strung between two posts. The air smelled of pinepitch and earth and the mixed fragrance of wildflowers.

She stood to the side of the open chamber, her face streaked with sweat, her hands lumpy with fireclay and sawdust from wadding the individual pieces so they wouldn't adhere to the shelving or fuse to one another in the heat. Behind her was an assortment of ribs, metacarpals, a pair of clavicles, a taloned foot, a femur, buffalo-sized vertebrae, a beaked skull, the hooves of an equid and a pair cloven, a single spiraled horn. Some of the pieces had wrappings of grasses and feathers that would burn away, adding texture to their surfaces.

"You sure you want to do this?" She was dressed in a tank top and shorts and lace-up workboots with her arms folded across her chest like some young archeologist posing by a newly unearthed ossuary. There was a breeze in her hair.

"I've always helped," he said.

"Just checking."

They built a starter fire and she latched the door closed, then sank down sideways in the hammock with her firing journal in her lap. He squeezed in beside her, the hammock sagging lower, swinging lightly. She recorded the exact time, noting that the kindling was damp. She could feel his leg pressed against hers.

"I got you a going-away present," she said.

She rocked back to get a hand in her pocket and held the small, black thing up in the evening light and he took it from her and pressed a button on the bottom that lit up its screen yellow and green, with lines forming to indicate the contour of the valley and numbers for their elevation and barometric pressure.

"I already loaded the maps of Africa," she said, feeling an unexpected calmness about his departure.

"I brought you something too." He struggled out of the hammock. "It's in the truck."

She watched him walk away, working at the GPS with both thumbs, and got up to tend the fire, intent on keeping it small and constant for the next five hours, candling the kiln so the ware would cure without cracking.

He came back with a skull balanced on a palm, its front teeth yellow as beeswax.

"Oh, my God," she said.

"The whole skeleton's up by the dams on Horse Creek, but this was all I could bring down without getting bucked off."

He set it on a round of fir at the edge of the pad and she knelt down to examine it.

"He felled a tree right on top of himself," he said. "Probably the wind caught it."

"They're related to squirrels. Did you know that?"

"Yeah, I did."

When she got up to check the fire he lay back down in the hammock, nodding off just before dark, and she let him sleep and at midnight lit two white-gas lanterns and hung them under the eaves, and the kiln's arch and chimney rose up out of the night in the lamplight, shadowed yellow and tan. She stacked in the two-foot lengths of pine, building the fire up all at once. She could hear the flames rushing back through the congestion of shelving and clay and thought of the accretion of fly ash upon the surfaces, the unexpected cocoas, ochres and terra-cotta colorings it would produce. She thought of the women he'd meet. Dark women, city women. She closed the front stokehole and looked back at his sleeping face. He was beautiful. The women would find him beautiful. Of course they would.

At one in the morning she opened the secondary vents a half inch, the mouseholes a quarter, and the fire breathed hotter. When she threw the door back to lay in more wood the flames folded, rushing from her like the burning wings of a dragon.

He raised his head from the hammock. "I'm good to go."

"I'm fine," she said. "I'll wake you later if I'm not."

He lay back to sleep.

It would be their bodies that knew, she thought, looking away into the darkness to search for the hands, breasts and thighs already dreaming of him. The patches of dampened hair. Sweat ran down her back, so she stripped her top off and wet it in the bucket before pulling it back on. She could hear the fire carrying the alkalies back against the ware, the flames licking out the sideports like bright horns.

At three she opened more vents, snapped on her welder's goggles and squinted through the spyholes, the flames lean at the rear of the kiln. She eased the damper down and watched them pulse yellow and white, fattening. She could hear the fire moan, hear the women's laughter bubbling against his body, her wet shirt steaming in the heat.

At four she took up the long-handled poker to stir the firebed, the draft thrown open so the ash and embers could ride the currents of gas and flame, settling more heavily on the ware. And there were the plans they'd made when they were younger, just kids—a family, a home. He shifted in his sleep.

At the five o'clock stoking she singed the hair off her right forearm, standing there watching the pieces shimmer on the top shelves, reflecting in the flamelight. What a fool she's been. Foolish in love. She rubbed the burned hair from her arm.

She turned the lanterns out at dawn, stacked in as much wood as the firebox would hold and opened the primary vents front and back, knowing that the pieces near the floor, where the oxygen was thinnest, would color purple and maroon. She was short of breath and gasped and watched him turn in his sleep, yawning, then blinking up at her.

"I can do this without you," she said.

She'd already seen cone six bending at the top back, and increasing the heat at a rate of three hundred degrees an hour will bend cone nine by noon. Tonight cone eleven, twenty-three hundred degrees. She could feel the heat rising inside her. And at midnight, just seventeen hours away, she will make the last stoke and seal up the firebox. Any hotter and the clay could flare and melt, running as though poured from the center of the earth, pooling on the floor of the kiln. That's when she'll sleep.

"What time is it?" He dug at his eyes.

She stepped to him, bending down to unbutton his jeans, working them loose from his waist. He arched his hips, wanting to help, and she knelt and took him in her mouth, but he tasted only of ash.

She gripped his hands, pulling him to his feet, and peeled her shorts down to the tops of her steel-toed boots, then fell back across the hammock and opened her legs, her knees winging out, guiding him into her. "The world tastes of ash," she said.

She shut her eyes.

# Twenty-four

He dreamed it was storming, the overgrown Russian olive at the corner of the house bending eastward in the wind, its topmost branches knocking against the eaves and gutter. He shifted in his half sleep, thinking he might as well get up, have breakfast and prune the tree back later in the day, and then Rodney was standing with his arm cocked against the truck's side mirror. McEban sat up in the seat, turning the key to put the window down, and Rodney reached a mug of coffee through. He was dressed in his bathrobe and hadn't yet combed his hair.

"I figured black," he said.

"Black's fine."

McEban blew across the top and took a sip and set the cup up on the dash, where it steamed a section of the windshield. He arched his back.

"If you want to come in I can fix you something to eat."

"Coffee'll be enough. Is Kenneth up?"

"Not yet."

McEban opened the door, sitting sideways in the seat and reaching for his mug. It was just breaking dawn. "How'd he like being in jail?"

"They didn't put him in a cell or anything like that. But they took his fingerprints, just to make an impression, I guess, and then he sat in a room and drank a Coke with a woman officer until I got over there." Rodney looked back toward the house, leaning into the side of the truck, scuffing at the pavement with a slippered foot.

McEban stepped into the street. "This is good coffee."

"Were you out here long?"

"Since about three." He checked his watch. "It seemed like a waste to rent a motel room for a couple hours, and I wasn't sure I was going to get to sleep anyway."

"It was my fault," Rodney said. "I thought he was having a good time."

"That's the problem with good times. They never last like they should."

A car passed, the driver craning across the seat, glaring at them like they were plotting a crime.

"What time's he get up down here in the city?"

"About now. I didn't sleep real well last night either, and then when I looked out I saw your truck."

"What's your wife think about all this?"

"I told her about the boy before we ever got married."

McEban nodded, running his tongue around his mouth. He pulled his Copenhagen out, offering him a pinch.

"I quit."

"Good for you."

"She's always said he was welcome down here. She did from the get-go."

McEban tossed the can up on the dash and finished his coffee. He handed Rodney the empty cup and they stood staring at it as a train whistled to the west.

"We'll work something out when he gets a little older. How's that sound to you? Where he can come down for a visit if he wants. Or next summer you could all come up. We got plenty of room."

"I'm a chickenshit when it comes to saying no to Rita," Rodney said. "I wish I wasn't, but I am."

McEban sucked on the tobacco, turning his head to spit. "We all are," he said.

He looked up when they heard the door slam and Kenneth was running across the street toward them without checking for traffic. He rocked McEban back against the edge of the seat, leaning in hard.

Rodney waited for him to get done, then helped him out of his backpack and tossed it over the sidewall onto the truckbed.

"Did you say your good-byes inside?" McEban asked.

Kenneth nodded, turning to the house. Claire was standing at the living-room window. He waved and she waved back.

"I guess we're ready, then."

The boy stepped forward and hugged Rodney, then ran to the other side of the truck and got in.

McEban extended his hand. "As far as Rita goes," he said, "we just have to try to think a step ahead of her." He winked, and Rodney smiled for the first time, and stayed standing in the street, watching as they pulled out.

For the first couple of blocks the boy poked quietly through the mess on the dash, finally finding a pair of yellow cotton work-gloves which he slipped on and held up against his face, and then dropped his hands into his lap. "Is my colt okay?" he asked.

"Sure he is, he's coming along just right. I've been working with him while you were down here visiting. Sacking him out a little bit every day, picking his feet up."

Kenneth was watching the houses drift by in the side window. "You think he remembers me?"

"He was asking about you before I left. He said to say yo." McEban could see the side of his face lift into a smile. "I probably shouldn't have, but I invited some girls to come over and stay in your room while you were gone. I got lonely."

"You did not."

"It was the Sherwin girls. I let them paint your ceiling pink and stick up a bunch of those stars that glow in the dark."

The boy was comfortable now, relaxing into the seat. "That's going too far," he said.

"Which part?"

"The ceiling part."

At a stop sign McEban said, "Your uncle Paul's moving to Africa."

"Right."

"He really is. To Uganda."

"Is he taking Jenny Sherwin with him?"

"I'm not kidding this time."

The boy screwed his face, locating the continent in his memory. "I did a report on Africa last year, but I don't know all the names of the countries. Is it close to the pyramids?"

"No, it's south of there. I'll show you in the atlas when we get home."

On the main drag there were mostly delivery vans, ranch and oilfield trucks. The boy lifted his gloved hands and scratched at the glovebox. "What's this look like?" he asked.

"An orangutan."

"That's what I think too. I went to Denver," he said, staring straight ahead.

"I thought they captured you in Cheyenne."

"I went to Denver first. I had a Denver omelet with a man, and he showed me where the Rockies play."

"Is there anything else you need to tell me?"

"What do you mean?" He pulled the gloves off, pairing them in his lap.

"This guy you had breakfast with in Denver. He didn't act funny or anything, did he?"

"He was a good guy."

"You could tell me."

"I would."

"Are you hungry?"

"Not yet."

He turned east onto the interstate. "How'd you get along with your brother and sister?"

"They're half."

"All right."

"I think I'll like them better when they get older."

McEban reached his chew off the dash and the boy leaned over to steer while he settled a fresh pinch under his lip.

"It's too bad Rodney married such an ugly woman, all wart-faced and bald and big-eared."

"Girls don't go bald."

"Some of them thin out a little."

"I think she's got really pretty ears."

"When was the last time you and me had waffles?"

Kenneth shook his head. "I don't think I've had waffles. Have you ever made any?"

"There's an IHOP over in Cheyenne. They'll put strawberries or blueberries or about anything you want on your waffles. And they got Frontier Days going on this week. I thought since we were over there anyway eating waffles we might take in a rodeo or two, maybe a concert if there's anyone we like."

The boy sat quietly and McEban thought he was picturing his breakfast, the week's possibilities.

"I'll be better next summer," he said. "I'll be a whole year older then, and three weeks won't seem like too long."

"You don't have to come down here next summer, or ever again, unless you want to. I told your dad they could all come and stay with us for awhile."

The sun was just off the horizon, the shadows long and dark to the west.

"What if my mom wants me to?"

"Have I ever lied to you?"

"No." He found the sunglasses on the dash and put them on. "Can you get waffles with a banana sliced on top?"

"I bet you can."

"I think that's what I'd like."

# Twenty-five

A HIGH, mottled cloudshelf was keeping the day cool, and Marin found she enjoyed driving the big flatbed north on I-90, sitting up above the passenger cars, Einar napping on the seat beside her.

He woke as she ramped down into Billings and told her where to turn, and they drove up into the Heights. They were looking for an antique store he remembered, and when they couldn't find it she pulled into a parking lot in front of a coffee shop. Einar craned around, looking out the windows.

"There should be a sign." He was alarmed, disoriented. "A big sign with red letters."

"I'm surprised," she said, "but the drive wore me out completely." She spoke calmly. She laid a hand on his thigh. "Can we go inside?"

He was staring at her hand, which seemed to anchor him. He nodded and followed her into the shop.

She ordered a cinnamon latte, got him to try a sip, and he ordered one too. They carried their coffees to a table by the front window.

"I know this is the spot." He sat staring out at the truck.

"I'm sure it was." She kept her voice soft and even, reaching across the table to pat his hand.

He pulled it away. "You're not sure at all." He held the hand like it had been stung. "You're sitting there thinking your brother's lost what little mind he has left."

"That's not true. Stores go out of business every day, Einar. When was the last time you were up here?"

"I was here with Ella."

"Well, for Christ's sake. How long ago was *that*?"

He took up his coffee cup in both hands, sipping. "I guess it could've changed owners." He looked toward the young man running the espresso machine. "Maybe it was that boy's father who sold antiques. Remind me to ask him if it was."

"I'll ask for their phone book," she said. "We'll find a good place, maybe even better than the store that used to be here."

He had a froth mustache and she tapped her own lip, but he didn't notice so she licked the corner of her napkin and leaned across the table to wipe his mouth. He let her.

"I'm sorry you lost her so young," she said.

"You mean Ella?" He was calming down now.

"I had Alice almost my whole life."

"I never understood how she could want a bald man." He turned his hat up on the end of the table, scratching absently at his stiff gray hair, and when he saw her looking at his head he said, "Charlie Newland's who I'm talking about. He and Ella sort of partnered up for awhile."

"You don't mean like bridge partners, or they went fishing together?"

"No. I mean the other." He sipped his coffee. There was a line at the counter now. "This is a nice place," he said.

"We'll come again if you like. The coffee's good."

"I don't really think I was ever what you'd call good help in bed, so she had it coming, I guess, and Charlie, he had that shriveled arm he got from having polio when he was a kid. Maybe he thought he had it coming too."

She started giggling, and that got him started, and finally a young woman waiting in line came over to ask if everything was okay, and Marin told her it was far better than that.

They found a used-furniture store downtown, where she picked out a walnut dresser and matching armoire after checking her diagram of the cabin to make sure they'd fit.

The owner and the large, docile boy introduced as his nephew got the pieces loaded up against the truck's cab with any surfaces that might rub padded with sheets of cardboard. Einar roped it all snug, the lines standing taut.

"I never could tie a knot worth spit," the owner said, standing back with his hands on his hips, still short of breath from loading the furniture.

"If you live around horses," Einar said, clearly pleased, "it's not something worth bragging about."

The man slipped a business card from his wallet, holding it out to Marin. "You folks drive careful, now," he said.

When they got in the truck she asked if he was hungry yet, and he said, "Fuddruckers."

"That sounds like a strip joint."

"Well, it's not, unless it's moved. Griff and I ate there last fall when we were up here delivering a bull to a man from Molt. They'll let you build a hamburger sandwich any way you want."

"Do they have salads?"

"They have lettuce and tomatoes and onions, I know that much. And they sell beer. It's been awhile since I've had a cold beer."

She was pulling into the street. "I'm disappointed it's not a strip joint," she said.

After she'd had her salad, watching him drink a beer and eat a burger as large as her hand, she checked a phone book again. They drove to a store on King Avenue, where they lay down, one after the other, on half a dozen mattresses before she found one that suited her.

"We ought to get you a comfy chair while we're here," he said. "Something you might sit in in the evenings."

He turned to find a clerk and felt the carpeting fall away, and a sudden panic rose, crowding the air out of him. He lurched to the side with his arms waving, thinking, *Oh, my God, not now, we were having such a good day.* There was a sharp and spreading pain behind his left eye.

He felt someone grip his elbow, and when he turned around an old woman was standing at his side, mouthing something in a language impossible to understand, some guttural phrase that sounded like a small dog barking, and he wondered if she was from a race of people who breed with beasts. "Where am I?" he screamed, watching her eyes fill with tears.

"Einar," she called, her mouth moving slowly, but at least she knew his name and she smelled familiar, like something from home. Unlike everything else in the store.

Then he was standing behind the foreign woman, the two of them watching the man she had by the arm stagger and fall, a standing lamp going over with him. All of it was as slow and silent as some movie with the volume turned down, but he felt unbounded and terrifically happy, and then he was on his side, the fluorescent lighting burning his eyes, every sound a knifepoint. He struggled to his knees and, with the woman's help, to his feet again. He could hear his teeth grinding, and he stepped away from her, one foot at a time, feeling for the edge of the world where it dropped off into darkness, the thin crust crumbling beneath him.

Since there were no windows in the room, he couldn't determine whether it was night or day. A tube was taped to the back of his hand, his arms and chest bare. His sister was asleep in a chair by the side of the bed. He tried to reach out to her, but there was an unexpected heaviness in his arm. His head throbbed, and he thought he must've fallen. The whole building hummed. He could feel it in his shoulders and back, in the back of his legs. He pushed up in bed, and when Marin opened her eyes and saw him, she stood out of the chair.

"I want to go home," he said. The words sounded like a slurred, off-key lullaby.

But she bent down over him, holding her cheek against his, her hand cradling his head. "I know you do, sweetheart," she said.

# Twenty-six

GRIFF HAD BEEN awake thirty-six hours and now it was after midnight again, the surrounding darkness flashing with unexpected bursts of pastel light. Mulberry, rose and amber. She's been this tired before.

She knelt at one of the buckets of water she'd carried up from the creek and immersed her head until she was out of breath and sat back gasping. She felt raw, jittery, like she might start cackling and not be able to stop.

She stared down at her forearms, expecting the skin to be split and weeping, but it was just spotted with pinesap, charcoal and clay. She pushed herself up against the rim of the bucket and shuffled to the front of the kiln, where the yellow bricks throbbed with heat.

At dawn he'd said: "You can sleep now. It's my shift. I'll stay."

"We already know that's a lie." She'd been standing by the hammock pulling her clothes back on. She'd meant it to sting. Then she asked him to leave. Well rested. Well fucked. This firing was hers.

She pulled on the thick canvas gloves, opened the door to the firebox and laid in the split pine for this last stoking. Her shoulders and knees ached and her ears rang with the fresh roar of the fire. The heat made her stagger.

When the box was filled she latched the door and stripped off the gloves and began mixing the sand and fireclay into a wet slop, one bucket at a time.

She circled the kiln, mudding up the spyports and ventholes and finally the firedoor, careful not to burn her hands. She shut the damper down. She could hear the wet clay sizzling against the metal door, the fire huffing for oxygen. Two days to cool, maybe two and a half, and the colors will be set into the ware. She was so tired she drooled, wiping at her mouth with the back of her hand.

She upended the remaining bucket of water over her head and stood there sputtering, shaking her head, trying for a last burst of clarity. Just enough to get home. She put the lanterns out and picked up her thermos and Einar's old black lunch pail. The kiln groaned in the dark.

She stumbled down the trail out into the meadow above the house and finally across the porch. She stood leaning into the front door, the exhaustion spreading like a drug, but when she stepped inside she could feel their absence like a second bucket of cold water. She didn't need to check the rooms, just stepped back onto the porch and swept the beam of her flashlight over the workyard. The truck wasn't there. Oh, God, she thought.

She stood weaving at the table in the hallway, staring down at the blinking message light. She pressed the button.

"Griff, this is Marin. Your grandfather's all right. He's had a stroke, but a very minor one. We're at Saint V's. He's resting now so please don't call back tonight. I'll call in the morning. About eight. I love you, and he really is going to be all right."

She sank to the floor, lying over on her side just a minute to rest. A shower would bring her back, a pot of coffee, and she'd be in Billings in three hours, tops.

She woke with the kitchen linoleum cool against the side of her face, then remembered where she was. It was just starting to get light. Five-thirty. She listened to Marin's message again and called Paul. There wasn't anyone else she could think of.

"It doesn't mean he's going to die," he said.

She held the receiver away, pressing it against her thigh, then sat at the kitchen table. She could feel her heart drumming in her chest.

"Are you okay?"

"I had to sneeze." She didn't want him to know her whole body was buzzing. Like it was filled with birds trying to fly out in every direction. "Marin said she'd call back this morning."

"I'm coming over."

"All right." And then: "Don't say anything to anybody. Not even McEban."

"He's in Cheyenne."

"Where's Kenneth?"

"They're together. McEban called yesterday afternoon. Said they had plans to tear up the town. He said they'd be home when they were done."

She could hear the morning downdraft rushing in the trees, the songbirds starting up. "I'm getting off now," she said.

She was sitting on the porchsteps when he got there, and they went in the house. She picked up the phone to check for a dial tone, then set it back in the cradle. "I need to clean up. I didn't want to get in the shower until you were here."

"I'll come get you if she calls," he said.

She stripped out of her clothes, and washed her hair twice, soaping and rinsing the woodsmoke away, finally standing braced against the side of the stall, crying until the water turned cold. Her eyes were puffy when she came out in her robe. She sat at the table.

He'd made coffee and poured her a cup, but her throat was so dry she coughed it back up through her nose.

She cleaned her face with a paper napkin, dabbing at the stains on the front of her robe. "Do you ever watch yourself?" she asked.

"Sure. Sometimes I do."

"I watch myself all the time," she said, "and right now I'm a fucking mess."

"I think you're doing fine."

She held a hand out between them. It was shaking. "You always think I'm doing fine," she said.

He took a cribbage board from a drawer and talked her into a game, but she had trouble deciding which cards to play. She folded her arms on the table, resting her cheek against a forearm. He reached over to rub her neck.

"Don't," she said.

"I wish you'd tell me why you're mad."

"I'm not." She puffed at her hair and it lifted, falling back against her face.

"Then how come you wouldn't let me help you finish the firing?"

"I wanted to see if I could do it myself. Straight through."

He tried to comb his fingers through her hair, moving it away from her eyes, and she sat straight up.

"I was tired of looking at you," she said. "Okay?"

He studied her face. Mostly she looked just tired. "Okay."

He took a carton of eggs and a package of bacon from the refrigerator and put a pan on the stovetop.

"I'm not hungry," she said.

"You could try."

"I tried a piece of toast when I was waiting for you. I felt like I was going to puke."

The phone rang and she was up and had the receiver even before he could turn toward the sound.

"Are you there? Hello?" Marin's voice sounded fragile.

"I'm here."

"I thought I'd call early. I thought you might be worried."

"Can I talk to him?"

"He's still asleep, but he's going to be just fine."

Paul was staring at her and she turned away, pacing with the phone.

"I can't picture 'just fine.' I don't know what that looks like."

"It means we were lucky to be up here in Billings. So close to a hospital. They did a CT scan and put him on a blood thinner right away. An anticoagulant. They don't think there'll be any damage. But he needs some rest, and they want to watch him a little bit longer. See how he does on the medication."

"Is that what the doctor said?"

"He said it was a wake-up call."

She sat down at the kitchen table. "That's such a bullshit thing to say. All it means is he's not dead yet."

"I think the doctor meant it to be more hopeful than that." Marin cleared her throat. "I need to lie down. They've put a bed in here for me."

"I'm coming up."

"You don't have to do that. Really. We should be home soon enough."

"Paul's coming too."

She looked at Paul and he nodded. She could hear a door open and close on Marin's end. Water running at a sink.

"The nurse just came in," she said.

"Do you need us to bring anything?"

"A change of clothes would be nice. A sweater if you can find one. They keep it cool in here."

"Toothpaste?"

"I got all that at the shop downstairs. But you could call Marlene Silas and see if she'll keep Sammy awhile longer." She cleared her throat again and said something to the nurse, but Griff couldn't distinguish the words. "When you get here," she said, "if I'm asleep just let me sleep. I haven't been able to yet."

The line went dead.

They gassed up Paul's car at the Mini-Mart, bought cans of Red Bull and a package of powdered doughnuts and didn't see a single cop on the Wyoming side or in Montana either, making the one-hundred-seven-mile drive to the hospital in an hour and twenty-three minutes.

He dropped her off at reception, and a nurse took her by the elbow and pointed her down the right hallway.

He was awake when she came in, and when she bent to kiss him he rose up out of the bed and wrapped her in his arms, gripping fistfuls of fabric at the yoke of her shirt, as though only the buoyancy of her young body was keeping them afloat. Then he fell away and lay there smiling.

"I thought your face might be crooked," she said.

The smile moved into his eyes.

"It's just his left arm that's weak." Marin was standing behind her. "And the leg on that side. Did Paul come?"

"He's parking the car." She took his left hand in both of hers and he squeezed lightly. Like a small child might.

"See." He swallowed. "It's not that bad."

She smoothed his cheek. "When can we go home?" she asked.

He looked toward Marin.

"We need to make arrangements for physical therapy," she said. "They're satisfied with everything else."

Griff straightened. "The doctor could show me how. Or the nurse could."

He squeezed her hand. "Marin's got it taken care of," he said.

Paul carried their lunches up from the hospital cafeteria and they ate together, and when Marin curled down on the other bed and Einar drifted off she found his doctor, asking enough questions to believe this was something they could do. And that he would improve.

The next morning at Costco, she bought pillows and a blanket and a CD of great performances by the New York Philharmonic, and they got him settled comfortably in the backseat. They played the CD twice on the drive home, Mahler and Vaughan Wil-

liams, Barber and Tchaikovsky, Paul following in the one-ton with
Marin's new furniture.

A physical therapist named Shawnee came up from Sheridan
on Thursday and by Friday afternoon he could hobble down the
hallway without the aluminum walker. Shawnee said she thought a
week of that kind of improvement and she could start tapering off.
She scribbled down her phone number, insisting it wasn't a bother
to drive up on the weekend if they needed her, and stayed for dinner when she was asked. They learned she was raised on a ranch in
Star Valley.

On Saturday morning he fell in the shower. Griff heard his
body hit the porcelain, heard him cry out and found him on his
side in the tub. He'd dragged the shower curtain off the rod and
was holding it over his groin.

"Where are you hurt?" She turned the water off, kneeling on
the floor. "Tell me where."

"Not you," he said. "Please."

"Get a chair." Marin moved her to the side and kneeled down
over him, and by the time she returned from the kitchen he was
up, sitting on the side of the tub, Marin holding him steady. They
got him into the chair with the shower curtain still across his lap.

"I'm going to call Shawnee," Marin said.

"Nothing's broke." He was still having a little trouble getting
his breath. "She doesn't need to drive over here just to look at
some clumsy old son of a bitch."

Marin draped a towel across his shoulders and he tilted his head
to the side, digging a finger into his ear.

"I hate getting water in my ears," he said.

He asked her to leave and Marin helped him into his bathrobe,
then down the hallway with his walker. He was only limping.

That night he called for Griff, and when she came in he had the
magnifying glass slung around and was holding a book open at his
waist. She sat on the side of the bed.

"I'm getting stronger. I can feel that I am," he said, and when she didn't respond: "I just fell on my ass. I've done that my whole life."

"You had a stroke."

"I've probably been having them for a year."

"What am I going to do with you?" Even to her the question sounded like a parent's.

"Right there's where I'm going with this," he said. "I want you to get out and do something with your life."

"Like what?"

"Whatever in the hell you want to do." He'd raised his voice, trying to sound mad, but it had no effect. "We've talked about this before."

"I've got plenty of time." She slipped the book from his hands. "It doesn't have to be this fall."

"Nobody's got plenty of time." He nodded toward the door. "She needs to take care of me," he said. "We both need it."

She closed the book and left it on the nightstand.


The next afternoon thunderclouds rolled down off the mountains and the wind picked up and the temperature dropped twenty-five degrees. Four inches of pea-sized hail fell in half an hour and then it rained like a levee had broken in the heavens. An icy mixture filled the borrow ditches.

It cleared overnight and got hot again the next morning, and the nose flies and deerflies swarmed thickly as gnats. The horses bunched in the shade shaking their heads, their eyes swelling from the bites, rubbing their faces into one another's shoulders. When they couldn't stand it any longer they pawed at the air and ran.

A den of snakes had been flushed from a dry hillside on Nameit Creek, and the kids there carried hoes when they went out to do their chores, and the clinic called a hospital in Billings to ship down a reserve of antivenom just in case.

She saddled Royal and trailered him over to the corrals and loading chute on Deep Creek. Paul was waiting for her on a well-mannered dappled gelding he called Mister.

They rode the leases up on the mountain, where the cattle were still scattered and edgy, and in the late afternoon they found a heifer and her calf killed by lightning. Their bellies were torn open, and a gang of coyotes sat in ragged order against the skyline just thirty yards away, their muzzles and chests stained with fresh blood. Crowding the treeline was an assortment of raptors and ravens, a pair of golden eagles and a mob of lesser birds drawn to the excitement.

She rested a forearm against the saddlehorn, leaning over it to stare at the dead calf.

"It could've been a lot worse." Paul took a notebook from his shirt pocket and recorded the numbers on their eartags.

"Not for them." She reined her horse around, and he fell in beside her.

"I took a job with the County Health Department in Billings."

She stopped the horse, the bird chatter almost making it hard to hear. "No more Africa?"

"You were right. It's too far away."

"And you're bailing on graduate school too?"

"I thought you'd be happy."

She looked back at the coyotes edging in to finish their meal, and snorted a laugh and spurred her horse forward.

"So we're done talking about this?"

"I have things to do in my studio," she said.

# Twenty-seven

JEAN STEPPED OUT of the shower, drying off with a towel she'd brought in from the clothesline. It was stiff and knobby and brought the blood to the surface of her skin. She turned to the side, examining herself in the full-length mirror mounted on the inside of the bathroom door. She sucked her stomach flat. Her arms and shoulders and legs appeared unblemished, darkened from working in the garden. She smoothed lotion on, twice on her elbows, knees and heels.

She sat in her terry-cloth robe at the vanity in the bedroom, applying makeup, returning to the bathroom to wash it off, settling on just a hint of eyeliner and a pale lip gloss. She didn't want the effort to show.

She drank iced tea and smoked four cigarettes on the sunporch waiting for her hair to dry, then went to the bedroom and shucked her robe off on the floor and brushed her hair until it shone, drawing it away from her face and securing it with a silver clasp. This was her best feature. Men stared at her hair even before moving their gaze to her breasts, her hips. Silver pendants in her ears. No necklace. She didn't want to break the long, graceful lines of her neck.

She slipped into the powder-blue panties and bra she'd bought at Victoria's Secret and stood in front of the mirror again, pushing her breasts up and together, drawing her hands away slowly. Her reflection was nodding.

She chose the jeans that made her ass look like she ran thirty miles a week, brown leather sandals with no heels, the beige silk-and-linen twinset that showed off her tan. She studied herself in the vanity mirror. This wasn't man-pretty. That was something entirely different. This was down-to-business pretty. Then she took his grandmother's pearl ring from her jewelry box and slipped it on, extending her hand to appreciate its simple beauty. She closed her hand into a fist.

She drove to the Hub with the windows up and the AC on low so she'd arrive fresh. There were a dozen cars and pickups in the lot, another dozen Harleys backed in against the concrete divider set in front of a hedgerow of caragana. She parked around the side of the log building and sat for a minute watching the tops of the cottonwoods to make sure the wind wasn't up. The women's bathroom wasn't well lit and she didn't want to have to fix her hair again.

She hadn't had a drink all day. With her eyes closed she could imagine the first one, the warm flush spreading across her cheeks like a shawl over her shoulders. But not yet. Right now it was all about attitude, about having the edge.

She walked in through the side door and stood at the end of the bar, leaning into the padded bumper. She loved the odor of bars, especially in the summer. Damp, cool and yeasty, like a sip of beer.

The men sitting near her stared and looked away. She watched their reflections in the mirror set behind the rows of bottles, the bikers and cowboys and businessmen.

The bartender slid a coaster in front of her, tapping it with a forefinger. "It's margarita night," he said.

He wore black slacks and a white shirt with a pleated front, black garters snapped above the elbows to hold the sleeves back. It's what passed for a uniform at the Hub.

"How's it going, Jamie?"

"Same old same old." He tilted his head back, his lips pursed like an old man's, studying her. "I'm glad to say you aren't looking your age."

"You're a sweetheart." But he was too young, and spent too much time in the gym to be interesting. She pushed back from the bar. "I'll order something with dinner," she said.

"You want me to send Crane in when he shows?"

"Who?"

"Your husband," he said. "If he comes in through the bar."

"If he does, I'd buy a ticket to that event."

She weaved through the tables, pausing in the archway to the dining room. Deep red carpeting, red draperies, flocked wallpaper crowded with pale watercolors, their prices printed on little white cards stuck to their frames. There was a banker and his wife from Sheridan she recognized, a real-estate agent working a client, a dozen families of tourists in their shorts and T-shirts advertising the places where they'd last vacationed. Helen sat at a table by the salad bar, both hands around a glass set on the red paper placemat in front of her. She wore a long-sleeved blue T-shirt and jeans. The scene held a strangely patriotic quality.

She walked across the room with her shoulders squared and her chin up. When she sat down she made sure her eyes were cold, and when Helen smiled she just stared.

A waitress appeared at her shoulder. "Would the lady like a cocktail?" She had an Eastern European accent.

"I sure would." Jean leaned toward the girl's nameplate— *Ksenia*—and wagged a finger toward Helen without turning to her. "I'll have what she's having."

"It's a gin and tonic." Helen held the glass up as a woman might in an advertisement.

"Bombay in mine." Jean lounged back in the chair.

"Yes, ma'am."

The girl backed away, bowing slightly at the waist, and Helen sipped her drink. She coughed, holding her napkin to her mouth.

"I don't normally drink," she said.

Her voice had been shaky on the phone when Jean called. Now it was just flat, but her body was sharp and shapely under the loose clothing. If she was nervous she'd made no effort to dress it down.

"I do," Jean said. "Every chance I get."

Helen nodded as Ksenia placed Jean's drink before her and took out her order pad.

"We're not ready yet," Jean said.

"Yes, ma'am."

They watched her backing toward the kitchen.

"They can't get American kids to work," Helen said.

Jean sipped her drink, then set the glass near the center of the table. Like shooting fish in a barrel, she thought.

"He's got Lou Gehrig's," Helen said.

"Right."

"I can't tell you how sorry I am."

"You're full of shit."

Helen's lips were still moving, but the words had become slurred, the music on the sound system slowing. Jean sat back in her chair and finished her drink in two gulps. She laughed. "You're telling me my husband's dying?"

"Yes."

"And he came to you?"

"I don't think he meant to. But yes, he did."

"Like an accident?"

"No. It wasn't an accident."

"And he couldn't tell me?" Helen's voice was coming clearer now, but Jean didn't feel like laughing anymore. "Did he tell you why?"

"I don't think they know why anyone gets ALS."

"Why he couldn't tell me."

"He said he didn't want to worry you."

"Really?"

"Something like that."

"He didn't think fucking his ex-wife would worry me?" This wasn't like shooting anything in a barrel.

"We never did make love. If that's any consolation."

"It's not."

Helen was folding her napkin into a triangle. "But we tried," she said.

"Did you hold him?"

"I don't understand."

"When you weren't making love. When you were trying to comfort him."

"Yes."

"Did he cry?"

Helen nodded.

"You know what this is, don't you?" Jean was searching the room but there was no Ksenia. "This whole fucking conversation? It's a Salvador Dalí painting. In the goddamn extreme."

"I thought you'd want to know."

"I wish he'd been fucking you," Jean said.

Her hand was on the table in front of her, the fingers tapping. They both looked at the pearl ring flashing dully. Jean brought the hand into her lap.

"I would too," Helen said. "If I were you." She stood, bringing her purse up from the seat of the chair beside her. She slung the strap over her shoulder and walked straight out without looking back.

Ksenia asked, "Would the lady like another cocktail?"

Jean pushed against the arms of the chair to stand, and when she lost her balance the girl caught her under the elbow. She pulled her arm away. "I hope you'll like this country," she said.

"Yes, ma'am."

Jean smoothed her hands over her hips, turning toward the archway. "The lady will have her next in the bar," she said.

Now the music was louder, and she was tapping the rim of her margarita glass and Jamie was coming toward her behind the bar.

"There's a fine piece," she heard, and turned with her elbows hooked back against the edge of the bar. She wanted to feel like a fine piece.

"So tell me, boys," she said, and when only the men at the nearest table turned she repeated it loud enough that they stopped playing pool at the end of the room, leaning against their cues. She brought the fresh margarita up for a sip. "So tell me, boys," she said again, pausing, "who'd like to fuck the sheriff's wife?"

They stared at her, then glanced at one another like kids at a dance, and she began to laugh and couldn't stop, didn't even try to.

# Twenty-eight

CRANE FORCED the county SUV along a rutted mining track, stopping at the edge of a gully where the road had washed out. He stood staring down at the collapsed and rusted body of the culvert, at the shabby remains of the company buildings just a hundred yards beyond.

He crossed the creek on foot, working up the north-facing slope through the sage and juniper, skirting the house-sized erratics of weather-paled basalt, stopping to look across the valley to the mineshaft—sealed now, but not until one of the Manon kids had fallen through the rotted planking. He'd been with the search-and-rescue team that had gotten her out. The sheets of muscle in his diaphragm clenched and he lay down against the sidehill, panting, waiting for it to pass. He wondered if God had spoken directly to the girl, lost for hours in the damp tunneling below.

When he gained the skyline he stretched out on his belly in the sweep of shade thrown by a stand of chokecherries, the ranch house and outbuildings just five hundred yards below. He brought the binoculars up from around his neck.

There were half a dozen parked trucks and cars, men emerging from the barn two and three at a time to start up their rigs and drive out through the log archway. More cars arrived, everyone going into the big, weathered barn but coming out too quickly to have been of any help.

At dusk a column of bikers rode in. They gunned their engines, then let them idle down, and Brady came out of the barn and stood there talking to them until a man pulled a pistol and fired into the dry brush along the creek. It was just dark enough to see the flames snapping out of the barrel and the house cat breaking from the undergrowth in a desperate sprint, disappearing through an opening in the masonry of the springhouse. Everyone but Brady was rocking at the waist with laughter.

He walked past the man, reached into a slash pile at the border of the drive and wheeled around with a four-foot length of pine scrap, catching the man full in the face, dropping him, then walked back into the barn. The downed man rolled onto his side and from there to his feet, staggering.

Most of the light had gone out of the day, and Crane sat back waiting for the moon to rise. He remembered hunting this valley with his father and old Jake Croonquist when he and Brady were still too young to shoot, sent ahead like eager hounds, circling, flushing the birds back toward them.

A covey of chukars was moving off the hillside behind him now, maybe a couple dozen in all, the accumulation of their low, harsh speech like the whispered conversation of anxious children.

It was late when he got back to town and swung past the clinic, pulling in at the curb. Dan Westerman was sitting on the front stoop.

"I didn't know you smoked," Crane said.

"I normally don't."

"You get a guy through here a little bit ago?"

"I just put thirty stitches in some simple son of a bitch's head, if that's what you mean." He dropped the butt on the step before him. "I hate fucking motorcycles."

"He going to be okay?"

"He's going to be fine, but I hope he's got a relative who's a dentist. How are you feeling?"

"A little sick to my stomach."

It was after midnight when he got home and found her car parked up on the lawn and looked in through the windshield to see if she was asleep on the seat, but it was empty. He could still hear the throaty rumble of the Harleys gearing down into town. The corner streetlight was out, the Milky Way leaving a smear of light across the night sky above him.

He went inside. In the living room his clothes were heaped in the La-Z-Boy with his toilet kit on top. Their bedroom door was shut.

He found clean sheets and a blanket in the hall closet and made up the couch, waking early the next morning. A man stood framed in the kitchen doorway, staring at Crane's pistol on the table at the foot of the couch. He was middle-aged, dressed in chinos and a golf shirt, a light jacket folded over his arm.

They both looked over at the bedroom door at the same time.

"It doesn't have anything to do with you," Crane said. "It's me she wants to hurt."

Some of the tension went out of the man's face, but he cut his eyes back at the pistol.

"This isn't a movie," Crane said. "You can go home now."

He washed his face and under his arms at the kitchen sink and dressed and scooped the clothes and toiletries onto the couch, folding the corners of the blanket back across them, then slung the whole works over his shoulder.

Starla was at her desk when he came in to work.

"You run this back to the far cell for me?"

"You bet." She didn't ask why.

Two highway patrolmen, and his undersheriff, Hank Kosky, were waiting in his office.

"You boys get any sleep last night?"

They all nodded.

"Good."

He walked back out to the wheeled cart by Starla's desk and poured himself a cup of coffee, stirring in the artificial sweetener as he returned to the office.

The senior patrolman said, "Goddamnit, Crane, it's not just baby-boomer accountants anymore. We've got some bad ones this year. Some Diablos and Angels on their way to Sturgis, I guess."

Crane sat down behind his desk. "You need more help?"

"I wouldn't mind it."

"I'll make a call."

The state cops shook his hand, telling him they appreciated his cooperation, and then lingered outside to gossip with Starla.

Hank was still in his chair. "I hope you know this thing's going to get somebody killed one of these years," he said. "Or raped."

"I agree with you, but it's the mayor you need to talk to." His back ached but the coffee was helping.

"I'm here to tell you I won't work that Iron Horse Rodeo. It ain't Christian."

Crane stared at him until the older man looked away.

"It's that weenie-bite event they run. Riding them women under that row of strung-up hotdogs and making 'em snap at them."

Crane came around the end of the desk and Hank stood out of his chair. He was puffed up, ready for a fight, and Crane looped an arm across his shoulders and guided him through the doorway. He could feel Hank soften.

"They're just hotdogs," he said. "And I'm not sure Jesus keeps that close an eye on any of us."


He drove to the top of the Bighorns, pulled into a campground and turned off the radio and slept in the backseat. He woke in the early evening, feeling more rested than he had in a week, and returned to the office. He cleaned up in the restroom while Starla warmed two Hot Pocket Ultimates in the microwave.

It was after ten when he double-parked at the corner of Ash and walked out into the milling crowd. There were two thousand Harleys backed into the curb for eight blocks along Main and two blocks back on Madison, Jefferson and Adams.

The volunteer fire department had lined hay bales through the crosswalks west of the main drag and the vendors had set up their tents and kiosks in the streets behind them. They hawked knives and cups of beer, leather clothing, Harley-Davidson patches sewn with silver thread. There were two tattoo artists and another offering hygienic piercings. A braut-and-soda stand. Burritos sold from a corner of the IGA parking lot, half the proceeds going to the Boys and Girls Club.

The Chamber of Commerce had mounted speakers and American flags on the corner lampposts and sixties and seventies rock and roll blared from noon until the bars closed.

He was standing across the street from the Spur when Brady came out. He watched him working the sidewalk like a politician, stopping to shake hands and clap shoulders.

Crane crossed at the intersection, following him east through a reeling street dance of curb-to-curb drunks and past the raised plywood stage where a band from Great Falls was butchering the chorus of CCR's "Fortunate Son."

Two blocks farther back, in the dirt and pigweed lot where Vorachek Saddlery had burned down, a gathering stood with their heads bowed before two sky-blue Dodge Power Wagons. The trucks were parked tailgate to tailgate, and in the bed of one a man paced back and forth wearing jeans and a leather vest, his beard grown to his waist. At certain points in his rant against Satan's onslaught of alcohol, drugs and fornication, the beard lifted away stiffly, exposing his naked chest. Brady sat at the edge of the congregation on a cairn of blackened bricks. He was drinking a beer, and Crane squatted down next to him. They watched a young woman get helped up onto the bumper of the second truck and from there into the bed.

"Haven't seen you in town in awhile," Crane said.

"I haven't been in awhile."

The preacher stepped over the tailgates, the woman sinking to her knees in front of him. He spread his hand against her forehead and intoned, " 'We have been buried with Christ by baptism into death.' "

Brady sang, " 'It ain't me, it ain't me, I ain't no fortunate son,' " then said, "I always liked that song."

"But you been doing okay?"

"I'm doing great. You look like shit, though." He took a pull from the beer.

The pickup bed was lined with plastic and filled with water that sloshed over the sidewalls and onto the dirt as the girl was lowered into it, the preacher cupping the back of her head and pinching her nose.

"That boy didn't have to die like he did."

Brady squinted through the weak glare of the streetlamp. "It wasn't my first choice either."

"Brought light and life to a formless world," the preacher said.

"Cooking that shit wasn't something he thought up on his own. He wasn't even twenty yet."

Brady swigged from his beer. "Hell, Crane, you don't have to look so sad about it. I knew him a bunch better than you."

The girl's head came up, sputtering, and the preacher proclaimed, "And Jesus said unto Nicodemus: 'No one can enter the kingdom of God without being born of water.' "

"We aren't kids anymore," Crane said.

"Amen," the crowd declared.

"It'd be a hell of a lot better all around if you turned yourself in."

"For you, maybe. I don't believe it would be for me."

"Do you repent of your sins, my child?"

The girl was shivering, her wet clothes clinging.

Crane stood.

Brady was looking up at him. "My guess is you didn't bring an arrest warrant out with you tonight."

"I wanted to talk first."

"Now we have." The light fell so completely from his eyes they appeared mere replacements a taxidermist might have chosen.

Crane unsnapped the leather strap over the hammer of his pistol as Brady stood up next to him, dropping the beer bottle. They heard it break.

"Go therefore and make disciples of all nations," the preacher said.

"This isn't just going away."

"For the love of our Savior, Jesus Christ." The preacher's arms were spread wide.

Brady lifted the front of his shirt. "What you've got to do now, old buddy," he said, gripping the pistol stuck in the waistband of his jeans, "is decide just how fucking Western you'd like this to get."

The worshipers were dispersing around them, a woman brushing past with a crying baby in her arms. Crane lifted his hand away from his side, and Brady turned with the crowd, pulling his shirt down over the gun.

"You be sure to call before you come out," he called back over his shoulder. "I'd hate like hell to miss you."

# Twenty-nine

CRANE WAS STILL awake when the light came on in the hallway outside the cells. He heard her footsteps on the tiles and then she was standing at the open doorway.

"You mind if I come in?"

He sat up on the cot and leaned back against the wall. "What time is it?"

"It's late." Jean checked her wristwatch. "A quarter after three." She sat on the cot across from him looking around at the graffiti on the walls, then set her purse on the floor. "Well," she said, "here we are."

"I guess so."

"I saw Helen," she said.

"She called. She said you two were thinking about starting a book club."

She wagged a forefinger at him. "You're funnier when you're homeless." She opened her purse, fishing around until she pulled out a joint. "You mind?"

"Pearl's out there."

"I don't have enough for her too."

He shrugged. "What am I going to do—put you in jail?"

"Twice as funny. You really are."

She lit the joint, inhaled, then reached it across to him. They sat for a moment, holding the smoke in, and he took another hit and handed it back.

He turned his head aside to exhale. "You think we ever were in love?"

"You were with me."

"Not the other way around?"

"I was in love with Griffin."

He felt removed from his body and didn't know whether it was the weed or something else. "Are you still?"

"He didn't live long enough to disappoint me."

"But you think about him?"

"Yeah."

His face felt unnaturally relaxed, heavy in the cheeks and around the eyes, and when she offered the joint again he waved her off.

"Are you fucked up?" she asked.

He nodded. He could hear his hair scraping against the cinderblock. "I snuck a little from your stash," he said. "About a week ago."

"I know. Addicts always know exactly how much shit they've got left."

"You aren't an addict."

"Don't you think it's cute, though? Saying I am."

He thought about it. "It's adorable."

She fished a can of beer from her purse and opened it. "I've got more in here," she said. "They're cold."

"I'm fine."

"It's weird." She sipped the beer. "But you dying's kind of sexy. It's like you're being sent on a secret mission, or to the front or something." She set the can on the floor, stood up and undid the top two buttons of her blouse. "I feel like if I came over there right now, something could happen for us."

She was only a step away, her hands at the waistband of her slacks. She had beautiful hands. "It's not going to work," he said.

"We could try."

"I'm not up to the humiliation."

She sat down, bending forward with her forearms against the tops of her thighs. Her blouse was open, and he stared at the rise of her breasts.

"I'm sorry about the other night," she said. "He was just the most adventuresome guy in the bar."

"I had it coming." He lay over on his side, still looking at her. She tilted the can up. He watched her throat as she swallowed.

"I want you to come home," she said. "Whenever you feel like it."

"I will in the morning."

"It's cold in here."

"It's the cinderblock. It holds the AC."

She finished her beer. "I'm going to take care of you."

"I don't want you to."

"How do you think it'll look if I leave you now?"

He was still lying on his side. He lifted his head, getting a hand under it. "It's what I'd do."

"No, you wouldn't."

"I might."

She placed the can on the floor and stood and stomped it flat, then put it in her purse. "Here's how it's going to be," she said. "Me and my girlfriends are going to go out every weekend and drink shots and I'm going to bitch about how hard it is watching you die. I might even let them pry it out of me that you tried to fuck your ex-wife."

"You don't have any girlfriends."

"I'll find some. It'll be the best time of my life."

When he closed his eyes she sat watching until his breathing deepened, then gathered up his clothes from where he'd folded and arranged them at the foot of his cot.

She turned off the light in the hall when she left, said good night to Pearl and put his things on the backseat of her car. She walked around and leaned against the trunk. It was raining lightly, enough that it made a purring sound. The air smelled of mown hay and sage and asphalt, and she didn't feel a bit tired.

She lit a cigarette and got in behind the wheel and backed out into the street. She put the window down, enjoying the mist of rain against her cheek. I can do this, she thought. She tried to remember when she'd been brave in the past. She'd done what she had to do. She didn't want to go right home, thinking she'd drive awhile before it got light, out toward the interstate, then turn around and go home and put clean sheets on their bed.

She shouldn't have said that about Griffin, made him out as someone special, unforgettable. We all have our shit, and it had been twenty years, and truly, she would've found something to hate about him if they were still together. She flicked the cigarette out the window. That's one thing she could change. If Janice Obermueller could quit smoking, how hard could it be? There were deer grazing the overgrowth of grass along the borrow ditches. Their eyes flashed red in the highbeams. Maybe she'd start exercising. She reached into her purse where it sat in the passenger's seat for a can of beer.

She popped the tab and took a sip, thinking she might taper off the drinking a little. Nothing drastic. No meetings, nothing like that, maybe just start later in the day, and this wasn't really like driving at all, more like gliding. It could be like that. She and Crane could have whole days together that were just this effortless. She could make it happen.

# Thirty

Kᴇɴɴᴇᴛʜ ʜᴀᴅ ᴏʀᴅᴇʀᴇᴅ a second plate of waffles and the ripest banana their waitress could find. He spread the pulpy fruit on like it was cream cheese and poured maple syrup over the whole works, closing his eyes when he chewed so he could concentrate on the flavors. After each bite he swished his mouth clean with a swallow of milk.

"I'm not sure we've ever taken a real vacation," McEban said. "Not that I can remember."

"We did when you broke your pelvis," the boy said. "When the roan colt fell over backwards and squished you like"—he looked down at his empty plate—"like a waffle."

McEban tapped the *Wyoming Tribune-Eagle* spread out on his side of the table where he'd been studying the program of events. "This might work out a little better for us," he said.

"I got to stay home from school for a whole week. And ladies brought food to the house and Paul and I played hearts. Remember? I drew pictures of horses all over your cast."

"I remember."

McEban folded his placemat back, borrowed a pen from the waitress and made a list of when the parade was going to run, the hours the carnival operated, when the rodeos and concerts began.

When they'd finished breakfast they stood out in the bright sun on the sidewalk.

"I guess first thing we ought to do is get a room," McEban said.

"Can we wash the truck?"

McEban pulled the toothpick from his mouth, staring down at the boy.

"In one of those places with the spray hoses," Kenneth said. "I've always wanted to."

They took a room with two beds at the Super 8 on Lincolnway off I-25, then found a carwash on Missile Drive. There were a few others but the boy liked the idea of a road named after something that got shot into the air.

He sprayed the truck with soapy water and clean, alternating between machine-gun and laser-sword sounds, and when they were nearly out of quarters McEban parked at the vacuum stands and sorted through the clutter on the dash while Kenneth sucked up the gravel, gum wrappers, dried mud and horseshit from the floormats.

On Capitol Avenue he stood at the curb waving to the people on floats and horseback, to the older kids in the marching bands, and when the men came zigzagging down the street throwing handfuls of candy from little scooters tricked out to look like turtles, he fell to his knees and filled his cap with packages of M&M's, wrapped taffy and miniature Baby Ruth and Butterfinger bars. There were people sitting on coolers and in lawn chairs, and at the corner a woman slouched in her chair cradling a baby in her lap. When she smiled he offered his cap, and she took a piece of candy.

"Thank you," she said.

Her shirt was lifted up from her waist and he could see the bottom curve of a breast, the baby's mouth pressed into her. She held a hand above his head to shade the side of his face, his cheeks contracting and relaxing as he suckled, an eyelid fluttering.

Then people were folding their lawn chairs and milling out into the empty street, the sidewalks draining. He looked around for McEban.

On the drive to the rodeo grounds he kept busy raking through his candy, finding the pieces he thought might melt.

"Did you get any Junior mints?" McEban asked.

"There's some SweeTARTS."

"I don't want anything sour."

He somehow got his cap back on his head even though it was still half-filled with candy. "Did my mom do that with me?" he asked.

A fire engine from the parade pulled alongside them, and the driver was drinking a beer.

"You mean like the lady at the parade?"

He nodded, feeling his face warming.

"Yes, she did."

He leaned back against the seat and closed his eyes. He tried to imagine what it must have been like, if his mother would've tasted different than other women, but the embarrassment only deepened.

The rodeo lasted all afternoon and they ate plastic boats of corn chips topped with cheese and chili, sipping cans of warm Coke.

They went to the carnival in the evening, and McEban bought a roll of tickets that allowed them to go on any ride they chose, and they tried the Kamikaze and the Gravitron, and felt pukey and brittle afterward and were satisfied to use the remaining tickets racing around and crashing into each other in bumper cars. The man who took their tickets at the gate had a tattoo of vines and flowers that covered his whole face and the sides and top of his shaved head, and Kenneth tried not to stare but he couldn't help it.

The next day they went to the parade again, then to the rodeo in the afternoon. It was two days now and they hadn't seen a single person they knew.

McEban tapped him on the top of the head. "You okay?"

They were walking back across the parking lot, weaving through the cars and the press of people, the sun glaring off the rows of hot metal.

"I don't remember where we parked."

"But you're having a good time?"

"It's harder than I thought it would be."

McEban stepped in front of him, squatting down so they were on the same level. "You need to go home?"

He shook his head.

"You look like you do."

He thought he must have the dumb expression he got sometimes. He made his face perk up. "I'm having a really good time."

"You're sure?"

He nodded, smiling, and when McEban stood up he took his hand and that helped. It made it not so noisy and crowded and hot.

That night they went to an outdoor concert to hear a singer named Taylor Swift and were surprised she was a woman. She had long blonde hair and wore cowboy boots and a shimmery black dress. She danced across the stage while she sang, at times so vigorously he thought it was a miracle the dress didn't fly off, or parts of her out of it. He especially liked her arms. They were thin and long and whiter than her pale hair, and when she reached up over her head while she was dancing it was like she was pointing out something special in the dark sky above them.

The next morning he had diarrhea, felt dizzy and weak, and his stomach hurt. McEban got him settled back in bed and told him not to open the door to anyone, that he'd be gone just a little while, and when he woke again McEban was sitting on the edge of the bed unwrapping a thermometer. There were plastic shopping bags on the floor between the beds.

He held the thermometer under his tongue while they watched the clock, and when he didn't have a fever they sat together at the table by the bathroom door, using plastic spoons to eat chicken noodle soup from white paper containers. Then he got back in bed.

That evening he felt well enough to sip a ginger ale and they went out for dinner. McEban made him order mashed potatoes and a chicken breast without the skin.

The next morning he was fine, but they decided to skip the rodeo and spent most of the day parked out on Happy Jack Road watching the jets take off and land at the Air Force base. In the late afternoon they sat in the back of a bookstore, taking turns reading in whispers from *King Arthur and the Knights of the Round Table.*

At dinner he told McEban he was ready to go home.

"I'm with you on that," the man said.

They were waiting for the lemon pie they'd ordered.

"I kind of mean now."

"Are you feeling sick again?"

McEban held his hand against the boy's forehead, and then the back of his hand against the side of his neck. "You don't feel warm."

"I don't want you to be mad."

"I'm not even a little bit mad."

The waitress set down their desserts and freshened McEban's coffee.

After she left McEban said, "I can't remember who we're supposed to go listen to tonight."

"It was Def Leppard." Kenneth finished his milk.

"Are they girl singers or boys? We got fooled last night."

"I don't know. I just liked the name." He was patting the meringue down flat with his fork. "I'm kind of sick of sweet stuff," he said.

"You don't have to eat it."

"You never said anything about the trouble I got in." He was sitting very straight in his chair.

"Was that one of the reasons you thought I was mad?"

"It was the main reason."

McEban looked over at their waitress, acting like he was writing on the palm of his hand so she'd know to bring their check. "I hate to disappoint you," he said, "but I pretty much forgot about you being an ex-con."

"Rodney and I stayed up and watched a prison movie one night. It was the only movie we watched the whole time I was there. Don't you think that's kind of weird?"

"Yes, I do."

"Did you know donkeys kill more people every year than plane crashes?" He was relaxing again.

"Was that in the movie?"

"It's just something Rodney knows about. Like Walt Disney being afraid of mice. He told me that too."

They went back to the room and took off their boots and napped for an hour. Then they packed and checked out and started north.

He'd stopped twice for coffee, and now the boy was asleep on the seat. His cell phone vibrated in his shirt pocket.

"Hello," he said, keeping his voice low.

"You're my hero."

"Pardon me?"

"For a lot of reasons," she said, "but tonight especially, for going down to get Kenneth. Really, Barnum, I'm thankful for everything you've done for my boys, and for me too."

He lowered the window a little more. He put the blinker on, taking the two-lane off the interstate. "I never did anything I didn't want to do," he said.

"Now you're just being modest. You've lifted us all on your shoulders, and you know you have. Or you should."

"Are you home?"

"You're the only man in the world who could've unlocked the universal love at my core. I'm sure I don't say that enough."

"You aren't at the ranch, then."

"I'm going to try harder. I've made a vow."

"Can you tell me what's wrong?"

"Nothing's wrong. Everything's better than I thought it ever could be."

"You aren't hurt?"

"I'm fine. Just a little bit stranded right now."

Kenneth shifted on the seat, but didn't wake up.

"You're broke down is what you're saying."

"The mechanic said it was going to cost seven hundred dollars to fix. Can you believe that? Him trying to take advantage of me?"

"Where are you?"

"Just over in Idaho."

"I'm not driving over there."

"It would only be maybe seven hours if you go through Yellowstone. Eight max. It'd be fun."

When he came around the bend by the river, a slant of light was cutting over the guardrail and into the trees across the highway, and he tapped the brake, slowing down.

"If you brought Kenneth it'd be like a vacation."

"I think there's been some kind of accident," he said.

"I know you'll come," she said. "I know you won't be selfish."

"I'm getting off now."

Kenneth came awake when he pulled onto the shoulder, and he told the boy where they were. He told him to stay put and handed him the cell phone. "Call 911," he said.

He ran past the skid marks and the splintered posts and stepped over where the guardrail was twisted and broken. He started down slowly, but the embankment was loose, slick from the rain, and he had to slide. There was the odor of gasoline and burned rubber, of broken sage and gouged earth, and at the bottom of the slope the car had come to rest on its roof. The windows were shattered, the domelight on, a side panel torn away. He recognized the car and now could smell the blood. Jean was on her side by the front fender, trying to drag herself away. She was talking quietly, not screaming or moaning, just speaking normally as if she were having a conversation.

She turned to him when he knelt beside her, her face so misshapen, so awash with blood, it could have been any woman in the world, he thought, but it was Jean.

"I'm right here," he said.

She reached out, the other arm wrenched back at an unnatural angle. "Crane?" She sounded relieved. Like he'd been gone for a while, and just now come home.

"Yeah," he said, trying to hold her still, but she was slippery with blood. "I'm right here."

"I so fucked this up." She relaxed into him.

"You're going to be fine."

Blood welled from her mouth, and she gagged and spat, but managed to take a deep breath. "I love you," she said. "I'm sure of it now."

He bent close enough that she could understand, each word spoken clearly. "I love you too," he said.

# Thirty-one

THEY WAITED A WEEK and held the memorial service at the
Horse Creek Community Hall off 343, where the borrow ditch
was shallow enough that people could line their outfits along the
highway's shoulder once the parking lot filled up. The sky was
dark, low-hanging and muggy enough to rain, but it never did.
Reverend Harrison from the Missouri Synod Lutheran officiated,
invoking the soul's reunion with the divine so effectively that a
good portion of the mourners felt a sense of ease, reasoning that if
Jean could be allowed entrance to heaven, they would be as well.
Marin selected the hymns. The crowd stood while they sang, the
men in freshly pressed jeans and sports jackets faintly smelling of
dry-cleaning fluid, their hats held at their waists, their foreheads
pale as ivory. Some had ties knotted around their necks. Some had
shined their boots. The women wore their best dark dresses and
the children fidgeted, stealing sly smiles from one another, their
thoughts reeling through the possibilities of a summer afternoon.
Einar sat very straight on his folding chair in the front row with his
hat turned up in his lap, Marin on one side and Griff and Crane on
the other. It was over at three.

Half the crowd followed Crane and Griff back to the house and
the women carried in their covered dishes, arranging them on the
table in the kitchen, slicing a ham and setting out buns and soft

drinks, brewing an urn of coffee. Crane had a keg of beer out on the sunporch, iced down since dawn.

They gathered in knots across the lawn and in the kitchen and living room, talking together about how Crane might get along without her, remembering funny conversations they'd had with Jean, laughing quietly, finally settling into observations about the weather, cattle prices, remodelings. Only Griff stayed back to help clean up.

"I should've had something to say." Crane was sitting at the table, his suit coat hanging on the back of the chair.

Griff was bent at the refrigerator, stacking the last of the casserole dishes inside and smoothing the strips of masking tape with the owner's last name printed out.

"I could've told a story about when we were first dating. Something like that."

She sat with him at the table. "You want another coffee?"

"Will you stay for one?"

She filled their cups at the urn. "That was a nice-looking woman you were talking to." She was stirring sugar into her coffee.

"I talked to a lot of women today."

"The one who was flirting with you. Wearing a blue dress." She stood and dragged the two black garbage bags leaning against the counter out onto the sunporch and sat down again. "Is she the one?"

"No, it wasn't her," he said. "And the one it was isn't anymore."

She toed her dress shoes off.

"Anyway, your mother and I lasted longer than you probably thought we would."

"You were the record," she said.

He got up, lifting the ham out of the refrigerator and peeling the plastic wrap back. He stood at the counter picking glazed pieces from the rim of the plate, nibbling. "I don't know why I'm still hungry," he said.

"Maybe that's why we never really tried very hard at the father-daughter thing." She sipped her coffee. "I guess you knew I didn't think she'd keep you around all that long."

"I could tell."

She filled her cup again. It felt good to have her shoes off. There were still red creases where the straps had cut across the tops of her feet. "She thought it would've been better if I hadn't lived out at the ranch."

"I could've made more of an effort, though."

She shrugged. "I didn't either."

"You were just a kid then."

"I never was," she said, "not really."

She stood again, reaching up under her dress, hooking the waistband of her pantyhose and pulling them down over her hips. When he realized what she was doing, he looked out the window.

"It doesn't mean I don't care about you." She was sitting now, wadding the hose onto the seat of the chair to her side. She crossed a foot up on her knee and scratched at the arch.

"You think you'd want this house?" he asked.

"Like to live in?"

"Yeah."

"Where would you go?"

He put the ham back in the refrigerator. "I'm retiring."

She was staring into the living room as if she'd never noticed it before. "I read somewhere," she said, "that you shouldn't make decisions after someone close to you dies. Not for a year. Not big ones, anyway."

"I was thinking about it before she died."

She switched feet.

"That would make who, Hank Kosky, the sheriff?"

"You never know who people might vote for."

She straightened her legs and held her feet together, stretching her toes. "You'd really leave?"

"I've been here most of my life."

She sat up straight in her chair, tucking her legs back along the sides. "I think you should keep it. You could rent it to somebody in case you changed your mind."

He sat down again. "She said she thought about what it would be like if I died." He tried his coffee and it had gone cold, so he carried the cup to the sink. "She said it like it wouldn't be the worst thing that could happen."

"That was just Mom." She lifted her purse from the table, opening it on her lap and stuffing her pantyhose in.

"Will you take some of this food with you?"

She stood up. "Not tonight."

"It'll just go bad."

"I'll get it tomorrow. I thought I'd come over and box up some things. Her clothes. Some other stuff."

"That doesn't have to happen right away."

"It'll make me feel like I'm doing something."

She had her purse slung over her shoulder and her shoes in that hand when she hugged him.

He kept his body very still, willing the tremors out of the muscles in his arms. He thought the beer had probably helped. "I care about you," he said.

She kissed him on the cheek. "Me too." She stepped to the door. "I'm not sure what I'm doing either. I don't think it's all hit me yet."


On Monday he talked with his attorney and had Griff made his sole beneficiary. He drew up a living will, called about his pension plan and Social Security, got his meager 401(k) switched over to her.

He thought about looking at nursing homes in Billings, then decided he needed to be farther away. The next day he drove to Denver. He found a place in Englewood he thought he could afford. It was clean and the staff looked like they'd seen so many people die it wasn't a shock anymore. That's what he wanted. Efficiency with no tears.

He got drunk in a downtown bar that night and had a seizure in the taxi riding back to his motel, then tipped the cabbie more than he needed to.

On the drive home he stopped in Sheridan for dinner and was just finishing when Helen and Larry came in. They turned away, speaking with their heads drawn close together, and then Larry nodded and she took his hand and they walked straight to the table.

"I'm so sorry about Jean," she said.

Larry shook his hand. "We should have come to the funeral."

"She drew a big crowd anyway."

They all nodded. There was laughter from a table by the windows.

"Will you join us?" She was staring down at what was left of his meal.

"I'd better get going."

"For a drink, then."

There were voices at the front of the restaurant. They turned and saw a young man in a wheelchair talking with the hostess, explaining something. Both his legs were gone, his jeans folded back at the knees, his haircut still high and tight. The girl pushing the chair stared down at him and didn't look up.

"I wish Dick Cheney was here," Helen said. "I wish he had to see a boy like that every day for the rest of his life."

Larry shook his head. "Know that Jean's in our prayers," he said.

"Thank you."

She hugged him. "I need you to believe how truly sorry I am," she said.

He nodded. He kept his eyes open, breathing through his mouth so he wouldn't smell her hair. She stepped away.

"Have a good vacation," he said.

"*Buenas noches,*" Larry said.

She stood between them with her hands laced at her waist, her jaw clenched, and they both knew this was the stance she took in public when she thought she might cry.

# Thirty-two

In the evenings, after eating his dinner at a café around the corner from the office, he'd drive out to the house and give her garden a couple of hours. Hoe the weeds, harvest whatever was ripe, turn the sprinklers on for a good soak. The first night after her death he'd carried a box of tomatoes, cucumbers, zucchini and bell peppers over to the next-door neighbor's, but they'd looked at him with such pity that he now brought the produce into the office, encouraging Starla and his deputies to pick through it. He learned there was far too much zucchini in the world and that he slept better on the cot in the cell. One night Pearl brought in a plate of cookies.

He thought he might buy a van and drive to Arizona. Have a look at the Grand Canyon, loop down into Mexico and poke around. But what if his condition worsened and he couldn't make it back? That's how it had gone with his grandfather. He'd been able to sit up at the table and mash his food around enough to swallow, then two weeks later was in a wheelchair, wearing a neck brace to keep his head level and sucking his meals up through a straw. Anyway, he couldn't imagine choking to death in a foreign country and didn't want some stranger he couldn't understand shoving a catheter in his dick.

He drove past the house before turning back south and out of town. The front door was propped open, Einar's truck parked in the driveway with boxes in the back. Griff passed in front of the living-room window.

The traffic was light. Ranch families, tourists, a tractor idling along the shoulder, a carload of teenagers coming into town going ninety. He could see the expression of alarm on the driver's face and watched in the rearview mirror as the kid stood on the brakes, locking them, damn near rolling it. He imagined their panic, their laughter, too young to honestly believe they'd been seconds away from dying, now pitching beer bottles two and three at a time into the borrow ditch, arguing who among them could walk the straightest line, contemplating how they'd get to school or get laid with no driver's license, what story they'd fabricate for their parents.

His dad had taught school. He'd also taught him how to roll the gauze pads and wedge them around the outside of his grandfather's bottom teeth, after plucking out the soaked rolls, the old man silently drooling. He remembered the apology in his eyes, unable by then to voice his thanks. Finally, the gauze wasn't enough and they had to knot a bath towel around his neck.

His dad had done the heavy lifting. In and out of bed and the wheelchair, on and off the shitter. He'd rigged a canvas sling from the bathroom ceiling, like a suspended lawn chair, to get his father in under the shower. He'd strip down and get in with him, soaping, rinsing carefully. And then it was just sponge baths on the bed, the old man's legs swollen red, purple and blue.

He turned off on Cabin Creek, stretching his mouth open wide, working his chin back and forth to relax the muscles in his jaw. He'd had another seizure last night, waking with it, biting at his tongue. He could still taste the blood in his mouth.

The tires rattled the plank bridge and he swung the cruiser around through the workyard, parking by the barn. There was only Brady's truck and the rusted hulk of a '52 DeSoto down on its rims, burdock and snakeweed growing out through the broken windows, the chrome hood ornament of Hernando's head hack-sawed off.

He unholstered his revolver, releasing the cylinder and turn-ing the barrel up, the cartridges falling onto the palm of his hand. The doctor—his name was Scott—had said it was a pulmonary embolism that killed the old man. It happened at dawn. Probably during one of the nightmares he'd begun having. The lungs fill with blood, maybe you cough in your sleep, thrash once or twice, and you're gone. Just that fast. Dr. Scott said if he had ALS it's how he'd want to go, but he hadn't been the one to clean up the mess. He thumbed the cartridges back into their chambers, all six of them, and snapped the cylinder home.

He didn't ease the door shut when he got out of the car but slammed it hard, flushing a party of gray jays from the apple tree in front of the house. A single horse was circling the corral, neighing.

Inside the barn it was just as the girl had said it would be. No hoofstrikes or the odors of clover or timothy or animal dung, only the scratching of packrats in the loft, the light falling in dust-filled shafts from the row of windows under the eaves. Stereos, televi-sions, computers and firearms stacked carelessly against the walls as high as a man could lift. The stalls overflowing with cameras, VCRs, DVD players, antique furnishings, saddles, chain saws, power tools, wrench sets, table saws, joiners, a planer and drill press. He didn't bother to part the sheets of milky plastic hanging from the rafters above the last stall. He knew what he'd find in there, his eyes already watering from the bite of ammonia, the mix of cooked chemicals.

"That you, old buddy?"

He turned to the granary door. He could feel the weak sunlight on his shoulders, on the back of his neck. It felt like a caress. "Right here," he called.

There was Brady's distinct laughter behind the door. "You want a beer?"

He slid his tongue against the roof of his mouth. Still the taste of blood. "I'm all right." He gripped the revolver, holding it at his waist as he stepped through the door. He felt relaxed, fluid, just a boy coming to see his friend.

"Well, look at you," Brady said. "Wyatt Earp–looking son of a bitch that you are." He was sitting across the room in a cushioned chair, with a floor lamp by his side, books stacked around the base. A hooked rug in front of the chair. A card table crowded with rows of bound bills, tens and twenties and fifties. "I've been waiting all day for this."

He bent over the arm of the chair and pulled a beer out of the cooler. The ice shifted. He offered the can and Crane shook his head. A pistol lay across Brady's thighs. "Suit yourself." A vein was pulsing in his pale neck, sweat dripping from his nose. "This is it? Just you?" He sipped the beer, wiped his mouth. "I was hoping for a SWAT team."

On the walls were framed photographs of their families mounted and moving cows. He and Brady at a branding, in a snow-drift with their schoolbooks.

"Remember when we tried to drop a new engine in that old DeSoto?" Brady asked.

"Greased lightning."

"That was us. Good times."

Crane nodded, and Brady was on his feet with the pistol snatched up off his lap, the muzzle blast knocking Crane back a step. He stood blinking, his hearing mostly gone, his head filled with a high-pitched shrieking. He turned and saw the hole where the bullet had struck the wall, and when he turned back he could see the spiral of rifling in the bore, the barrel level with his face. "You have the right to remain silent," he said.

Brady swung the pistol just inches to the side and it bucked again in his hand, the concussion again like a blow. He could smell the burning gunpowder and thought blood might be running from his ears, his skull and shoulders now vibrating.

"Anything you say can and will—"

Brady fired once more, just over the top of Crane's head, his hand trembling. "Can't you just fucking do this?" He was pleading. "Pretend I'm on fire." His voice cracked. "Pretend I'm screaming so loud you can feel it in your teeth."

Crane slapped him in the temple with his service revolver and Brady's head snapped to the side but he didn't go down. He just smiled like that's what he'd needed all along, the blood sheeting the side of his head, as smooth and bright as new paint.

Crane leaned forward, lifting the pistol from Brady's hand, and cuffed him. He didn't struggle being led from the barn and folded into the backseat of the cruiser. He just bled.

# Thirty-three

GRIFF CAME OUT in stocking feet, cotton pajama bottoms and a T-shirt a size too large, found where she'd left her boots on the porch, and sat on the top step to pull them on, watching the moon rise. When it cleared the horizon she started across the workyard staring into the sky, understanding she wouldn't see the stars this clear and sharp for some time. Her arms prickled and she drew them back through the armholes, hugging herself inside the shirt.

When she ducked between the corral rails Royal nickered softly, his voice deeper than the others, a dozen of them milling around or standing in their sleep. She could just distinguish where he stood by the water trough, the night settled darker on his body, and when she got closer the outline of his head came clear in the moonlight, his ears pricked. The gate stood open. They'd come in from the pastureland to drink, perhaps finding some comfort in the shadows of the barn. A horse snorted, the stamp of a hoof reverberating in the ground. Another coughed.

She circled his neck with her arms, water dripping from his muzzle back into the trough, rippling the moon's reflection. He nickered again, and this time it tickled her cheek.

He followed her to the barn. They all came, thinking of grain, but she latched the door behind her and stepped out through the tackshed holding a bridle against her side. They edged away, cautious as deer, and she wondered if it was the leather they smelled or if something had changed in her posture, revealing she wasn't just another animal sharing the night but a woman wanting something from them. Only Royal did not care. He stepped to her and lowered his head.

She looped the reins around his neck, offering the bit and slipping the headstall over his ears. She buckled the throatlatch, turning to grip a handful of the dark mane at his withers, and swung onto his back. He stood straighter, the night changed for both of them.

The others moved away, coyly at first, then out through the gate at a run with her and Royal among them, the rhythm of their hooves striking the earth in a tremendous, continuous roar, the bunch of them moving at once together and apart, much as clouds shift. They swept down and across the creek, the surface breaking up in thin sheets that fell back into her chest and face, making her gasp. Once through the cottonwood and into the pasture, they separated and slowed, only she and Royal maintaining the pace.

He crossed the irrigation ditch that bordered the sage in a single jump and worked upward along the fall line, warming between her legs. She lay against his neck, a breast on either side of his neck, his body straining beneath her, lunging, and at the crest of the ridge she reined him in. They turned, looking back at the moonstruck valley below them, its long shadows falling westward. There was no wind, only the sound of their breathing. They seemed to be floating, as we float in our dreams.

She stood in the hallway outside his room, listening to the ticking of the old windup clock he preferred. "Are you asleep?" she whispered.

"I thought I was." There was the rustling of bed linen. "I'm not sure I can always tell the difference anymore."

She skirted the foot of the bed and stretched out on top of the covers beside him, the ticking even louder now.

"You used to come in here all the time when you were little. I forgot how much I liked it."

She found his hand. "Me too." His grip had gotten stronger.

"You smell horsey."

"I was saying my good-byes," she said. "I decided to go to Chicago. For the clay residency."

"I was hoping you would. I would've been disappointed if you didn't."

The wind gusted and a series of pinecones fell against the roof, rolling into the gutter.

"They've got every kind of kiln you can think of," she said, "and a gallery, and Marin said Paul can almost walk to school and I can take the 'L' down to Oak Park."

Another gust of wind and more pinecones on the roof.

"I never said so, but I didn't think Africa or Billings, neither one, would work for him." He cleared his throat and pushed up higher against his pillows. "We're going to manage here just fine. I don't want you to worry."

"I'm going to."

"Then try to limit yourself," he said. "Maybe just an hour in the mornings."

She turned onto her side. "You don't think Marin bribed them, do you? To accept me for the whole year?"

"She just sent the pictures she took."

"You're sure?"

"Marin wouldn't do something like that." And then, as though it had just occurred to him: "You aren't taking them along, are you?"

"No. I made them for you."

"I've gotten fond of that little snake-faced girl," he said. "The others too."

She slipped up against him, her head on his shoulder. "I'll miss you."

"I know you will." He stroked her hair. "Why wouldn't you?"

# Thirty-four

Hᴇ ʜᴀᴅ ᴀ ʙʀᴇᴀᴋꜰᴀꜱᴛ of cereal and skim milk. A breeze was coming through the window, and he sat listening to the notepaper snapping against the cabinet door. She always taped it up to the left of the sink, a printed-out reminder that she loved him, every day since they'd come back from the hospital. He thought he'd have a look at it later.

When he returned the milk carton to the refrigerator, he slid the meals she'd stacked up in casserole dishes to the side. Two plain, saltless lunches and dinners. Nothing fried. No sauces. He'd gotten used to them, but she was gone for the day and he'd made other arrangements.

She believed in reincarnation, and they'd agreed to come back as brother and sister again. He told her that if he got to pick, he sure wanted another run at it.

He drank two cups of coffee from the thermos she'd left on the counter, rinsed the dishes and positioned himself in the center of the kitchen. He swung his arms around him, cocking his hips left and right, and everything seemed to be working better than it had for some time. He felt an uncommon clarity and didn't hurt anywhere, so decided not to take his pills. He wanted to see what would happen.

He dressed, sat down by the new phone she'd bought and called McEban, running a finger over the little strip of duct tape she'd stuck on the console next to a button that would dial her cell phone in case he had an emergency. He'd promised her he would, but that was a lie. He wasn't about to ruin her one night away.

Then, when he'd made his plans with McEban, he called Curtis Hanson. "I'm ready," he said, and hung up.

He picked up his cane, put on his hat and started down the drive. It was a fine, late-summer day. The sun warm, a light breeze. He could hear the grasses rustling alongside the road and whistled a few bars of his favorite birdsong, and a meadowlark sang back.

When he reached the turnout at the mailboxes he could hear the Cummins diesel idling, throaty and even, and Curtis helped him up into the cab.

"I didn't make you wait too long, did I?" he asked.

"No. I just got here myself."

They eased down through the borrow ditch and out across the pasture in four-wheel-drive, listening to the sage scraping against the undercarriage. They could smell it.

He dug the folded bills out of his pocket and held them up between them. "I need to give you something for gas."

"I'm your neighbor, for Christ's sake."

He put the money away. He could feel the warm press of sunlight moving across his chest as Curtis turned them in a slow arc, then backed around.

"That level stretch there?" Curtis asked. "Just south of Mitchell?"

He nodded. "It's where I pictured it."

Curtis dragged a shovel off the truckbed, and Einar stood leaning into the fender, listening to him hacking away at the prairie grass. Then the squeal of the gin poles pivoting back, Curtis locking them in place.

Einar started back along the side, above him the cable groaning in its pulley, the electric winch whining. He laid his hand open against the steel edging of the flatbed and felt the truck squatting against the torque.

"You might want to take a step back," Curtis said.

"Am I in your way?"

"You're standing where you needn't be if this cable snaps."

He worked around to Curtis. "It'd be a funny way to die, wouldn't it," he said, "squashed by a gravestone?"

"It'd damn sure make a good story if a man could tell it right. Here, reach out to me." Curtis guided his hand onto the winch lever. "Just ease her off a little when I say something."

He stood waiting.

"Just a tad now." Curtis grunted, shouldering the marble into the slot he'd dug, and then the chassis rose up off the leafsprings. "That's got it," he said.

He joined Curtis at the back of the truck. "Have you pulled the tarp off?"

"I just did."

He knelt in front of the black marble, fingering the lettering and whispering: *Alice Conners Clark, born March 2, 1927, died April 14, 2007, beloved & remembered.* He sat back on his heels. "Thank you," he said.

"You ready for your dinner now?"

"I've been thinking about it."

Curtis got him settled in the shade on the old weathered chair, and sat with him, leaning back against the cottonwood, and they ate their corned-beef sandwiches and pickles, sipping cans of cold beer.

"Miss Clark there"—Curtis was talking with his mouth full and coughed—"I don't believe I ever met her."

"You never did. She was a friend of my sister's."

"I'm glad to hear it," he said. "I was afraid she was somebody I'd forgot." He carried their trash up to the cab. "You want me to run down and fetch Marin?"

"She's up to Billings, her and Marlene Silas. For the aviation show."

"How's she know Marlene?"

"They met at that yoga class for seniors at the rec center." He pushed up out of the chair. "I guess they started talking and found out they're both off their rockers for airplanes."

"So this here's like a surprise?"

"That's it, exactly."

Curtis dropped him off at the house in the early afternoon and he napped for an hour, then woke thinking he'd heard Sammy wanting out. He was already standing in the hallway before he remembered Marin had taken the dog with her. He held his breath, listening harder, but whatever made the noise had now stopped.

He sat in the living room listening to a scratched 1955 recording of Her Majesty's Regimental Band and Massed Pipers. It was a favorite of his and Mitch's that they used to play on winter evenings when the wind howled under the eaves and the house groaned like a floundering ship. They'd turn the music up loud, sipping bourbon, smoking cigarettes and joking that bagpipes were the only way to fight back against the weight of the long, cold nights. There wasn't a drop of Scots blood in either one of them.

In the late afternoon he wandered into Griff's room eating the piece of chocolate cake Curtis had left, his free hand cupped under his chin to catch the crumbs. He licked his fingers clean and felt around in her closet, finding a hooded sweatshirt that smelled of her perspiration, of clay and horses, of the lightly scented perfume she wore. He sat on the corner of her bed holding the thing to his face, inhaling. He expected this would make him feel maudlin, but he didn't. He felt simply loved, as though she were still there, whispering something comforting, saying something funny.

He put the sweatshirt back and sat out on the porch thinking he was experiencing a kind of breakthrough in his health, then pressed that speculation away, to the very edge of his mind, keeping it pushed up tightly there until it fell away altogether. He couldn't see wasting whatever time he might have left on nonsense.

In the early evening when McEban and Kenneth arrived, he explained which horse he favored, and they stood together at the pickup, his hand on Kenneth's shoulder, both of them relaxed and warm in the last shafts of sunlight.

He couldn't make out much more than the glare of sunset over the darker rise of an uneven landscape, now and then a flash of paling color, but it was enough to mark the end of a good day. When he looked down, the boy was merely a smallish shadow. "You're going to be just fine," he told him.

They were listening to McEban in the corral, the horses circling. The boy didn't respond.

"I'm saying you've turned out first-rate so far." He squeezed the boy's shoulder. "It ought to carry you through."

"Yes, sir."

They heard McEban come through the gate, the latch click, the hoofstrikes in the workyard.

"I just felt like I needed to tell you something," he said. "Like I actually knew something."

"Did you know a duck's quack won't echo?"

"I guess I hadn't thought about it."

"It's something Rodney told me."

"Well, thank you. That's a good thing to know."

McEban tied the leadrope to the bumper and they got in with Kenneth between them, then swung around and idled up the track behind the barn. The songbirds had grown louder, agitated by the coming rain.

"How's that horse doing?" McEban asked, and the boy knelt on the seat and looked out the back window.

"He's doing fine," he said.

"It won't rain for awhile yet," Einar told them. "Not until after dark."

"And then what?" McEban asked.

They parked in the pine and cottonwood and McEban picketed the horse at the edge of the meadow. Kenneth helped Einar to the bench and ran back into the timber, snapping off any dead branches he could reach. He made a dozen trips, carrying arm-loads of them back, working the dry limbs in at the bottom of the pile of antlers and bones, McEban circling behind him, sloshing kerosene up into the mess from a five-gallon can. When it was empty he sat down beside Einar and lit a cigarette.

"I didn't know you gave up chewing," Einar said.

"I'm doing them both now."

He was watching the boy skirt the north edge of the bone heap, disappearing behind it, coming back toward them from the other side.

"Can I bum one from you?"

McEban handed him the cigarette he had going and lit another, staring at the figures where they stood away from the mound. "I could tip those creepy sons of bitches over," he said. "Drag them in close enough to burn, if you wanted."

"They're better left where they are. I like the company."

"I guess I've never known what to think about 'em."

"I think they're cool." Kenneth was squatting to the side of the bench.

"If you just wanted to get out of the house we could've gone into town." McEban turned to look toward the darkening sky in the west. "I don't know why you'd want to be left out here."

They could smell the dampness and ozone in the air, hear the rumble of the storm.

"It's a celebration."

"Burning this heap of shit up, you mean?"

"It was something Griff and I talked about."

"You ought to wait for her, then. Till Thanksgiving or Christmas."

"I'm not sure I can."

"Well, damn." McEban looked to where the boy was bent over digging in the ground with a stick, and then back. "You're not thinking you can swing up on that horse when you're done, are you?"

"I thought I'd turn him loose. Hold on to his tail and let him lead me back to the corrals."

Kenneth was standing now. "I could stay and help," he said.

"Maybe we all ought to stay."

"You aren't invited."

"Why not?" McEban laughed, gesturing toward the boy. "I didn't hear you invite him either."

"We'll have more fun without you."

"You're probably right about that." McEban dropped his cigarette, grinding it out under a boot tip. "I'm going to leave a shovel here with the boy. In case that grass starts up. And a flashlight."

"You're a good neighbor, Barnum."

"There's something else you're right about."

They could feel the pressure of the storm gathering, turning back upon itself like a large, dark animal circling into its night bed.

"You're going to get soaked. I hope you're not kidding yourself about that."

"That'll be part of the fun. Won't it, Kenneth?"

"It'll be like an adventure," the boy said.

McEban carried the empty kerosene can to the truck and returned with the shovel and flashlight. He slipped his cell phone out, then put it back in his pocket. "I didn't think there'd be reception up here." He knelt down by the boy. "You call me when you're done," he said, "when you two get back to the house. If I don't hear from you in a couple hours, I'm driving out here to find you."

"I promise," Kenneth said.

McEban stood. "You want another cigarette, Einar?"

"No. I enjoyed the one I had."

McEban took the flashlight from the boy, turning it on to check the batteries, and gave it back. It was nearly dark.

"Goddamnit, Einar, I wouldn't be doing some screwball thing like this if I hadn't known you my whole life."

"I wouldn't have asked."

"You owe me at least a dollar," Kenneth said.

"All right, then."

McEban kissed the top of the boy's head, and they heard him walking away, stopping to look back, and then the sound of the truck pulling out and the rolling approach of thunder.

"You want to light it up?"

"Can I?"

Einar drew a pill bottle of wooden matches from his shirt pocket, shaking them out into the boy's hand, and he circled the pyre, lighting the kerosene around the perimeter, and came back. It was very still, and they sat listening to the fire gather and spread.

"I better check the other side." Kenneth picked up the shovel and disappeared behind the pile.

Einar could feel the heat now against his face, and thought that maybe Marin was right and this was only one in a succession of lives, a thousand of them, and then the heat increased and he could distinguish the oranges and reds and yellows, labile and rising into the darkness. "How we doing?" he called to the boy.

"Great."

He could hear the boy's laughter.

Lives of deformity, there had to be those, the losing of limbs. He felt the first drops of rain. Lives of brutal commerce, lies, lying with neighbors' wives. A chanter of hymns. The beater of slaves, his years marked by the chains of slavery. He glimpsed the boy weaving through the figures at the edge of the dark night, at times wildly lit, in and out of shadow, circling, thrusting the wooden shaft of the shovel ahead of him. Lives of hopelessness, beauty, decency, charity, body after body consumed by fire. Kenneth came back into view again, the figures on that side of the fire seeming to move along with him.

The rain hissed in the flames, the air alive with sparks, and he wondered how many times he's been an old man sitting at a fire in the night, a horse looking on, in a dark rain. Good men and bad, through the grind of centuries, and then there was Ella, who he imagined he could see dancing in her girl's body, their son holding her hand, Mitch Bradley and Ansel Magnuson. He heard the accretion of their laughter rising from the flames. The rain fell in sheets, the fire sizzling, snapping.

"Are you out there?" he called.

"I'm over here."

The boy was passing in front of the wolf-headed figure.

"How about a rooster?" he asked. "Can you get an echo out of one of them?"

The boy sat down beside him. "I only know about ducks." He smiled, his eyes shining with the last of the flames.

Water ran from their faces.

"You think you can get me and that old horse back to the house?"

"Yes, sir." He stood and stabbed the shovel into the ground. "I know I can."